TERMINUS²

....

BLACK FANTASTIC TALES FROM THE ATL

EDITED BY MILTON J. DAVIS

MVMEDIA, LLC
FAYETTEVILLE, GA

MVmedia, LLC
PO Box 143052
Fayetteville, GA 30214
www.mvmediaatl.com

Publisher's Note: This is a work of fiction. Names, characters, places, and incidents are a product of the author's imagination. Locales and public names are sometimes used for atmospheric purposes. Any resemblance to actual people, living or dead, or to businesses, companies, events, institutions, or locales is completely coincidental.

Cover art: James Mason
Cover Design: Uraeus
Book Layout ©2017BookDesignTemplates.com

Ordering Information:
Quantity sales. Special discounts are available on quantity purchases by corporations, associations, and others. For details, contact the "Special Sales Department" at the address above.

Terminus 2/ MVmedia, LLC. -- 1st ed.
ISBN no.: 979-8-9857336-1-7

Contents

To the Phoenix. Keep Rising.

"Nothing Was About To Happen Until Something Happened."
—*Atlanta*

The Washer
By
Jessica Cage

The soft orange light highlighted her form as Jakai stepped into the shadowed corner. When the light faded, she tapped the face of the gold band on her wrist to send the homing signal back to her command post. A group of women crossed her path laughing about something she hadn't heard. She watched them closely making sure they hadn't noticed her there. The civilians couldn't be allowed to see her. There were already too many conspiracy theories about aliens floating around as it was. She didn't want to add to it.

The band on her wrist lit up and the three beeps sounded in her right ear, confirmation that home base received her communication request. She turned her attention from the raucous group to her mission.

"B5713, checking in. Transport to sector six successful." She reported in and waited for verification of her objective.

"Copy, B5713. Locate subject in initiate termination sequence." Marcus, her assigned technician, spoke around a mouthful of food. The man was always eating something.

"I've been gone for five minutes and you're already stuffing your face again?" Jakai could almost picture the orange dust coating his fingers from whatever cheese flavored snack he'd pulled from his nibble drawer the moment she stepped into the pod. She only had herself to blame. She was his supplier, always bringing him treats back from her trips to Earth.

"Hey, I'm a growing boy." He joked, and his deep chortling laugh filled her head.

"You're not growing." She corrected him. "You're expanding, horizontally."

"Yeah, yeah, but the ladies still love me." She heard the series of key taps and beeping in the background as he did his job locating her subject. "Your target is nine clicks away. Her favorite spot."

"Right, time to get to business. Adjusting appearance." She tapped the band on her wrist again and brought up a holographic wardrobe. She flicked through the options until she found something she was comfortable with opting for skinny jeans, a leather jacket and a pink crop top and wedged sneakers. She chose a pink mohawk style to show off her afro. The color popped against the dark skin that was typical of her people.

Jakai had to change her look any time she touched down. She wouldn't exactly fit in with the crew of women who wore body-con dresses and heels higher than her ankles, but her new attire was much more fitting for the new environment than the standard white jumpsuit the washers wore.

"Young woman, right?" Jakai confirmed more details about who she was there to find.

"Yes, mid-twenties." Marcus responded. "Full figured, blonde hair, and green eyes."

"Got it." Jakai stepped out of the shadows and headed down the street. She walked carefully, making sure to stay aware of her environment. "What's this make, twelve this month? Numbers are high."

"Yeah. The subjects aren't responding as well to treatment anymore. Signs that the strain is evolving. Lab is working on a solution." Marcus crunched on another chip. "They say we should have a new serum soon."

"Not soon enough." She scoffed. "You know this used to be a cushy gig. One or two washes a month and the rest of the time I got to hang out at the tearoom."

"One day, we'll get back there." He said, hopeful even though it would mean fewer treats for him.

"Wishful thinking Marcus? That's not like you?"

"Well, you're Miss Doom and Gloom today. Someone has to bring the optimism."

"Right. Well, I'm checking out. Need to stay alert. I'll let you know when I make contact."

"Steady movements." Marcus said, then the three beeps sounded again, ending their communication.

Jakai was a washer, a medical scrubber for her people. The Elementals. Theirs was a species that had evolved passed the limits of humanity. Their connection to the earth and other elements allowed them to ascend to a plane separate from the Earth.

For centuries the elementals lived in peace, abundance, and happiness. Not only did they evolve but so did their technology. With it, they returned to Earth in hopes of improving the world of their ancestors, whose roots were planted in the place now known as Africa, though in their text it was called Alkebulan. They had hopes to restore their home to its former glory as the origin of all life. Unfortunately, returning to their former home resulted in the introduction of a bacterial virus to their new homeland.

At first, it seemed like nothing to be concerned with—a few sick people here and there. But eventually, it became so much more. The infection not only made them sick, but if left unchecked for too long, it changed them. And those people, the elementals who lived in light, turned into something horrible. Darklings.

First it started with a cough which was the telling sign that something was wrong. Elementals never got sick. Soon after the cough, the virus spread through their body, changing everything about them on a molecular level. Eventually, everything good about them was transformed and the energy they held, the power, was corrupted. The darklings trusted no one and only had one thing that motivated them: the destruction of others. Entire families were wiped out by a person they once loved.

The darklings had to be taken out or they would destroy everything the elementals had achieved. Eventually, the healers discovered that sending those who were infected back to Earth slowed the effects. And while they were on Earth, it gave them more time to produce medications to fight off the infection.

Each elemental that was sent back was put under a form of hypnosis. A medically induced mental state that temporarily erased their memory of their home. Each subject was given a new life, one that would feel as if nothing was wrong. They did this because it made it easier on the subject. If they didn't know that they weren't home, they wouldn't miss it.

When a subject was determined to have fully recovered from their infection, they could return home. Unfortunately, it had been years since anyone reached a point of complete recuperation and in the recent months, the number of darkling transitions had only increased.

That's where the washers came in.

It was her job to do the thing no one else wanted to. She would find the subject and then inject them with a toxin that would break down their magic, both the light and the dark. Unfortunately, to destroy an elemental's magic was to kill them.

Jakai preferred the title, Washer. It felt more like she was there to clean up something rather than to destroy a life. Other people, the members of the families of those who were washed away, had another word for her. Deathbringer.

She walked down Peachtree Street and had to remind herself that not everything was as it seemed. Yes, the humans she passed were real, but some of them were a part of this simulation. There were elementals who had volunteered to return to earth so that they could watch over those who were sickly. They were a part of the reporting system. If an elemental took a turn for the worst before the healers realized it, one of the volunteers would sound the alarm.

She rounded the corner walking into the Atlantic Station. Apparently, it was one of the subjects' favorite locations. She met a friend there shortly after her arrival and it became habit. In the middle of the outdoor mall was a small green yard with a large screen that displayed nothing more than ads for clothing. Jakai spotted the woman from behind. Just as Marcus said, her blonde hair blew in the wind, and her full hips spread over the edge of the seat designed for someone with a narrower frame.

As always Jakai would make it seem like a casual encounter. This would be nothing more than a stranger bumping into someone along the way of her normal day. She never pretended as if she was lost or in need of directions because she found that most of the subjects would avoid giving out directions. No, she needed an opportunity to get closer.

The brief information provided on the woman only gave a physical description and general location of where she could be found. No picture, which was weird but not unheard of. Which meant Jakai needed to rely on the woman's learned habits to connect with her.

"Are they planning anything good tonight?" Jakai slid into the seat next to the woman on the screen.

"Excuse me?" the woman asked, her blond hair still moved wildly as the wind kicked up. She didn't look at Jakai, probably nervous about the new presence at her side.

"I was told that they played movies out here some nights." Jakai repeated what little she knew of the area. "I didn't catch what film they were showing tonight."

"Oh, sorry you wasted your time coming out here. Unfortunately, this isn't one of the nights that they're gonna show anything. I just like to sit here and for some reason it brings me a lot of comfort." She pointed over her shoulder to the building behind the courtyard. "If you want a movie, the theater is just there. I was thinking of catching one myself."

"So, this is like one of your happy places?" Jakai changed the topic focusing more on her than the movie.

"Happy place?" she asked, still not turning her head so Jakai could see what she looked like.

"Yeah, you know a place where you can go just to get away from all of your thoughts. I used to have a couple of those back home."

"Are you new here?"

"Yeah, I am. I just moved here not too long ago. Brand new from Chicago." The city was always the location she chose. She liked their pizza and therefore it was her chosen earth-based home.

"I love Chicago. I haven't been there in years though." The woman spoke of a memory that wasn't real.

"You should definitely go back again." She turned and offered her hand tell the woman to introduce herself. "I'm Jakai."

"Gem." The woman offered her hand back turning to face her for the first time.

Jakai shook her hand and as she watched the wide smile stretch across the woman's face her heart stopped. The subject gave her the name that the healers implanted in her brain but that was not her real name. Jakai knew her name as well as she knew her own.

"Jaylee?"

"I'm sorry?" The woman shook her head. "What?"

"I, uh." Jakai hesitated as she tried to come up with an explanation for why she just called this woman by a name that was clearly not the one she'd given. "Sorry you just you look so familiar."

"Oh, I have one of those faces."

"Yeah, right. I'm sure." Jakai stood from her seat. "I need to go. It was nice to meet you."

She hurried away from the woman who stared at her in disbelief. Her pulse raced and her hands became clammy with sweat as tears formed in her eyes. She tapped the wristband and waited. Three steps later she heard the three beeps. Two steps later she heard the crunching of potato chips.

"Tell me you didn't know it was her." She didn't allow Marcus to speak before blurting out her thoughts.

"I did. I'm sorry, but that is why I sent you. I figured you would want a chance to have a few last moments with her. I know this is difficult, but if you don't do this now, you know what will happen, what she will become." Marcus was only focused on the task at hand, not the heartbreak that she was experiencing.

"Difficult? Talk about an understatement Marcus." Jakai held back the curses that flooded her mind. "I can't. How could you ever ask me to do this? How could you want me to do this? You sent me here to end her life!"

"I didn't think you would want anyone else to do it." He gave the simple explanation.

"Marcus, I didn't even know she was here." Jakai stumbled over her thoughts. "How could no one tell me she was sick? How did this happen?"

"I didn't know that it was a secret kept from you." He paused. "I'm really sorry. I just assumed you knew. I left out her photo and other details so no one would question it."

"How long?"

"You know I'm not supposed to tell you that information it only makes the job harder"

"Marcus, don't play diplomatic with me right now. How long has she been here? She is my sister!" Jakai's voice broke with preemptive mourning, but she pressed the issue and when he didn't answer she repeated herself. "Tell me the truth. How long have you known? How long has she been here?"

"Six months."

"Six? Six months?" Tears fell freely as she tried to understand how six months had gone by without talking to her sister. How much longer than that had it been? "How could you keep this from me."

"I thought you knew. Figured you just didn't want to talk about it. This job is hard enough without having to consider washing away our own."

"No. I'm not doing this." Jakai refused to do what she was sent there to do.

"You know you have to do this. If you don't they will send someone else."

"I'm not gonna kill my own sister Marcus. She's my flesh and blood." Jakai shook her head as she watched a family walking together. They shared ice cream and laughter and it broke her heart.

"I understand that." he said. "But she is just like the rest. She's going to change."

"I don't care. I'm not gonna do this and you can say whatever you want. This isn't happening. My sister is not going to change and I'm not gonna be the person who ends her life." She wiped the tears from her eyes. "That's not how this is going to go."

"What are you going to do? You can't come back empty handed." Marcus's voice lowered meaning there was someone nearby that he didn't want to hear their conversation. "You know what that will mean."

"I'm not coming back." Jakai admitted plainly.

"What?" Marcus asked. "Jakai you can't do this."

"If they want to kill her, they're gonna have to find her first."

"Don't do this. It's suicide Jakai. You know that."

"No. It was murder when you gave me this assignment." She tapped the band on her wrist and ended the call.

Jakai turned and ran back to the courtyard, but her sister was no longer sitting in the narrow seats. She frantically searched the area until she saw her yellow hair entering the movie theater. She ran until she caught up with her on the escalator.

"I know this is gonna sound crazy, but you have to come with me." Jakai said as she ran up the moving steps. "We have to leave this place now."

"I'm sorry, what?" her sister frowned. "Look I'm sure you're nice and I know you're missing home and you said that I remind you of someone but I'm not going anywhere with you."

"You have to trust me. There are people coming for you. They want to hurt you. I'm here to help you." Jakai tried to explain herself, but her thoughts were jumbled, twisted by her own emotion which of course made her look like a psychopath.

"Okay. I don't know who you are, but you've lost your mind." she pushed past her to try to walk down the stairs. "You should get help."

Jakai couldn't leave anything to chance. If Jaylee got away from her, there was no telling if she would ever be able to find her again, and if Marcus was doing his job, soon another Washer would be on their way to take over the job. Quick thinking, she did something she never did.

From the side of the belt wrapped around her waist she pulled out a small pen with a little liquid in the chamber. Will look like a regular writing utensil was more than that. She popped the top revealing a needle that she then slammed into the arm of the woman who tried to get away from her.

"What the hell?" she looked back at the needle in her arm before she fainted.

Jakai looked around to make sure no one could see them. When she was sure they were clear, she used her power to shift them away from the theater. As an elemental she could blend with the natural world and use it to travel great distances. It was how the watchers did their job. Everything in nature was connected, a web of linked data. Elementals learned that by mixing their magic with the advanced technology, they could better work those connections in their favor.

When the women reappeared, they were in a hotel room. Jakai laid her sister on the bed and waited for her to come to.

"What's going on?" her sister grumbled, touching the sides of her forehead as she sat up on the bed.

"Jaylee? Do you remember who I am?" Jakai wasn't sure if the medicine had enough time to work on restoring her memory. The longer a subject was under the hypnosis, the longer it took to get them out.

"Jakai?" she said less than confident before she shook her head and frowned. "Of course, I do. Why would you ask me that? Where are we?"

"Earth." Jakai answered honestly. "In a hotel room, not sure which one."

"What? Why are we here? Is everything okay?" Jaylee panicked and touched her sister's face, concern in her eyes. "Oh no. Are you okay? I always thought this job was too risky for you. Coming face to face with the virus so often. Now you're sick?"

"No, it's not." she placed her hand over Jaylee's and leaned into the familiar touch. It was the same thing her sister always did when she was upset. "I have to tell you something that's gonna be hard for you to understand. But I need to know that what I'm about to tell you is true."

"You're scaring me. Just say what it is." Jaylee frowned. "You know I never liked the lead up to bad news."

"I'm not the one who is sick, Jaylee. You are." She watched the horror in her sister's eyes as she tried to process the news. Jakai thought to add more to the explanation to help. "Six months ago, you were sent to Earth to heal, but the virus has progressed, and you've only gotten worse since you've been here. I was sent here to-,"

"To do your job." Jaylee's hand dropped. "They sent you here to kill me."

"Yes, but I'm not going to do that. I can't. You're my sister, there's no way I'm letting anyone end your life. I mean I don't know what we will do yet. I'm still working out the logistics but, but we'll find a way to survive. We can get away from this place. I'll take you somewhere safe and you'll be okay."

"Jakai, what are you saying?" Jaylee listened her sister's desperate planning and sighed.

"I'm saying I'm going to take care of you."

"Jakai I love you but if what you're saying is true there's no way you can take care of me. If they sent you here to do your job it means that soon I'm going to turn into a darkling and there is no taking care of me if that happens." Jaylee leaned back against the headboard. "It's pretty messed up that they sent you to do this."

"It was Marcus. Trying to do me a favor. He said he wanted to give us more time together." Jakai sobbed. "Jaylee, I didn't even know you were here until I saw you today. I feel so horrible about that."

"Why?"

"You're my sister. You got sick. I should have been there for you."

"Don't do that to yourself. It's not good. Being there wouldn't have stopped me from getting sick. Besides, it was like I made some great effort to keep in touch. We both sucked at being sisters." She laughed. "Boo to us."

"I just," Jaylee grabbed her sister's hand and held it between her own. "I've miss you so much."

"I've missed you too. And well, thanks to Marcus, in some sick way, we get to have more time together before-,"

"No. That's not happening." Jakai still denied what they knew was inevitable. "They're working on something in the labs right now and soon they'll be able to fix you. We just have to keep you safe until then."

"Keep me safe from a virus that is currently changing who I am internally?" Jaylee shook her head. "No."

"You have that annoying responsible big sister look going on right now and there's no way that's gonna work on me. You're my sister Jaylee. I have to do something. I have to try."

"I know I am and you're mine. And I love you so much for even thinking of taking the risk that you are now. But ultimately if I am sick, I'm gonna become a darkling. But I won't allow you to do anything that will ruin your life once I'm gone. And I'm not letting you put everything you've worked for in jeopardy for me. Not now. Not when I need to know that you're okay. Because I won't be here to take care of you."

"You want me to do what they sent me here to do?"

"I think you have to." Though she smiled, tears fell from her eyes. "I prefer it be you than some faceless shadow. Isn't that how you're supposed to do this?"

"Not my style." Jakai shrugged. "I haven't seen you in two years because of work. I thought I was protecting my family by doing this job. You know, I was helping the greater cause and somehow buying us all some good karmic energy, but I've missed out on so much. Now you're here in front of me and I should be so happy. This should be a moment that makes me smile, but I can't be because I can't do this."

"How about this? How about this? We have an opportunity to make up for all the time we've lost. We will watch pointless human television, as dad would say. We'll drink liquor, here on earth is really fun. I think my memories are kind of blended but I'm pretty sure there were a couple times where I landed ass up on the sidewalk and I had so much fun doing it."

"Jaylee-,"

"I know it's not what you want to hear. I know that you are looking for something better from this, but ultimately this is the end for me. And I should be upset. I should be angry, but I just I feel this sense of calm. You know, my memories are coming back, and the last thing I do remember is the fear that I would be alone in the end, but I'm not alone. You're here and if there's anyone I would want spend the rest of my life with it's you."

"You really want me to do this?"

"I really want you to do this because if not you, there will be someone else and they won't just be coming for me. I need you to take care of me and then take care of yourself."

Jakai thought about her sister's words, then gave in. She was right. No matter how hard Jakai wanted to fight it. If a washer was called in, it meant the woman was too far gone to survive and if she let her sister turn and hurt anyone, Jakai would be next on the washer's list.

She hit the band on her wrist initiating the three beeps again and waited for the crunching of potato chips.

"Marcus."

"I didn't put the call out there yet." He calmed her fears.

"Thank you. This one is gonna take a while though."

"I figured it would. Take all the time you need to. Wouldn't you know it, just when you left, we got the alert that it's time for a system update. You know those things really can take quite a while."

"I really appreciate this." Jakai smiled. "I'll bring you back more snacks."

"I need you to come around to do that." Marcus tapped the keys in the background. "Oh, and Cheetos. I don't care what they say here, those things are heavenly."

The sisters did everything that Jaylee said. First, they changed their outfits and Jaylee forced her sister to pick something more fitting for a night out on the town. And then they did all the things together that they never got to. The first night, they went to the club and danced until they were kicked out. The next night they stayed inside drinking wine and watching chick flicks, crying every time the girl inevitably got her heart broken and cheering when her knight in shining armor arrived. And the next night, just as the pizza arrived, Jaylee took a turn for the worst.

"I know you said you wanted anchovies but there was no way how I was getting that." Jakai returned to her sister's role in the small rental house she lived in, but instead of finding her sister sprawled out across the bed still chomping on the sweet and spicy jumbo sunflower seeds, she found her crouched down in the corner face hidden in her hands.

"Jaylee, are you alright? What's wrong?"

Her sister gave no words, only snarls and growls as she started to pull out her own hair. It was then she realized her sister's arms and hands were covered in scratches. This was the first phase of the change—the disconnection from self and the inability to feel the pain that they caused themselves. The darklings devolved quickly, first destroying their own body before turning on those around them.

"Jaylee." she said her name once more, but Jakai knew it was too late. Her sister, whatever form she knew once, was no longer there.

As she promised her she would, Jakai pulled out the vial that had the toxin. She loaded the needle with the black fluid that would breakdown her sister's magic, severing her connection to the elements, and end her life.

Carefully she approached, needle poised and ready for injection. Jakai tried to administrate the toxin, but her sister attacked. She slapped and pushed Jakai, knocking the needle out of her hand. The next thing she knew, she was in a fight for her life. Jaylee punched, kicked, and clawed at Jakai who only worked to defend herself from the attacks as she searched for the needle.

She tapped the band on her wrist but there were no three beeps this time, only silence. System update. She knew she couldn't let her sister get out. There was nothing she would be able to do if that happened, so she locked the door hoping to contain her in the room, but her sister was strong even before the change and she phased through the door, blending with the material for a moment to step out whole on the other side.

Jakai spotted the needle on the floor beneath the bed, retrieved it then ran out of the bedroom, where she saw her sister staring at a photograph hanging on the wall. She charged her and tried to administrator the toxin again, but her sister felt her coming turn and smacked her so hard that she fell against the wall and cracked it.

"Jaylee if you're still in there please help me. I'm trying to take care of you like you asked me too." Jakai spit blood from her mouth.

When she looked into the woman's eyes, Jakai realized that her sister was no longer there. All that was left was the beast. And maybe that made it easier. She charged again, this time with force. She kicked Jaylee's legs from beneath her and quickly pinned her to the ground plunging the needle into her chest. The dark liquid disappeared into her chest and soon Jaylee's fight ended.

"Jakai?" her sister said her name as her body seized.

"Jaylee." Jakai sobbed, fresh tears rushing down her face.

"Thank you." Jaylee managed a small smile before the light faded from her eyes.

Three beeps sounded in her ear as Jakai held the limp body of her sister.

"B5713, checking in."

"Copy, B5713."

"Subject terminated."

Consecrated
By
Gerald L. Coleman

'Never was there a clearer case of stealing the livery of the court of heaven to serve the devil in.'
-Frederick Douglass

Yes, it was partly the bourbon. But mostly, it was that it was two in the morning and early autumn. The night was cool. The air smelled like cut grass and discarded charcoal briquets. It was so late on a Thursday night, or early on a Friday morning depending on your philosophy of telling time, that the street outside the coffee shop was empty. That was part of it too – fully lit streets, stoplights turned to flashing, but no one in sight. He loved it. Maybe it was also that fall always reminded him of the first week of a new college semester, which meant old friends and new acquaintances – and now he was self-aware enough to know that feeling was really about new possibility.

Drexel tossed the butt of his cigar in the cigarette pail next to the door. The windows were long since darkened but the employees didn't care if you sat at the stone tables out front after they were gone. The parking lot in the front was the size of a deck of cards so he parked down the street. A crescent moon, that hung so low in the night sky that it was like a tree branch you could reach up to and pluck an apple from, cast a glow so luminescent the hundred tinier lights around it strained to be seen. It was as if they were jealous of how much sky the moon took up. The soft clap of the leather soles of his boots on the sidewalk was only interrupted by the jarring infrequency of a car rolling by. It was so quiet. It was like that moment between when the orchestra finished a piece and the audience decided to applaud. It felt like the whole world belonged to him.

Drexel saw a flicker of movement from the corner of his eye and froze. The rear parking lot, nestled behind the shops like a backpack between the shoulders, was only open to deliveries and employees unless you wanted a three-hundred-dollar tow bill. *Had he really seen something or was it just really late?* He shrugged it off and started walking again. Drexel made it three more steps before he heard a muffled cry.

His mother had raised him to stick his nose in. He eventually learned it was also naturally in him. When you're on the mat or in the ring, and you get hit, you learn something about yourself. Your instinct is either to step back or step in.

Drexel was also, always, incredibly aware of being a large Black man. Any time he forgot, even for a moment, someone would remind him by moving their purse to the other side of their body, locking their door at a stop light, or refusing to get on an elevator with him. So, he made sure to stay in the light and move slowly. He put his hands up as he rounded the corner.

The other thing was to mentally dial for a light tone and raise his voice from its more naturally deep one. God forbid it was a white woman doing some crazy shit. He did not need to have to explain to cops why he was in the back lot after midnight with a scared white woman.

"Hey, no need to be afraid. I just heard something as I was walking by and I'm just checking to make sure everything is ok."

Did that sound friendly enough? Was it unthreatening? Ease inducing? This shit was exhausting.

He moved to his right so he would round the corner from the middle of the lot and be in plain sight. Hopefully they would be able to see him clearly.

"I have my hands up. Let me know you're ok and I'll move on. I was just heading to my car. Hello?"

Nothing. Fuck, he thought.

If this was going to be a thing he was going to be pissed. This was America though. One moment you're living your Black joyful life and the next you're carrying the weight of all of America's bullshit. In the back of his mind a small voice was saying move the fuck on. But the louder one was saying someone might be in trouble. He quickly considered and then tossed the idea of pulling out his phone and recording. Darkness, the late hour, and something in his hand, would be a pretext for some scared white person. And they'd get away with it. The last thing he wanted was to be a hashtag or have his name on a fucking tee shirt.

Drexel stepped around the corner and stopped dead. The smell of sulphur hit him like a cloud of joy-smoke at a house party. The first thing he saw was the black cap-toe brogues. They were glossy with polish. The suit was sharper than a thumb tack. It was slim-cut, royal blue, and chalk striped. The white guy wearing it was average height with close-cropped black hair. He was holding a white guy in jeans, a checkered shirt, and work boots with well-worn soles like he was a limp ragdoll. And his chest was torn open.

"Hey!"

It was instinct more than anything else. Drexel had barely processed what he was seeing. He took three quick steps toward them. The guy in the perfectly pressed suit dropped the dead guy. The body made a soft thudding sound when it hit the pavement. Then, suit-guy turned toward him. When Drexel got a good look at him, he instinctively threw his hands up, covering his face and chest. It was suit-guy's face. It summoned something primordial in Drexel, a defense mechanism that was deeply biological.

The rest of suit-guy should have matched his face – like claws, fangs, or a misshapen body. But it didn't. He looked like a wealthy businessman with a five-hundred-dollar haircut and a three-thousand-dollar suit. The incongruity was blood dripping from his lips onto his chin and the heart he was holding in his hand, which was still beating. And then there were the eyes. His eyes were completely black.

Drexel was frozen to the spot. He could not move. It felt like something was holding him there. A small voice, in the back of his mind, screamed. It said, *run*! But he couldn't move. He wasn't even sure if he was breathing. What the fuck was he looking at?

Suit-guy went from standing twenty feet away to right in front of him in a weird jump-cut, like a scene out of a Jordan Peele horror flick. But Drexel still could not move. His nose filled with the smell of sulfur. His mouth tasted like copper.

In an odd moment of clarity, the kind where you feel like you're standing outside yourself watching, he realized he was going to die. It was a calm, clear, rational assessment. This was how it ended. The man reached out a manicured hand to grab him. Drexel watched the world slow to a crawl. His mind raced. His mom wouldn't know what had happened to him. He would miss the next Black Panther movie. He would never get to find out what might have happened between him and Olive. And then creepy suit-guy howled.

The sound of it made Drexel's heart beat faster and his head pound. Suit-guy shrieked and pulled his hand away. Suddenly, Drexel could move. Before he could run, a jagged slit of red light appeared a few feet away and creepy suit-guy stepped through it. In a flash, he was gone.

Drexel stared at the spot where he disappeared for a moment. *What the fuck just happened?*

Then he looked down at the dead white guy, glanced around the parking lot, and said, "Oh shit."

He should run, he thought. No, he should slowly, but quickly, walk away. If he was found with this dead white guy, they would put him on death row. No one would believe that he didn't kill him.

"Interesting."

Drexel nearly jumped out of his skin. He spun around to see another Black guy leaning against a pole, a few feet away, under the building's covered walkway.

"Yeah, you should be as dead as that white dude."

* * *

His skin was dark brown, and he was nearly as tall as Drexel. While Drexel sported a thickly curled afro with a close-cut beard and mustache, the man was clean shaven – head and face. Right away he noticed the short-sleeved, black, polo sweater with waist band, slim black jeans, and black, Italian, dress boots. Drexel had an eye for fashion. It was casual but he still looked like he'd stepped out of a page of Gentleman's Quarterly. Drexel also clocked the black Rolex, large gold ring, and Zulugrass bead bracelets stacked on his wrist. The beads were black with green, red, and gold interspersed in the stringed circles. But it took him a few moments to register the black 1911 handgun, covered in strange scrollwork, and the knife with the curved hilt tucked in his belt. It was also covered in decorative scrollwork accompanied by glittering blue and green gemstones.

"You can put your hands down."

His voice was even deeper than Drexel's.

"Uh, are you sure?" he said, indicating the gun with a nod of his head.

The man glanced down at his hand and said, "Oh, yeah, sorry. This isn't for you. It was meant for the Infernal."

Drexel cocked his head to the right and said, "Infernal?"

Azriel slid the gun into a leather holster, tucked inside his jeans, on the back of his right hip.

Then he smiled, extended his hand, and said, "I'm Azriel."

Drexel's hand shot out before he could stop it. It was such a socially ingrained habit that the man was already holding his hand before Drexel could decide if having him in his personal space was wise. He had a strong grip.

The moment where a normal handshake would end passed but Azriel did not let go of his hand.

Instead, the man stared at his hand and said, "Hmm. I see."

"You see? What does that mean? And what's an Infernal?"

Azriel released Drexel's hand, pulled out his phone, and held up a finger while he dialed.

"Hey, this is Azriel. We've got another one. I'm pinging the location. Get some Cleaners over here immediately."

He lowered his finger, hung up the phone, and said, "Look, you've got a lot to catch up on and very little time to do it. Come with me and I'll explain what I can. Unless you'd rather stay here and hope nobody catches you with that poor guy's body?"

Drexel glanced over at the guy lying prone on the ground and tried to avoid staring at the gaping wound in his chest.

"Oh, hell no. Do you know what kind of shitstorm would follow being caught with a white boy's mutilated corpse? As long as you've got someone coming to deal with it, I'm good. Someone should call the cops – but long after I'm gone. You know those assholes. A slight breeze and they're gunning you down in the street. Frightened bitches. You'd think if they were that scared they'd find another job."

Azriel nodded and said, "Yeah. Facts. But don't worry. After the Cleaners are done, I'll call a new friend of mine. She's an F.B.I. Agent. And this won't be her first time dealing with something like this."

* * *

Drexel rode in silence all the way to what he assumed was Azriel's house. He thought about the car to keep his mind from spinning out of control. It was a classic – a nineteen sixty-six mustang Fastback. But it was custom. Drexel loved a beautiful car and this one was choice. The paint job was a unique blue-gray with a black hood, roof, and grill. Bits of red ran through the detailing as highlights. Large wheels with satin-black rims, red brake calipers, and matching red rotors, finished the look. It roared. Whoever worked on it dropped it, giving it a lower aggressive profile. He guessed there was an Edelbrock crate engine under the hood making his seat rumble beneath him.

The house was as beautiful as the car. It was spartan grays and creams. The furniture was contemporary, like the stuff you saw in the modern houses with concrete and glass interiors in gentrified neighborhoods. The kitchen was all stainless and Drexel spied a four-thousand-dollar espresso machine on the counter. It was way too late for coffee but as he leaned back on the leather couch, Azriel handed him a heavy crystal whiskey glass with two fingers of the smoothest bourbon he had ever tasted in it.

Drexel emptied the glass with a single tilt. Azriel must have known because he was standing there with a matching crystal decanter and poured another two fingers in his glass. He sat the decanter on the glass coffee table with a soft *thunk* and dropped into the oversized chair across from the couch. He took a sip and stared at Drexel for a moment with slightly narrowed eyes.

"What do you know about your ancestors?"

Drexel slowly rotated the glass in his hand as a half-grin spread across his face.

"Huh, you know the conundrum, right? Our guess is Madagascar. But short of giving a company I don't trust a DNA sample there's no way to know for sure. Even that would only give you a region. It wouldn't tell you about your people. That's a part of the crime perpetrated against us. Our names, family history, generational knowledge – all lost to time and barbarity."

Azriel nodded and sipped.

"Are you in the clergy?"

Drexel tilted his head to the left. Took another swallow and said, "I was. For about fifteen years. I tried to help people be better versions of themselves, to follow the philosophy of the brown-skinned, Mediterranean Jew people claimed to believe in. But it was all smoke and mirrors. People just wanted to be excused so they could continue to be who they already were."

"Yeah, he would be disappointed."

Drexel noted the odd tone. It was the way you talked about someone you knew personally. But that was obviously not the case. So, he shrugged it off.

"I get that reasoning, Drexel. What I'm trying to ascertain is whether you were consecrated?"

Drexel shrugged. "Sure. Twice, in fact. Once, as what the church called a Deacon and the second when I became an Elder."

Azriel made a satisfied grunt. "That's it then. I suspect you are from a long line of Guardians."

"Guardians?"

"Yes. They had many names depending on the region of the Continent. The Yoruba called them *Babalawo*, while the Igbo used the term *Dibia*. The Maasai called them *Laibon*. But behind the veil, a small number of them were recruited from across the Continent to serve as Guardians."

Drexel said, "Ok. I'm with you so far. Guardians of what?"

Azriel sat there for a moment, took a deep breath, and placed his glass on the table.

He stood, crossed over to the couch, and said, "There's an easier way."

He touched Drexel's forehead with his finger and the world went white.

* * *

They stood on a small outcropping. The ground stretched out, unendingly, before them. It was sandstone and rocks for as far as the eye could see with a singular exception. A few hundred yards ahead was a mound that filled the rest of the horizon. The only sound was the wind blowing across the empty plain.

Azriel's now familiar voice broke the spell.

"It's called the Eye of Africa and it's as old as life itself."

Drexel had heard of it. It was so large it could be seen from space. It looked like a giant blue bullseye from orbit. He had no idea it was so old.

To his right a short line of men and women made their way to the mound.

"Who are they?"

Azriel glanced over at the handful of people and said, "They are why I brought you here."

"So, where is here?"

Azriel smirked and said, "More when than where."

"Huh!? What do you mean when?"

Drexel twisted around at the thought of it but there was nothing to see except more rocks and flat earth.

"For as long as there has been memory, the Infernal scratched at the veil that separates their world from this one. And sometimes they find a thin place where their efforts are rewarded."

"And this is a thin place?"

Azriel looked up at the sky. He put a hand over his eyes to shield them from the sun.

"In the present, people think the Eye is the result of geological factors like pressure and movement. Before that they thought it was the aftermath of a meteor strike. They would never believe the truth. The Infernal have been scratching at this spot for millennia hoping to break through. And the only thing that kept that from happening were the Guardians."

Azriel indicated the small of group with a nod of his head.

Drexel said, "So how did they do it?"

"Simply put? Magic."

Drexel immediately opened his mouth but Azreil held up a hand and continued, "Now, before you say something asinine like magic doesn't exist, you need to understand that its just a word. It's a word that has been used to describe forces that people didn't understand and, as is the human penchant, that frightened them. It's a shorthand. Rather than trying to explain the use of energy, direction, and intention to you in a few minutes let's just say, magic."

Drexel's mouth clamped shut and he nodded.

Azriel continued. "They created a set of wards that reinforced the veil in this spot, making it impossible for the Infernal to break through."

Drexel watched the small group of men and women climb the mound and begin making strange motions in certain spots.

"So, what happened?"

Azriel nodded again. "Good question. You surmised that the wards failed and some of the Infernal were able to scrape their way through into this world, including Hardgraves."

"Hardgraves? Is that the name of the one I encountered to-night?"

"Yes."

Drexel continued to watch the Guardians do their work.

"So, how did they break through?"

Azriel sighed. It was audible and long. Drexel looked over at him and saw the sadness painting his face like the ravages of a long-fought sickness.

"They broke through because sometime in the early to mid six-teen-hundreds the Guardians stopped making their yearly pil-grimage from across the Continent to strengthen the wards."

Azriel hardly finished his sentence before Drexel said, "What? Why would they …."

He did not need to finish the sentence. The rest of the words caught in his throat. A chill washed over him. He knew exactly what had interrupted the work of several thousand faithful years – a work that kept what he could only describe as evil at bay. Heart stricken, he turned and looked at Azriel.

Drexel swallowed hard around a lump in his throat and forced the words out.

"The slave trade."

The disgust in Azriel's voice was just as evident.

"Yes, the slave trade."

The Trans-Atlantic Slave trade had wholly disrupted the lives of millions of African people, destabilized the African continent, and caused horrors like rape, child abduction, murder, and all kinds of brutality against Black people at the hands of white.

Drexel had never liked the term Trans-Atlantic Slave trade. It masked who was responsible for it, namely white people in Europe and the Americas, and it dehumanized African peoples by labeling them slaves. They stopped being Mandé, Gbe, Akan, Wolof, and Makua, with rich histories and innate claims to humanity and became chattel. He preferred using the term Euro-African Enslavement Trade. It had destroyed language, culture, family history, and traditions that were tens of thousands of years old. And now he knew that one of those traditions had been guarding the world against evil. It made sense that one evil had made a way for another.

Drexel said, "We should go tell them what is coming so they can prepare."

"We can't."

Drexel looked at Azriel with scrunched eyes and his mouth agape.

"Why not?"

The world turned white again and Drexel jerked upright on the couch.

"Because we weren't actually there. I'm an immortal not a time traveler."

It took him a moment to adjust to the softer lighting in Azriel's living room.

His mind flitted from the mound, to the guardians, to what he had just experienced and – "Wait. Did you just say immortal? You're an immortal? How is that a thing?"

Azriel smirked, "It's a curse, really, but that's a story for another time."

He slumped into the chair across from Drexel and wiped his hand across his face.

"You know, there is so much about the world that would be better without the sins of Europe. That's not to say that the world would be a garden of peace and tranquility – because I don't think human beings are capable of that. But so much of the world's ills can be traced to how they rampaged across the map without a conscience – and believe me, I've seen it firsthand. But that's not our immediate problem."

"And what's our immediate problem?"

"Our immediate problem is that the Infernal, particularly Hardgraves, now know about you. And you are ill-equipped to defend yourself."

Drexel leaned forward. "But he wasn't able to touch me."

"Oh, he'll find a workaround. And as dangerous as Hardgraves is, there are more dangerous things that go bump in the night in this city."

Drexel's lips pressed together firmly, and he said, "So, what do we do about it?"

Azriel stood up and said, "The amazing thing about Black folks, the real magic, has always been the ability to reinvent ourselves on the other side of the horror of enslavement. We find ways to mend what was broken."

* * *

The seat beneath Drexel stopped vibrating when Azriel turned the key. They sat outside a barbershop on a narrow street next to a tattoo parlor. It was still so early that the streetlights continued casting their warm glow at the darkness. A street cleaner whirred by blowing leaves against the car window. Azriel waited for it to disappear down the street before hopping out of the car. Drexel followed him across the empty thoroughfare and onto the sidewalk in front of the barbershop. The windows were dark. The street was quiet.

Azriel looked left, then right, before ducking around the side. The walkway between the two shops was only wide enough for one person at a time. Halfway down it they had to squeeze past garbage cans. It ended in a brick wall.

Azriel paused and turned back to look at Drexel.

"There's no easy way to tell you this so I'm just going to explain it very briefly. You'll be tempted to ask questions, but don't. We don't have the time."

Drexel grimaced and said, "Hardgraves."

Azriel nodded and said, "Hardgraves. And probably his boss."

Drexel opened his mouth and Azriel said, "Ah, ah, ah, no time."

He stared at Drexel until he threw up his hands up and nodded.

Azriel returned the nod, took a deep breath, and said, "There's another city behind the one you've always lived in. It's a place where the gifted, the cursed, and the Other live their lives just out of the corner of the eye of human beings. Our hotels, bars, grocery stores, and coffee shops, are just behind theirs. And *behind* is just a figure of speech."

Azriel reached out to the wall and turned a knob that had not been there. The wall opened like a door and he ushered Drexel in with a wave of his hand. When the door closed behind him Azriel pulled back a thick crimson curtain and Drexel's eyes widened. It was part barbershop, part tattoo parlor. But he knew there was nothing on the other side of that wall but a hedge, a driveway, and the first house in a small neighborhood. Where was this place?

The shop was empty save for one woman hunched over a table with a lamp beaming over her shoulder. She was working on a tattoo gun.

She didn't even look up when she said, "Well, well. The cursed immortal who found his way. What have you dragged in off the street demon hunter."

Azriel said, "He's one of the Ashkandar. Confused, bewildered, and untrained – but a Guardian of the Old Blood none the same. I need to speak to Oshun."

The woman spun around in her chair. Her sleeves were rolled up revealing dragons, sprites, and something with wings coiling up her arms in brilliant colors. Her hair was done up in Bantu Knots and her skin was as dark as Azriel's. She reached down and opened a draw in the table. After rummaging around in the draw with her hand, she pulled out a monocle and held it up to her left eye. She looked Drexel up and down and then tossed it on the table.

"Yep. Poor bastard. Just living his life and now the world has been pulled inside out. But what's the hurry?"

That, she directed at Azriel.

They both said, "Hardgraves."

And Azriel added, "And likely his boss. Medusa, you know what they can do if they get ahold of him before he's been trained."

Drexel shot a hard look at Azriel and started to ask what he meant by *what they can do* but the immortal held up a hand and Drexel swallowed the question. He did, however, mouth the word *Medusa* to himself and tried not to stare at her. She looked like she could've come from Atlanta or Brooklyn, not a mythical tale.

Medusa said, "Ok, ok. Bless his heart. Hold on."

She disappeared through another curtain in the back before Drexel could get his mind to stop spinning. Even he could tell he was spinning out. He managed to get his shit together by the time she returned. She was leading a small, bald, black man. He was wearing a white shirt—buttoned to the top—a vest, and pants in a green, gold, and black striped pattern. Drexel thought his black, dress boots were John Varvatos. The man was, as his uncle used to say, clean as the board of the health.

"May the sun shine upon you."

His voice was deep but comforting. His eyes were brown, and his handshake was warm.

Like Azriel, he held his hand for a bit, looked him in the eye, and then said, "I'm sorry you found your way to us like this. Has the immortal explained to you how your hereditary line was broken?"

Drexel nodded. "Yes. He ... he showed me. I used to think that watching movies like Mississippi Burning or video of cops killing Black folks in the street was the most infuriating thing I could see. But I was wrong."

Oshun shook his head and said, "I understand. So much of what we knew and how we held the world together was lost during enslavement. However, we believe in finding ourselves again.

Even here, in this blood-soaked country. Their sins are theirs. Refusing to take up the mantel of what was lost to us would be ours."

Azriel said, "That's my cue. Good luck, Drexel. I'll see you on the front lines."

Drexel watched him go. The things he must know - all the amazing things he must have seen. One day he'd have to visit Azriel again, when there was time for questions.

He turned back to see Oshun waiting.

"What now?"

"Now, we begin your training. There are things to be hunted. But one last thing before we get started."

Oshun produced a small knife with a curve as wicked as the smile he was wearing.

"Have you been circumcised?"

Drexel looked from the knife to Oshun's smile and said, "Fuck."

1

The Observer
By
John Darr

"I think beyond the immediacy of this moment's observation to understand the deeper, long-range outcome."
Third Cardinal Rule of an Imperial Observer

-1-

The Black Economic Zone (BEZ) Number Six, Atlanta, Georgia is unlike most other zones and not just because of its hover lanes crisscrossing the skies above the elevated highways below. It is the heart of the Eight Guilds and the Zones, the advanced scientific and cultural enclaves in which we live.

I gaze out on the busy vista that never ceases to impress me. Since it isn't often that I venture out of my lab in southern Maryland to come south, I linger at the view from the slanted, two-story windows.

Standing between two Sweet Olive trees, the fragrant scent of the flower clusters tickling my nose, I can almost forget my junior researchers waiting nearby. They will not interrupt me, the Director of the Science Guild, Research and Development Branch. If I want to remain indefinitely, I can. But enough is enough. Deeply inhaling the almond scent one last time, I turn.

Behind me, throngs of people move along the Grand Concourse of the Guild's Worldwide Headquarters, located in the AUC section of the zone. Functionaries, councilors, Congress people and Guild members, all going about the important business of managing the Eight Guilds.

Sentry Agents, clad in their royal blue uniforms and posted along the corridor, are more ceremonial than for protection. The zones are free of any meaningful crime. With a silent signal, I send my group ahead to the shuttle bay. I want to take my time strolling there.

Half a dozen steps along the corridor, I catch a glimpse of a young man watching me from the meeting room side of the concourse. Pausing, I peer through the sea of brown faces, but the man is gone. No one else offers me more than a cursory glance or occasionally, a slight dip of the head in acknowledgement of my respectable position.

A sudden chill runs down my back and I clench my fists. I can only wonder why my heart rate spikes until I take a few deep, calming breaths. Maybe it is just my imagination. When I face the windows again, I spot the young man nearing a section of low-slung benches primarily used by visitors and tourists to take in the view.

Tall and well-built, the young man's ebony skin radiates the abundant health that all members of the zones exhibit. His charcoal grey suit is immaculate and the coat is cut in the latest Guild style. Curiously, the suit is plain with no sash or emblem to hint at his particular Guild affiliation.

"Excuse me, young man."

He turns to face me with a curious expression. "Yes?"

With an almost unconscious tugging on my light-blue sash, I nod to him. "Which Guild do you call home?"

"I do not belong to any Guild."

I blink hard at hearing that. "Are you a tradesman? I would have guessed you attended one of our colleges."

"I am not a tradesman. I am a chief organizer with the Cooperative."

My brows draw together. "What kind of organization is that?"

The young man scans my face as if searching for something. I don't know what, maybe to see if my ignorance is real.

"It is... " He pauses and then continues, "it's a movement."

"And you're a chief organizer?"

"Yes, I am."

"So," I begin slowly, slightly offended by his statement, "you don't believe in the saving graces of the Guild system?"

"No, we believe there is danger of stagnation in the present model."

My smile changes to a frown and my formally relaxed

posture becomes defensive as my muscles tighten. My back is rigid. By the time I ask my next question, even my tone has become harsher. "What is your movement about?"

"The Cooperative resists the rigidity of the Guild system. We believe this setup, despite its operation for nearly two-hundred years, is stifling growth. People should be able to choose their own life paths and change them whenever they want."

In my mind, I sense the beginning of a cognitive dissonance, but I can't help myself. "How can you not believe in the group economic system?"

The young man focuses on me with almost inhuman intensity. "Tell me, Doctor, why do you need to believe in that system?"

The question is devoid of any sarcasm, yet I grow increasingly agitated.

"I - I believe it. I have to believe it, otherwise all would be lost. We would be lost! Can't you understand that?" I shout the last sentence. Others turn our way. A Sentry Agent speaks into his vid-com while eyeing us. He moves from his post but I raise a hand to wave him off. The agent obeys, but remains vigilant.

"Doctor, I understand," the young man says, sounding so reasonable, it angers me even more.

A heat rises inside me. "We would be lost in a miserable existence," I practically wail.

He lifts his hands in a placating gesture. "I did not mean to upset you, sir." He glances at his chrono. "I have a shuttle to catch. Please, accept my apologies." With that, he leaves.

Pacing back and forth, alternating between tightening and relaxing my fists, I ignore the curious glances of the passersby. My ears ring and my breathing is heavy for several minutes before I can calm down. When I do, I sink onto one of the comfortable benches and stare out the window, but I don't see the Atlanta zone around me. It's all a blur as my sight focuses inward. I'm shocked at my own visceral reaction to the young man's simple questions. Even now as I replay the exchange, I realize he never lost his composure. Why did I react so strongly? And where did the sense of being lost and without hope come from?

As I stand up, I hastily smooth out my coat and sash. When I'm sure I can walk without my legs collapsing, I head for the hangar bay, far away from the unsettling encounter.

-2-

After a week of hiding in my lab, I need a diversion, and to my surprise I decide to go south again. Within fifteen minutes of disembarking at the Atlanta Zone Travelport, I'm down on street level in the zone, walking through central district. It is huge, dizzying, bustling with residents, Zoners. The borders of the zone begin along Northside drive to the east and extend west and south, going right through Vine City and Ashview Heights, past the HBCU's and onward to include large swaths of the surrounding southwestern neighborhoods and schools.

The welcoming aromas of various foods and southern delicacies reach my nostrils. The music is varied and mixed, causing my heart to race in time with each unique rhythm I encounter. The Zoners are vibrant and excited. I feel so enriched as I study the architectural stratification in the buildings. The original businesses were carefully preserved and renovated when the idea of the zone was implemented. Higher, modern buildings and condo complexes were added later. Those extend into the sky like spires. Each layer represents a different time from our past.

Taking in more and more of the sites, I eventually approach one of the VR Gaming Cafés. Garish, multicolor lights flash, drawing visitors like moths to a flame. I step through the entrance. Music blares from speakers while vid-screens blast high-def images of the latest sports games or videos. The energy in the establishment is almost palpable. The bass from the music literally rattles my bones as I move toward the gaming rooms.

Groups of young people prep to enter the simulators. They consult holo-screens, scrolling through options to pick the weapons, powers and other devices they will use as characters in the game. All wear the patented full-body suits with the VR goggles dangling from the clamps at their sides.

My contemplation is interrupted when I sense someone beside me: the young man from the Cooperative. I tense up at once; this couldn't be a coincidence. No doubt the young man wants to recruit me. *Or taint me.*

My voice is low and dangerous when I speak. "Are you following me?"

The young man blinks but doesn't seem wary. "We have a rally today and I was preparing the location when I saw you walking down the street."

That sounds probable, but the young man reignites a dread inside me. I slide a hand into my right pocket and grip my vidcom, ready to call a Sentry Squad.

Unaware of my discomfort, the young man nods toward the kids. "Have you observed how the young people immerse themselves in the game even before they enter the arena?"

"What of it?" I blurt out, caught off guard by his innocuous observation. I also hate to admit he is correct.

The young people are in character; talking and reacting to each other as their avatars within the game. Guild psychologists warned us that people would require time to transition back to the *real* world, hence the mandatory cool-down periods after each adventure.

Hearing a slight accusation in the young man's voice, I seek a rebuttal. "I've heard of actors in the fantasy holos who remain in makeup just to stay in character. It's quite similar here."

"Actors are always surrounded by the production crew and the real world," he replies. "These young people are totally engaged and become game pieces as they lose themselves in the environment. They forget they are players. As such, they are at the mercy of the programming and the probabilities contained therein."

"Probabilities?" The word ignites something inside me and my hand tightens around the vid-com.

"They are like the Zoners under the Guild system," the young man continues, "locked inside a program."

"Ah, I should have known you'd connect it somehow to your Cooperative ideology," I say, nodding. "Look around you, the system works."

"And a game simulation also works. What would happen if the players never woke up and simply lived out their lives according to the program?"

I'm stunned. "Is that all you think of the Guilds and zones? Just lifelong programs designed to put our people to sleep?" It is utterly astounding and all I need to hear. Yanking the vid-com out of my pocket, I raise it to my mouth to make the call.

The young man's hand snaps out so fast, it's almost a blur. He snatches the vid-com from my hand, actually injuring my finger. I recoil from his unexpected strike and the subsequent explosion of pain in my hand.

An emotion flits across his face: embarrassment. "I am sorry, Doctor. I didn't mean to hurt you. But I can't let you make that call." He squeezes the vid-com in his bare hand until it cracks and breaks. Pieces of the electronic device fall to the ground.

My feet are already moving on their own as I back away from him. The music is so loud, no one will hear any call for help. I need a Sentry. Even a Street Sentry would do.

"Doctor, please." The young man steps towards me.

I ignore the man's calls as I spot the side exit door. Hitting the release, I charge into a stairwell. A metal gate blocks the downward steps, so I head up the stairs. Perhaps I can evade my pursuer on the second floor or even by taking the maintenance walkways above the main floor.

But that door is locked.

"Doctor Ghee!" The young man's voice is surprisingly close.

Panic propels me onward. Using my entire body, I plow into the next door. Agony explodes across my shoulder, but the door swings wide and bangs against the side of the exit. Bright sunlight blinds me as I tumble out the door onto the roof.

The music from inside is a distant thump below as I regain my balance and move away from the door. Nearing the roof's edge, I look back, fully expecting to see the young man exit. He doesn't because he simply appears before me and grips my arms.

I struggle. "Let me go!"

Having learned the basics of self-defense, I catch him below the chin with an upward thrust of my right hand. Bad idea because it's still injured. Intense pain rolls up my arm. But the blow shocks the young man.

It's the opportunity I need, and I twist free of his grip only to slip. In that horrid moment of realization, I know I've fallen over the edge. There's nothing beneath me but a three-story drop to my death.

-3-

Excruciating pain explodes inside my head. I open my mouth to scream, but I can't hear my voice. But I'm alive, I assume, lifting to hand to rub my forehead. With a start, I remember falling, open my eyes, and jerk upright. I'm reclining on a low chair and not laying in the alleyway behind the café.

The room is large, possibly inside a home judging by the look and feel of the stylish furniture. Massive columns flank either side of the entrance and an embossed winged-sun disc is carved into the stone directly above. It's also reminiscent of an ancient temple.

Glancing down at myself, I notice the flowing priestly robes. I run my hands over the plush garments done in light blues and tans. Lifting one of the billowing sleeves to my nose, I sniff. It's neither cotton nor synthetic. *Mir.* The word comes unbidden to my mind. Mir is the native plant of this world.

Through a huge window, a pale sun slips lower as it sets. The sight stirs my memories. I'm on Menes Prime, the oldest colony of the Mu Empire, inside my family home. Rising from the chair, I cross over to the window, my sandaled feet making little sound on the soft stone floor. The sparsely populated planet still retains large swaths of the ancient, alien forests my ancestors discovered upon first settling it. This estate hugs the edge of a beautiful ravine.

The fading light of the sun casts its final rays through the large, multicolored windows, forming a giant Navigator's Wheel on the south facing wall. At night, the stars align with the coordinates programmed into the complex design of the wheel. I brush my hand along the patterns and it all comes back to me.

I'm reliving a memory, but why this particular one? I pull back my sleeve to expose my wrist and see the bio-chrono attached there. One look at the date and more details of the memory flood my mind. Today I had addressed the High Council to voice my opposition to the revisions to our history. As a member of one of the oldest houses, I led the charge.

My performance didn't sway the High Council, so I had returned home to await their final decision. Peering out the massive window, I focus on a particular star in the southern quadrant, a tiny, yellow orb that so many in the Empire would rather forget.

But why this memory? Why am I an observer as well as a participant of this recollection at the same time? The duality causes my head to painfully throb, but I sense it's imperative so I allow the memory to play out.

What's next? I wonder. *Ah, yes.* The Chief Attendant to the Supreme Imperial Observer will come to deliver the news. Right on cue, my niece, Noni, leads the tall, powerful man with deep ebony skin into the hall.

The Chief Attendant is clad in the standard, all black, military-style uniform with gold piping. His cap, with its pyramidal shape and gold-lined sides, frame his face, but in an odd way. I've always thought those caps looked rather uncomfortable. It bobs slightly as the man glances around the receiving hall.

Every Imperial Observer in my family, dating back more than twenty-five thousand years, is pictured on the walls in holos. At one time, Imperial Observers were the right hands of the King or Queen. As the kingdom and later the Empire expanded, along with our confidence in technology, military might, and predictive algorithms, the status of Observer gradually waned until the office of Supreme Imperial Observer lost all of its importance and grandeur.

Most of us are little more than historians and record clerks now, working close to the Inner Core. Remote, crewless listening posts on the frontiers conduct most of the direct observations now.

Crossing back to my chair, I sit and wait. The Chief Attendant is so engrossed, he's caught short by a signal from my niece. She's very professional and reveals no amusement as the man recovers before facing me.

Waiting a long beat, I finally ask, "What is the decision?"

"The High Council has proposed that all theories about the ancient star numbered 196525," he glances at the Navigator's Wheel a moment before going on, "be expunged from the official history of the Mu Empire. The approved and accepted explanation of our origin is that the Mu people arose from the local star sector twenty-five thousand years ago. Our Honorable King signed that clarification into law."

My fingers curl into claws, threatening to shred the chair's fabric. "So, our ancestors didn't flee here, trying to evade an ancient enemy?"

The Attendant shudders at my provocative words. He holds up the message cylinder in a shaky hand. It's archaic considering all the other ways of modern communication. But the Supreme Imperial Observer insists on important messages being presented this way. It was the man's pitiful attempt to hold onto a heritage he never understood. My lower lip twists in contempt.

Noni, displaying more common sense than I, retrieves the octagonal cylinder from the Attendant and crosses over to me.

"Here, Uncle," she whispers as her deep brown eyes burn into mine, pleading with me.

"Thank you," I finally reply. She nods, steps back, and stands tall. At my touch, the holo message appears mid-air: a large, semi-transparent rectangle of scrolling text.

I read and my frown deepens. "Why me and why this planet in the heart of the forbidden star system? Are trying to entrap me?"

The Chief Attendant glances around the chamber. "The Supreme Imperial Observer has been given dispensation to allow you to *indulge* your morbid curiosity about the so called Lost Ones a final time before travel to that sector is permanently banned." A smirk tweaks the corner of his mouth. Seeing my reaction, he tries to cover it up.

I shut off the holo-message with an angry click. "It's so far away! I'll have to cryo-sleep for nearly twenty cycles." I glance at my niece, who will be fully into adulthood by the time I can return. *Over forty cycles away!* Advancements over the millenia have increased the average life span of the Mu to well over three hundred cycles.

Even so, my niece will have changed considerably by the time I return, probably with a family and children of her own. I tap the cylinder against my thigh in irritation. It's clear my enemies want the most vocal member of the oldest family out of the way when the silent change happens. Why else send me so far beyond the range of the kingdom's explorations and military?

With effort, I pull back to watch the memory as an impartial observer. Something vital has been lost in the hearts and minds of the Mu people. I didn't sense it that day, but I'm detached enough to see it now. We've changed in a fundamental way that will lead to our inevitable decline.

The Chief Attendant clears his throat. "I'm sorry, but it's an order from the Supreme Imperial Observer."

Once the man leaves, my niece kneels beside my chair and places a hand on my forearm. "Should I call the others, Uncle?"

Our eyes meet. She's the image of her mother, my oldest sister. Already, she's poised to join the Expeditionary Ranks and journey to the farthest sectors of the realm.

As I smile at her, a massive headache overwhelms me and I sink to my knees. My vision blurs with the pain, forcing me onto my back before darkness descends.

* * *

I awaken in a cryo-chamber. Once again, the intense pain forces me to keep my eyes and remain still until it slowly recedes to a dull throb. When the nausea finally passes, I open my eyes while allowing the memories to return until I feel more settled in the strange duality of an observer and participant.

The chamber's inner display reports that nineteen-point-eight cycles have elapsed during my slumber. Of course. I'm on my ship. The journey to star 196525. As the chamber indicators switch to Cryo-Recovery, I'm suddenly reminded of unpleasantness of the process.

My legs and arms feel feeble and my chest seems sunken. The sudden change of position creates the instant pressure to relieve myself, which is something I never understood. After rehydrating myself, I shuffle into the cockpit. On the screen, an unremarkable, yet beautiful, orb rotates. Our world of origin. Already, I can tell they are primitive. There're no orbital platforms, no ship traffic, nor satellites. Nothing challenges or detects my sudden appearance in orbit.

"Prepare the probes and move into a stationary orbit." I feel the ship complying as the view changes and the planet looms closer. Moving to the record crystals, I access a location from a truly ancient family database. The destination is one of the largest continents on the planet.

"Position us over this location, Ship."

Leaving the details to the craft, I kneel in the center of the cockpit, bow my head and repeat the Cardinal Rules of the Imperial Observer. When I rise, ready to begin the long work of observation, the blinding headache returns. Only when my head smacks against the deck do I manage to register that I fell. I'm helpless as the agony and darkness overtake me.

* * *

Flashes of light. I glimpse the young man again. My eyes meet his and I plead, *Kill me and end this.* However, he doesn't acknowledge my request.

* * *

Analysis confirms we have arrived in what the inhabitants term the early nineteenth century.

Ship's announcement penetrates the darkness and my mind. I open my eyes and blink hard, looking around. The memories come quicker and I settle into the flow. Working my dry mouth, I say, "Repeat that, Ship."

Analysis confirms we have arrived in what the inhabitants term the early nineteenth century.

It's on the screen, I remind myself, scanning the data for a few more seconds. Right. We're in eighteen-nineteen, to be exact. The Lost Ones have survived. But my elation soon evaporates when I review the footage of their horrid living conditions. Their former highly advanced civilization crumbled as their collective knowledge dimmed. All the ancient abilities went into hibernation. And now the Lost Ones are truly lost. They are literally slaves: conquered, belittled and ruthlessly exploited.

The very thought of people who look like me being subjected

to the will of others is nearly overwhelming. We know nothing of this type of existence in the expanse of the Empire. Genuine tears fill my eyes for these forgotten people.

I am a Imperial Observer, I chide myself. Still, the data is numbing. Sudden pain stabs my forehead and the memory shifts. I'm an island at the center as everything else blurs. When my surroundings stabilize, I know this is the memory of the day I was to begin my journey home. Despite the depressing information I amassed, oh, how I longed to leave this sector of space.

Moving with the memory, I secure data crystals and re-enter the cockpit. I've satisfied my curiosity and theory. The Lost Ones survived, but perhaps it would have been better if they hadn't. Drawing in a deep breath, a say, "Take us home, Ship."

Yes, sir.

A profound sadness gnaws at me as I gaze at the sad planet below. Soon we will move away until it shrinks to no more than a pinpoint of light. Perhaps it is best we forget our true home. Guilt wells up inside me at the prospect of the long sleep and respite after dealing with this dismal world.

Without warning, the ship jerks and vibrates so hard, I lose my footing and tumble to the deck. "What's happening, Ship?"

We've developed a problem in the hyperdrive engines.

"How?"

That is not known.

"Why didn't you diagnose a problem before now?" Pulling myself back to my chair, I note the planet moving closer. "Ship, why are we moving toward Earth?"

We are caught in its gravity. The engine failure is cascading.

"Give me the controls," I order before maneuvering us through the atmosphere and into the thick cloud cover. The ride is rough and jarring but eventually we break out of the clouds. An expanse of blue-green, sparkling ocean appears below. I steer us towards the nearest continent. "Ship, find us an uninhabited destination!"

Located.

Using the coordinates, and with the ship's help, I bring us in low over the land and skim the tops of trees in what appears to be an almost endless forest. In the distance, a mountain range looms closer. As we reach the low hills, I take us down in a controlled crash landing. Loud creaks and groans announce our arrival as the craft settles on the uneven ground.

"Evaluate the vessel for more damage," I order, unbuckling myself. "I want to check the engines."

Yes, sir.

A thorough analysis of the engines confirms want I feared.

The engines were sabotaged, Ship reports.

Rage and disbelief battle inside me now that I've been betrayed and stranded on the other side of the galaxy. The memory of failure is as painful now as it was then. The scene blurs and moves while I remain still until the memories stabilize. On the center table is a set of data. I recognize this memory and my mouth moves without me having to think about it.

"Ship, open the predictive subroutines." Most Imperial Observers couldn't do that, but I was trained in the process.

The kingdom's scientists developed the predictive algorithms and field-tested their output over thousands of years. Once their accuracy was confirmed, they began employing the time projections after gathering data on other civilizations. While the first Cardinal Rule of an Imperial Observer forbids us to interfere, Mu military leaders used our analyses to predict, prepare and protect the Empire when eventual contact occurs.

I run a time projection with Ship, focusing on the Lost Ones. I want to know if they will develop a brighter future. It's all academic, of course. There's no one to peruse my results. But what else can I do?

Time projection complete.

Eagerly, I review the report. While current conditions for the Lost Ones will improve, eventually they will experience near total extinction, something that reignites my barely contained panic.

The memory shifts around me again. Now, I'm bent over the time projection results and poised to do something a Imperial Observer should *never* do: introduce changes into the time projection. The memory shifts over and over with increasing speed as multiple phantoms of myself test thousands of false starts with equally grim results.

When the memory ends, and my phantoms converge into one person, the disorientation is so severe, I have to lean on the table and take a deep breath to quell my queasy stomach. My eyes focus on the latest result. It is the one change that actually worked. Falling into the memory flow, I send the simulation to the mind-projector chamber.

May I remind you, sir, you are a Imperial Observer?

"I know, Ship. But I want to see the simulation from the inside." I enter the chamber, making final adjustments to the simulation before sitting in the chair. As I lean back, light emitters activate, one aimed at each temple. They will facilitate the exchange of data directly with my mind.

"It's research," I explain to Ship. "Activate simulation 123048."

* * *

Darkness, again.

"Sir?"

Ship's inquiry enhances my senses. I can feel the hard pavement beneath my body and I smell the wet odor of recent rain falling on the pavement. Strangely, I can hear nothing but my own breathing. Not even the young man's movements are discernible. Slowly, I open my eyes to stare at a cloudy sky above.

"Sir? Let me help you."

The young man helps me sit up. Looking around the alley behind the Virtual Café, I don't see any people. That explains the lack of standard noise. I twist around to peer at the wet ground. Water, not blood. Even so, I touch the back of my head. Though it still throbs, my skull isn't fractured.

The young man patiently waits as realization washes over me. "How long have I been in the simulation, Ship?"

The ship's avatar smiles. "A week, Imperial Observer S'Kenkique."

The news shocks me. "I could have starved to death." My throat rasps with a burning sensation like I haven't used my voice in days.

"Your body has been conditioned to store necessary nutrients in the event of unexpected long periods without food. You are not at the critical stage, yet."

I close my eyes and swallow hard to moisten my throat as I try to alleviate the soreness. Beyond the burning hunger in my stomach and the rawness of my throat, there's the shame of losing myself in my own mind-projection.

"End the simulation."

The world around me disappears to reveal the dark metal surface of the Mind-Projection room. Two slender arms, their ends still shining with brilliant, bluish light, recoil from me.

As I flex my stiff fingers and move my sore arms, a slot in the floor beside the chair opens and a cup of liquid appears. I sip the warm stimulant, letting the moisture coat my throat until it doesn't ache as badly.

The avatar remains since we are still inside the chamber. "You accessed my personal memory projections. Why?"

"As you know, if a person dies inside a simulation, while believing the simulation is real…"

"They die in the real world. I needed to understand where I was and what was happening."

"Correct, sir."

I shake my head and try to stand. My legs are weak from non-use. I grip the headrest on the chair to steady myself, pausing to re-set myself in the real world. Maybe I need my own cool-down period after the simulation. Eventually, the stimulant works its magic and a slender finger of energy begins to flow through me. I hobble to the door, which opens at my approach.

Turning to the avatar, I say, "I'm tired of this chamber."

-4-

Over the next few days, I spend time reviewing the data collected by the ship remotes. Like a ticking clock in the back of my mind, the countdown to the nexus point approaches. It's the precise moment in the simulation when I introduced the change that lead to a brighter future for the Lost Ones. But that was a mind-projection. Can I intervene in the real world to initiate a new time branch? I'm a Imperial Observer. We don't interfere. Not ever.

Suddenly, I recall Ship's words in his guise as the young man. Am I reacting to my own programming? Can I move beyond that limitation and ritual drilled into my kind over thousands of years by ceremony? Or is my reluctance to act rooted with indifference to the plight of the Lost Ones? As Imperial Observers, we tended to ensconce ourselves in our codes while observing the plights of others from a superior position and never offering help.

Now, in extremis, stuck on this primitive world, and cut off from all the trappings of my civilization, will I abandon my vaunted Observer Codes to save myself? Is that it?

"Ship? What if I choose to live among the Lost Ones?"

You would have to live as they do, suffer as they do, and not introduce any changes into the timeline.

"Or, I could continue my job as a Imperial Observer until I die in this..." I look around myself, "vessel."

Yes.

That option doesn't appeal to me. And going into cryogenic sleep for hundreds more cycles in the hope that the Earthlings will progress far enough to help me isn't an option either, according to the time projection.

While I don't voice my decision, my actions reveal it. I'm making preparations, the first of which is to move the ship. Scanners reveal a cave near the base of a nearby mountain. I fly Ship into that and, using the limited weapons on board, collapse the opening behind me. It takes me a little time to burrow a shaft to the outside and fabricate a concealed doorway.

That done, I assign Ship the job of producing period clothes, locating a place for me to live, and providing the money and credentials I'll need to launch my plan. I know where my contact resides and have already developed a cover story. I'm ready for the nexus moment.

Most people think a nexus moment has to be a great act. That's not true. Time has an inertia factor and the biggest events are the most difficult to change in a direct manner. The best way to effect change is with minor course corrections. Over time, that process can yield a huge difference in destination. In the minutia, I chose from a small number of correction points, one that could best affect everything else to my needs.

Once the new time branch is in motion, I'll retreat to my ship to sleep. At several pre-selected times, I'll resurface under a new persona and make sure the path is secure. The estimate is two hundred Earth years. Even with my kind's extended life-span, it's better to use the cryo-chamber to preserve myself. I was already one-hundred-and-fifty, by Earth reckoning, when I arrived.

The day comes for me to leave the ship. I collect my things and place them by the exit. Last of all, I remove my badge of vocation. I'm not a Imperial Observer anymore, not in the true sense. Besides, I can't take it with me.

"It may be a few weeks before I contact you again."

Understood, sir.

I gather up my bags, exit the ship and start walking up the passage to the surface. The bright sun feels warm today when I open the concealed hatch to the outside world. In fact, the sun is almost blinding after the dim confines of my ship. Taking one last look around me, I step away from my cocoon into a new future of my own making.

One hundred and ninety-eight years later...

The day is clear and I gaze out the large window at the sky lanes over Atlanta's zone. My vantage point, a guest office on the twenty-eighth floor of the Guild Headquarters Building, the *real* building, is spectacular.

Closing my eyes, I whisper the third Cardinal Rule of a Imperial Observer. "I think beyond the immediacy of this moment's observation to understand the deeper, long-range outcome."

By the third repetition of the admonition, calm returns to my thoughts. Everything is so fragile at this stage that I need to remain clear in order to focus on all that has been accomplished.

The Eight Guilds were created and the economic zones for blacks were erected around the country. The Lost Ones have lived and thrived in these strongholds of culture and group economics for nearly two-hundred years, all protected by a dedicated force: the Sentry Corps. One day soon, their science will advance enough for me to repair Ship and return home.

That thought excites as well as worries me. What will have become of my family after two hundred cycles? How much will the Empire have transformed in my absence? Will I be considered an enemy of the realm? They banished me here. How will the High Council and the King respond when I appear with Lost Ones?

Of lesser concern to me is the violation of my oath as an Observer. A change has come over me while living among the Lost Ones. They are truly my kin. And they will be a great people, perhaps greater even than the Mu people.

At long last, I begin to understand the reasons our civilization chose to forget its origins, beyond the communal shame of our only true defeat. Our leaders, well, all of us actually, wanted to avoid a collective sense of guilt for leaving the Lost Ones behind. It remains a twenty-five-thousand-year stain on our consciousness.

The cosmos knows how these people survived as long as they did, in this harshest of all training grounds. They are a new creation, long beyond what their ancestors were, and dissimilar to the current citizens of the Mu empire. These Lost Ones are unique because of what they had to endure.

I see my crash landing as the will of the Universe. It was time to quicken their progression and bring them home. Whether I live long enough to see it happen or not, one day, they will overtake their brethren among the stars.

Impundulu
By
L. M. Davis

The sky was that wide expanse of purply periwinkle only imaginable in that part of the world. A color somehow still possible despite everything else that had changed.

White light, bursting from an untraceable source, arched across the sky. It could have been from a storm hundreds of miles away or from the heavens themselves. It touched ground at some unseeable point in the distance and a boom of thunder followed.

The lightning did not stir the oldish woman, who puttered in the sparse garden in front of the shotgun house that was little more than a glorified shed. She had long grown accustomed to flashes that never ceased, day or night. The thunder, however, made her jump. Her partner, who watched from the shade of the covered porch, laughed.

"Dang near twenty-five years, Elise, and it still gets you every time."

Beneath the wide brim of her straw hat, Elise scrunched up her face at the gentle ribbing. She had not always been afraid of the thunder, but two and a half decades of daily lightning storms had whittled away at her calm. Not the lightning. That was no threat. They always knew exactly where it would land—within the city limits—and what it would destroy—anything it struck. The thunder, though, that was sometimes so fierce and loud that it shook the house, the ground, hell the whole world around them, even though they were more than thirty miles away.

Elise stood and turned toward Atlanta. She wiped the film of sweat just below the rim of her hat as she gazed toward the skyline that was little more than a ghostly gray outline of decimated buildings.

"Seems like it's happening more frequent the last few days, don't it?" she asked. She turned toward Lyn who was now leaning against the banister. "They never did figure out what it is, hunh? All those geological and meteorological surveys and not a clue?'

Lyn's eyes lit up and Elise knew exactly why. It was not often she got a green light to muse about the lightning storms. Strange as the lightning was, both in its constancy and destructive capacity, after twenty-five years, everyone around just accepted it as a matter of fact. For Lyn, it would never be that simple. She had been born and raised right in the middle of the city. She was a refugee from the lightning when the always smoldering fire made the city too dangerous to live in. Too perilous to protect.

Before Lyn even said a word, the light drained from her face. A cloud, the only one for miles around, settled over her features. Her next words were a whisper.

"Elise. Get over here now."

Elise didn't hesitate even for a moment. Thirty years of living with and loving Lyn had taught her to read the woman like a book. She started to walk slowly toward the house, something in Lyn's voice urging both calm and haste simultaneously. Fear leapt to life in her breast as Lyn's concern coalesced into a low-grade terror. She did not look at Elise, but rather the woman's gaze remained trained on something behind her.

As soon as she reached the bottom of the stairs, Lyn grabbed Elise, snatching her into her arms. Lyn's heart pounded wildly, and Elise could see and feel the way she trembled. Her arms went around the woman, her own fear subsumed by her need to comfort her love.

"It's okay," she soothed. "I'm okay."

Lyn's grip slackened. Not much, but enough for Elise to look over her shoulder to discern the cause of the woman's fear.

A dog-like creature—a bewildering amalgam of brown, hair-like fur and stripes, snout and claws—stood fifteen yards from them. Elise's heart jumped. She turned to apprehend the animal more fully, which carefully considered them in turn.

"Is that a…hyena?"

The creature perked up, seemingly at the recognition.

"How on earth did that get here?"

Terminus[2]

* * *

The hyena didn't know how it had gotten there either.

Standing on the line between soil and the hard, circular, black road that dead-ended at the house, it had no memory before that moment. No memory before the word hyena, partly a question, tethered its consciousness to this plane, this reality, this body. Where it had been before, what it had been, was ether.

It studied the women entangled with each other and sniffed the sharp tang that wafted from them, making them smell like food. White light crackled overhead....

...Different limbs, dark and sinewy, intertwine. Not just arms but also legs. Skin smoother than velvet and darker than the night sky....

...Thunder boomed. So loud the pebbles between its toes quivered. Pain lanced through the creature. That and the shaking ground was almost enough to bring it to its knees. Its anguished howl rent the air.

The women jumped and the mouthwatering smell grew stronger. The hyena considered them again, its eyes tracing the contours of their interwoven limbs, but its curiosity had diminished. A different kind of hunger called it now.

The one not called Elise backed toward the house. Without taking her gaze from the animal, she yanked open the screen door and shoved Elise inside. In the same motion, she reached for the shot gun that always rested near the door.

But before she could even get the chamber loaded, the hyena was already gone.

* * *

As much as it could, it stayed within the trees, away from the humans and the sounds of racking shotguns, tracking toward the place where the lightning touched the ground. The lightning summoned it, and this confounded the creature as much as the mystery of its own existence. Still, it followed that instinct. The only one it knew.

Lightning glinted....

...Feathers as white as the lightning, maybe made
from the light itself, rustle around the hyena, pulsing like
a cocoon. They dance across its body, tickling everywhere they touch....

...Thunder rumbled. The hyena laughed, the eerie sound fill-
ing and echoing through the twilight dark. It laughed for the loss
of the vision that tickled and teased the half-forgotten memories
that wounded both body and soul. The hyena wanted desperately
to grasp them but shrank away from them at the same time.

* * *

Its pace was dogged. It should have been tired. It could not
remember the last time it had slept. It should have been hungry.
Had it ever eaten before? But its body could not rest or pause.
Something deep beneath the level of subconscious spurred it forward.

Houses and streets flashed by, a blur in its peripherals. It
could not even see what was right in front of it. Not really. The
terrain just did not register. Its tunnel vision focused wholly on
something it could not see but knew was there.

The nearer it drew to the city, the more frequent the lightning
came. White light traced jagged patterns across the moonless
sky, the thunder's boom almost simultaneous with the flares.
Each sequence carried a new fragment of memory. Each sliver
more vivid, more telling, than the last.

Lightning flashed and flashed....

...A gown, white as the feathers, hem red from the
clay in the dirt. A body in ecstatic communion with ancestors and gods. A dance like the swooping, the gliding,
the diving of flight....

58

…Faces. So many different faces. All the colors of the African lands. The deep black of the Dinka and the gold of the Berbers. The sienna of the San, the dark amber of the Amhara, and the umber of the Xhosa. All present on this ground, the soil red as though it had been watered with blood. They bow at the red-stained hem of the white gown. They carry offerings and promises. They plead for vengeance. In the homeland, they never would have come, but here they needed power more than a scapegoat….

…Thunder clapped.

The hyena's pace was erratic. Each memory was like being struck by lightning. They jarred, plunging deep into its body and exploding cells. They flashed behind its eyes rearranging molecules until it wondered if it might survive. Lightning turned the black night gray….

…The city is on fire. Burning to the ground. Soldiers dressed in navy wield torches not guns, but all around them, lightning rains. The lightning does not stop for three full days. Nothing is left behind….

…A sobbing woman. A small sepia print in her hand. On the card, the image of a man, her husband, whose limp feet point toward the ground they will never touch again. She will have her vengeance too, though it will take its time. This is the promise she receives….

…Thunder roared.

Every nerve ending fried, and every synapse sizzled. The hyena burned from the inside out. It lurched a few steps more, its body went rigid, and its heart stopped.

* * *

I am changed when I awake. Still a hyena. Still in pain. My body and mind are all together fragmented and bonded. Through the night, the visions have given me new form and shape. New understanding too; I know now what is calling me.

My bodies, because there are more than one, move with new purpose. Now I know I am going to the place I have always been since I have come to this new world. I am going home, and I will find my most precious treasure there.

The lightning still streaks, each serrated arch bringing another memory or vision. Many bring grief and longing, not just my own. But some carry joy. They hurt less because I am hungry for them. I embrace them greedily, devouring each new piece of me that is returned.

I reach the river.

* * *

The line of demarcation is clear because the lightning adheres to a celestial mathematics. On this side, life of all kinds. Above me, leaves shiver in a breeze that does not reach the ground. Around me bursts of wildflower color peeks from beneath the thin cover of recently fallen leaves. Behind me, the sounds of cars, the ring of voices, and the buzz of humanity.

On the far side, not death but desolation. Across the way, ghost-gray skeletons of trees dapple a barren hill. Nothing moves or scurries either on the ground beneath the timber carcasses or in the world beyond. It is silent, but silence on a precipice. Silence waiting to roar.

Perhaps this is my doing. Vengeance is a slow brew and cannot be recalled no matter how much times have changed. Perhaps this is just decades upon decades, centuries upon centuries, of chickens coming home to roost.

I step into the water. Lightning lances the waves that lap the distant edge. The jolt ripples across the surface....

....Grief hits like a hammer. This is not my memory nor is it something we shared. This is years of separation. This is decades of searching and sorrow....

My heart, just beginning to mend, breaks beneath the weight of it. I was right and wrong. This is my doing, but this is not reprisal. This is loss, confusion, and fear. This is a longing as old as time and the despair of its constant frustration. This is all for me.

I am so deeply sorry.

*   *   *

I swim toward the far shore. It hasn't all come back to me, but I understand I have been gone too long. I can't remember how I died the last time, but I must have been unprepared for my memories—my entire sense of self—to be so completely lost.

The lightning dances along the edge of the water. The strikes less chaotic, less of a rage of sadness and loss. It knew I was here. It knew that I had returned, and the joy in my heart is its joy as well. As soon as my paws touch the sand of the shore, lightning rains down. The whole world goes white.

> …A flash of a smile. Another kind of brightness; a different sort of electricity. Everything I have longed for regardless of my form….

> …Kisses, sweet and searing, stolen from the gods in the moments we occupy the same plane in harmonious bodies….

These visions hurt but heal. The fragments that were my mind and my spirit meld together and I am almost whole.

*   *   *

The wholeness is all that it takes, and the hyena body can no longer confine me. I keep it though because its sure paws serve. I hurry up the hill, out of the woods, and on to the road.

Atlanta is in shambles. Charred and exploded bits of tree clutter my path. Pillars of smoke from buildings smolder on the horizon. Even in the middle of 75, at the peak of rush hour, I am safe. The chaos of my absence has made humans scarce. They dare not even use the roads to cut through town. The burned-out husks—cars that have failed in the attempt—litter the lanes.

Each lightning strike is fuel that makes me indefatigable. Fast as any car, I sprint between lanes, dodging abandoned vehicles before exiting on the ramp at the center of the city. I don't slow even for a moment as I turn east and trot beneath the overpass.

I am in my element, on the ground that has been my home since before the city had a name, when the land still belonged to the future generations of Mvskogee* and Aniyvwiya* who never, ever ceded it. It is mostly the same as it has been for more than a century; the brown-bricked storefronts interspersed with churches as majestic as its folks could build, which was quite grand. I remember these streets crowded with people bursting with jubilance. At the same time, so much has changed since last I stood here, that I don't even recognize it.

The neighborhood is a ruin that I can only partially claim. These abandoned buildings, these trash strewn streets are the legacy of decades of disregard that was never quite repaired. This somberness, the forsakenness, these streets have seen that before too. The memories layered one over the next like a veil.

New buildings, in similar shades of brown, show jagged, grinning, funhouse mouths where their beautiful multistory windows used to be. Colorful bits of stained glass that formerly graced rose windows bite into my paws as I pass. These and the blackened facades of buildings hollowed by fire and then decay, the bitter scent of burning rubber, and the smell of ozone are my responsibility alone.

The lightning flashes, tightening the perimeter around me. Each time I change my course and go to the place where it touches the ground. But I am behind before I even start to run. So, at MLK's memorial I stop. Without a target, without me as a guide, the strikes remain imprecise. He will land when and how he can, but he will find me. I just have to be still.

Terminus[2]

* * *

Patiently impatient, I wait. Twenty-something years have delayed my return, I can wait at least this long. Lightning lands and I mark it in my periphery …

   …A warm vise encircles me now that the
   work is done, our souls intertwine in a communion that sustains us; that allows us to do the work
   that we only do for others and never for ourselves. This bond makes it possible for us to go
   on.…

   …Glass, from a window long shattered, tinkles as the world and not just the ground rumbles.

My body changes with each burst, straining to become the being that can receive and return such caresses. The memories have done their work. I am malleable inside, and I use the thoughts I need to reshape this flesh.

* * *

Behind me, a blinding light flashes. I whirl to see the white arch of outstretched wing and the deep black sinew of shoulder and neck. With the dimming of the light, he is gone.

My heart is louder than the thunder. It—and not the quaking ground—shakes my entire being. He is not a memory, but the tool of my craft in the flesh. My familiar. My lightning. My god. My love.

I follow the strikes to catch glimpses. The broad, deep chest. The smooth, hairless head. The avian gaze that pierces to my core. The smile so wide, so joyful, that tears spring to my eyes and the same smile curves on my lips.

The air around me sizzles. The fine hairs that line my now human arms stand on end. The sky overhead crackles. I look up as the energy coalesces. At its center, he is a winged darkness. The light races toward the earth. I reach out to grab it.

* * *

Elise and Lyn sat on the porch, gazing toward the city.

"How long's it been?"

Elise looked at her watch. "About five hours."

It might have been longer than that. They had awakened late that morning.

"What do you think it means?"

Elise shook her head and frowned. The periwinkle dome arched overhead, unbroken by white light for the first time in more than a quarter century.

"Maybe it will finally be safe again."

Elise reached for Lyn's hand. Together, they watched the sky.

THE END

This story is inspired by South African lore about the Impundulu or the Lightning Bird. Just as the Africans who came to this country during the transatlantic slave trade came from all across the continent, so too might their supernatural beings. And as Africans were changed by their experiences with the institution of slavery and its aftermath, this story imagines how those beings might have changed and what they might become in this land.

Carnival
By
Milton J. Davis

Antwon was late. He rushed out his Peachtree Street flat as he summoned a Rideout and the electric transport appeared moments later, scanning the young mixer for his ID and payment. Antwon jumped in and the door closed.

"King Center Art Gallery," he said. "High priority."

"Insufficient credit," the car replied.

Antwon slammed his fist on the empty seat.

"Scan for ride share options," he said.

The car hummed before answering.

"Ride share confirmed. Please buckle your seat belt and thank you for choosing Rideout for your transportation needs."

Antwon buckled up then leaned back into his seat, pissed. The latest song by Prince, Inc. filled the cabin as the Rideout lifted into aerial traffic. If his account was short that meant Antwon's payment didn't go through. That was the second time. There wouldn't be a third.

He tapped his band and the holoscreen hovered before his eyes.

"Damarius Taylor," he said.

The screen pulsed for a moment before an image Damarius appeared a wide grin on his brown bearded face.

"There he is!" Damarius said. "Man, this shit is ice!"

Damarius took off his shirt then extended his muscular arms. His tats illuminated then danced about his body. Antwon did do good work. He tapped his band and the tats went dark. Damarius looked stunned.

"What the fuck?"

"Dee, where's my cred?"

Damarius was still staring at his torso.

"Your what? What the hell just happened?"

"Mufa where's my cred?" Antwon shouted.

Damarius glared at Antwon. "You shut me down? You shut me down! Man, I paid your ass!"

"My account is short the same amount you owe. You didn't pay me kaka."

"Quit fucking with me Twon," Damarius said. "I made the trans while you were walking out the door!"

"I'm not arguing with you, bwoi." Antwon shut down the comm. The Rideout rose to the fifth level then eased down on a condo plat. The door slipped open and an umber woman wearing a tight-fitting kente dress and matching headwrap entered the lift and sat beside him.

"Piedmont District," the woman said.

"Thank you for choosing Rideout," the lift responded. The door closed and the lift maneuvered into the swirling traffic.

"Nice outfit," Antwon said.

The woman turned to him and smiled.

"Thank you . . .oh my ancestors! Antwon Green!" The woman squealed then clapped her hands. "I'm sharing a lift with Twon the Don!"

No matter how many times it happened Antwon was always flattered and somewhat embarrassed when people recognized him. The woman opened her purse and her phone emerged, rising over her head.

"Look y'all! I'm riding a Lift with Twon the Don!"

Antwon waved. "Hello friends of the woman in the fiya dress."

"Kecia," the woman said. "My name is Kecia Thomas. I was at your Solstice set two years ago. It was my life!"

"I'm glad you enjoyed it. It was hot."

"So, what you doing for Carnival?" Kecia asked.

"Can't tell you," Antwon replied. "All I can say is that it will be unforgettable."

"Better than Solstice?"

Antwon smiled. "Life ending."

"Piedmont District" the lift announced.

Kecia opened her purse and her phone descended into it. They stared at each other in silence. Kecia finally blushed.

"This is my stop," she said.

"Yes, it is," Antwon replied.

"You know, my plans are flexible."

Antwon laughed. "Mine aren't. It was nice meeting you, Kecia."

Kecia lunged at him, wrapping him in a tight hug. She smelled of mangoes.

"You are so ice!" she said. "I can't wait to see what you do for Carnival!"

The lift door slid open and Kecia climbed out of the lift.

"You have a nice day, Kecia," Antwon said.

Kecia waved as the lift door closed. Antwon's phone buzzed; he looked at it and saw Kecia's number. He quickly deleted it. The phone buzzed again and Damarius's face appeared.

"Check your account," he said.

Antwon punched up his account. The creds were there.

"Thank you, bwoi," Antwon said.

"Now turn my tats back on," Damarius said. "I got a date to-night."

"Done," Antwon said. "And never call me again."

Damarius's eyes went wide. "Wait, bruh! You ain't gonna . . ."

Antwon cut him off, deleted his number and blocked him.

"Broke ass," he whispered.

The Rideout descended to ground level, landing wheels drop-ping as it touched pavement. It rolled to a stop before the King Center Art Gallery.

"Thank you for choosing Rideout," the car said. "Have a blessed day."

Antwon skipped to the Center door, which slid open when it recognized his ID.

"Twon!"

Marissa jogged up to him and gave him a warm hug and a quick dap.

"You're late," she said as she passed him a joint. Twon took a deep toke then coughed.

"Shit! Where'd you get this?"

"Rocky Mountains Hydro," Marissa answered. "Only the best for the best."

She grabbed his arm then dragged him across the gym floor to the dance hall.

"Kye and Dame have been going at it since daybreak," she said. "They killing it."

She extended the joint to Antwon and he waved it away. One drag and he was probably going to be high the rest of the week. When he entered the dance hall he smiled. The room shook with old school soca and like Marissa said, Kye and Dame were killing it. He almost began dancing but didn't. He was as bad a dancer as he was a good DJ, and he was the best DJ in the world.

He watched them dance for few more minutes, his smile matching his high. Kye and Dame were money well spent. Carnival was going to be so ice.

Kye was spinning when she saw him. She stopped then glared at him.

"Music off," she said. "Where have you been?"

Antwon walked toward Kye, his arms outstretched for a hug. Kye hit him in the chest with the palm of her hand.

"Where are our costumes?" she said.

Antwon dropped his arms to his side and made an exaggerated sad face.

"What? I've been waiting all day . . . oomph!"

Kye hit him in the chest again, this time harder.

"Stop playing with me," she said. "We're only a month away from Carnival. We should be dancing in our costumes right now. And what about the holos? I hope we didn't get these implants for nothing."

"The costumes are on the way," Antwon promised. "I talked to JaBarr and Dean two days ago and they're almost done. As for the holos, let's see how they work."

A smile broke like sunshine on Kye's face.

"Put on your skins," Antwon said.

Kye skittered across the floor, grabbed Dame then dragged him into the dressing room. They returned a moment later, the dance skins clinging to their every contour. Antwon lost concentration staring at Kye's perfection. Her hands went to her hips and she frowned.

"Twon, concentrate," she said.

"What . . .oh yeah, right. Lights!"

The lights dimmed. Antwon pulled up his shirt sleeve, revealing his touchpad on his forearm. It was old school, but Antwon liked tapping the screen in time with the music. This task, however, didn't require rhythm. He punched in the code and the holo costumes appeared. Marissa almost dropped her joint.

"Ice!" she exclaimed.

Kye and Dame hurried to the nearest mirror.

"What do you think?" Antwon said.

Kye shrugged. "It's alright. I've seen Trinnies with better."

Antwon chuckled. He knew Kye was going to say that.

"Music," he said.

Kye and Dame took the queue. They danced, the holo-costumes synching with their every move. Antwon tapped the buttons and the costumes changed colors in rhythm with the music. He saw a smile come to Kye's face.

"This is better," she called out. "Can't win with this, though."

"You haven't seen it all," Antwon called back.

"When?" Dame said.

"Carnival."

Kye and Dame kept dancing with angry faces. Antwon laughed.

"Don't worry. It will be amazing. You just keep doing what you're doing. I'll handle the rest."

He swiped his hand over the pad, sharing the code with Kye.

"Keep practicing. I'll be back in a few days."

"Where are you going?" Dame asked.

Antwon looked at Marissa. "Where am I going?"

"Mile High," Marissa answered.

"Really? Ice!"

"Mile High!" he yelled out as he and Marissa walked away.

He turned back to Marissa.

"She's in Mile High? You sure?'

Marissa shook her head. "No. Nothing's sure with her. It's the best lead I got. The note said go to Mile High. Once you get there check into the Snowcap Hotel. She'll find you from there. If she wants to."

Antwon gave Marissa dap. "I owe you."

Marissa grabbed his arm. "Hey, why don't I come with you? We can finish this." She patted her pants pocket.

"Not tonight," Antwon said. "I got to lay some tracks tonight then pack. Rain check, okay?"

Marissa looked crestfallen. "Okay, cool. Next time."

"Solid."

Antwon summoned a Rideout as he left the building. He laughed out loud as he waited. If Marissa came to his flat with weed and let those dreads out, there would be no tracks and no Mile High for at least three days. He couldn't be distracted. Everything was about Carnival.

He jumped into the Rideout to his building. Antwon moved two years ago when his former flat became too small. He needed more terabytes for his business and the burb flats didn't have the capacity. So, he put in a request for a Flat in the Pit. He thought it would take longer than it did, but celebrity has its privileges. The Rideout dropped him off and security scanned him in. Seconds later he was on the 52nd floor bouncing to his room, the tracks floating together in his head. By the time he entered his flat, he had at least three tracks. He didn't make it to the bedroom, dropping everything on the floor as he went directly to his tables. His fingers flowed across the board, the music running like sweet water. It was going to be a long, beautiful night.

* * *

Antwon's alarm shoved him out of the bed at exactly 12:30 pm. He lay still, his eyes opening to the graffiti mural on his ceiling. Last night's session went way too long, but he was feeling it and couldn't let go. And Marissa showed up anyway. There was no saying no to her, especially with her dreads loose. He sat up to look at his bed then smirked. Marissa was gone. The only sign of her was the lingering smell of weed and cocoa butter.

Antwon stumbled to the shower. He called up the Tube schedule to Mile High as he showered. He had two hours before the next ride, which was plenty of time. The jets dried him as he called up last night's mixes then swiped them to his waiting clients. The crypts showed up in his account seconds later. He was looking in his closet debating whether to pack or buy clothes when he got to Mile High when his forearm buzzed. It was Kye.

"What's up, beautiful?"

"Hey, handsome. Me and Dame were up all night working on the routine. We made a few changes."

Kye's image was replaced with the duo working it out, holo-costumes and all. Antwon's eyes teared up.

"That's amazing," he said.

"It could be even more amazing if I knew what to expect at Carnival," she said.

"Just keep doing what you're doing," Antwon said. "It will all come together. I promise."

"C'mon Antwon!" Kye pleaded. "Give me something!"

"Can't," Antwon said. "Trust me."

Kye scowled then broke contact. Antwon shook his head. He wanted to tell her; hell, he wanted to tell everybody. But there was no such thing as a secret once a word's been spoken. Truth was he didn't know if things would come together. He wouldn't know until he went to Mile High.

Antwon arrived at the Tube ten minutes before departure with a small bag. He decided he didn't want to take the time to shop, and who knew what the trends in Mile High were? He was not going to be tacky. Each Urb had its own flavor, and Antwon preferred Aytee-El's.

The tube was crowded but not packed. Antwon killed the four hours working on new mixes and tracks, ignoring the people staring at him and trying to get his attention. He was relieved when they reached Mile High. He rushed to the exit with his single bag and jumped on the escalator to the surface. He was greeted by a stunning view of the snow-capped Rockies. In five more years, if all went well, people would one day be able to visit them again. Antwon was looking forward to it.

He pulled up directions to the Snowcap Hotel while paging a Rideout when the signal was interrupted. A face filled the screen; a brown-skinned woman wearing hoop earrings and shades with a flowered headwrap smiled at him.

"Hi Antwon. Welcome to Mile High. There's been a change of plans. I need you to go to the Environmental Transition Office. A Rideout is on its way to pick you up."

"How do I know this is legit?" Antwon asked.

The woman smiled. "You don't. But you've come this far. You might as well go all the way."

Antwon was about to reply when the Rideout appeared.

"Fleek!" Antwon whispered as he climbed inside.

"Welcome to Mile High, Antwon Green. Thank you for choosing Rideout."

The Rideout whisked him to the city. Antwon was disappointed he didn't have time to sightsee, but he was there for business, possibly the most important business of his life. Carnival was always important; it was the biggest audience for his skills. But this one was special. He was betting all on this one, and he was in the Mile High to make sure it was beyond his best.

The Rideout climbed to high traffic as it continued through Mile High. They were passing through the main city and into the urbs. Antwon drummed his fingers on his thigh. Where exactly was this thing taking him?

"Rideout, confirm destination," he said.

"That information is confidential," the EV replied.

"Confidential? What the fleek do you mean confidential?"

"The renter has requested that the location remain confidential. If you feel threatened, you can terminate the service at any time."

It was decision time. If he walked away Carnival was fleeked. If he stayed Carnival still might be fleeked. He threw up his hands then slumped in his seat.

The Rideout took him to the skirts, landing before a small windowless square building. The door lifted and Antwon was blasted with frigid air.

"Thank you for choosing Rideout. Have a blessed day."

Antwon took his bag and stepped out the EV. He was so cold he shook.

"Somebody needs to turn it up!" he shouted.

The door to the square building opened and a woman he recognized from his cell emerged. She ambled up to Antwon, extending her hand.

"Antwon Green?" she asked.

"The one and only."

"I'm Kadisha Simone. Follow me."

"Where are we going?" Antwon asked.

"Outside," Kadisha replied.

Antwon laughed. "Yeah, right. Look Kadisha, I didn't come all the way here to play games. Just take me to Set. We got business."

"If you want to meet Set, we have to go Outside."

Antwon stopped. "We can't! Rangers only, remember? What kind of krak is this?"

"I'm a ranger," Kadisha said. "So is Set. And today, you are, too."

Kadisha entered the building. Antwon didn't move.

"Antwon?" Kadisha called out. "You're wasting time. I thought you didn't want to do that."

"Fleek!" he said. "Fleek, fleek, fleek!"

He picked up his bag and followed Kadisha into the building.

"Here." Kadisha swiped her forearm and his cell vibrated.

"What did you just give me?" Antwon asked.

"Credentials."

The inside of the building was sparse, a few scattered chairs with screens displaying scrolling images of Outside landscapes.

"What is this place?" Antwon asked.

"Excursion travel center," Kadisha replied. "I take it by your question you're not a fan of Outside."

"Never had a reason to be," Antwon replied.

Kadisha sighed. "Typical."

"What?"

"Nothing."

They reached a door at the end of the building. A light flashed and the door slid open. Antwon could see the landscape over Kadisha's shoulder. He tried to move his feet but couldn't. Kadisha turned around.

"What are you waiting for?"

"I've never been Outside," Antwon confessed.

Kadisha rolled her eyes. "Gods!"

She grabbed Antwon's arm then dragged him through the door. The cold air hit him, and he shivered. Kadisha looked at him and sucked her teeth.

"It's warm in the EV," she said.

Antwon bolted to the vehicle, opened the door then jumped inside. Kadisha climbed inside, taking the front seat. She pressed a button on the console and the EV came to life. Antwon watched puzzled as she grasped the circular object in front her.

"What are you doing?" he asked.

"Driving," Kadisha replied.

"What?"

Kadisha pivoted around then chuckled.

"I'm driving," she said. "None of that self-steering stuff on the Outside."

Antwon swallowed. "Is that safe?"

"Sometimes," Kadisha replied. "It gets interesting when the weather gets bad."

She turned around then pulled out on the road. Antwon made sure his seatbelt was fastened as he waited for the EV to lift off. Five minutes later they were still rolling on the ground.

"Is this thing broken?" he asked. "We're still on the ground."

"It doesn't fly," Kadisha answered. "We're restricted to ground travel near Mile High. Airborne EVs are only used to reach remote areas."

The rocking over the uneven ground was making Antwon queasy. He held his stomach.

"Don't throw up in my ride," Kadisha said. "We're almost home."

They rolled over a wooded hill. As they crested, Kadisha's home came into view. The cube shaped structure looked like someone had torn a flat from Mile High and dropped it in the forest. Antwon let out a sigh when Kadisha pulled next to the building and shut off the EV.

"Home," she said.

Antwon followed Kadisha into the home. It was a one room studio with a large patterned rug in the center. Antwon was expecting to see something resembling the old Westerns he watched on the pirate channel, but Kadisha's flat was nothing unusual. She pulled a chair from the small dining table then sat.

"So, what do you want from me?" she said.

Antwon sat. "I don't want anything from you, except taking me to Set. When will we do that?"

Kadisha smiled. "You're talking to her."

Antwon gasped. "You? You're Set?"

Kadisha nodded. "Talk fast. If I'm not convinced in five minutes the answer is no."

Antwon stuck his hand into his pocket and pulled out an object. He tossed it to Kadisha.

"I don't need to say a word. Everything is on this."

Kadisha frowned. "You brought me a file on a flash drive? I didn't think these existed on the Inside."

"Took me a fortune to get that one."

"Why?"

Antwon smiled. "Because we both know there are no secrets in the cloud."

Kadisha grinned. "Smart man. Let's see what we got."

Kadisha tapped the tabletop and a panel slid open. She inserted the flash drive into the port.

"Screen," she said.

Code filled the space over the table. Kadisha reached into the hidden compartment, pulled out a pair of VR specs then put them on. She studied the code then whistled.

"You got some skills," she said.

It took everything in Antwon's power to keep from jumping to his feet and pumping his fist. A compliment from Set/Kadisha was nothing to take lightly.

"Thanks. So, what do you think?"

Kadisha removed the specs. "This is buck wild crazy. Most of this is theory, and if it does work, you will have broken so many laws I don't think you'll ever see the light of day again."

"But is it possible?"

Kadisha smirked. "Yes."

"So, you'll do it?"

"Yes, but for twice of what you're offering."

Antwon's hand slapped his forehead. "Twice? Fleek!"

"Hey, this is some serious dope," Kadisha said. "I'll have to change my life if this works. You will, too. Which leads me to ask, why are you doing this? You're the top DJ in Aytee-El and one of the best on the grid. You don't need this."

"Why do you hack?" Antwon asked.

Kadisha smiled. "Because I can."

Antwon winked. "Same reason."

"Yeah, but you're set," Kadisha replied. "I can screw something up then hide. I'm adaptable. You're plugged in. You might lose everything."

"It's the challenge," Antwon said. "I didn't get here by being safe. I take chances all the time. I push the boundaries every opportunity I get. And when it works, the rush is incredible. There's nothing like it. Not even sex."

"That's debatable," Kadisha said. She stood then strolled to her fridge. "You want something to drink?"

"You got rum?"

"No, but I got wine."

"That'll do."

Kadisha took a bottle of red wine from her cabinet and poured them both a glass. She handed a glass to Antwon.

"Let's go out back," she said.

"It's cold out there!" Antwon protested.

Kadisha went into her closet and emerged with two heavy woolen blankets. She tossed one to Antwon then exited the back door. Antwon wrapped the blanket around his shoulders then followed Kadisha out onto the small patio. They sat in cushioned chairs, a small table between them. Kadisha took a sip of wine then sat her glass on the table. Antwon did the same. He stared at Kadisha, waiting for her to restart their conversation.

"Don't look at me," she said. "Look at them."

"Who?"

"Not who, what." She pointed to the snow-topped mountains. Antwon glanced at them.

"Okay, I looked. Now can we finish . . .?"

"Shhh," Kadisha said. "Drink your wine and look. I'm thinking."

Antwon slumped in his chair then sipped his wine. The blanket did a good job keeping him warm. He stared into the distance, focusing on the mountains. They were beautiful, towering higher than anything humans had yet to build. The quiet was unnerving at first, but as he settled in, he realized it was quite calming. He saw something drifting in the sky and thought for a moment it was an EV. It wasn't, of course. It was some kind of bird. He sat up, straining his eyes trying to make out the details. Motion out the corner of his eye caught his attention; he looked in the woods before him to see a four-legged beast come into view. It looked at them briefly then began munching the grass in the clearing.

"I'll do it."

Antwon jumped. "What?"

Kadisha smiled. "I'll do it. I'll meet you in Aytee-EL in two days."

Antwon was elated and concerned at the same time.

"Two days? We need to get started now."

"Two days," Kadisha said. "I'll contact you when I arrive. We're not to be together unless it's absolutely necessary."

"You say I got skills, right? It took me a long time to develop this code. I can be useful."

"I'm much better than you. That's why you're here," Kadisha replied "Two days. Now finish your wine and I'll take you back to Mile High."

They sat in silence as they finished their wine. Nature had its effect on Antwon the longer he observed it. It was truly beautiful.

"You think they'll let us out again?" he asked.

"I hope not," Kadisha answered. "We almost killed everything the last time."

"But we're different now."

Kadisha laughed. "No, we're not. I'm a ranger, remember? Every day we catch somebody trying to cut down a tree, murder an animal, or dump a toxin in a river just for the hell of it. Mother Earth won't survive a second round of us. So, we stay on the Inside. That's the law."

"I don't know," Antwon said. "I mean, we're part of nature, too."

"We stopped being a part of nature when our greed overtook our common sense," Kadisha said. "We're a cancer determined to kill our host and we've been quarantined, not cured. It's going to take a few more generations for that."

Kadisha turned up her glass, finishing her wine.

"Let's get you back to civilization."

Antwon took one last look at the mountains then followed Kadisha inside. The ride back to Mile High was subdued. Kadisha was silent, Antwon kept looking back at the mountainous landscape. The sun was setting behind the western peaks as they reached the transition building, the city lights awakening to challenge the encroaching darkness. Kadisha held the door open to the city for him.

"Two days," she said. "I expect the first half of the payment in my account by the time I get back to my house. Otherwise the deal is dead."

Antwon's fingers ran across his forearm. Kadisha glanced away then back to him.

"Thank you. It's still early. Mile High is lively at night. Nothing like Aytee-El, but you might find something to do."

"Right," Antwon said. "See you in two days."

Antwon hailed an EV. The vehicle descended and he stepped inside, his mood sour. He thought he'd be happy. Set said yes, which meant Carnival was going to be spectacular. But his mood had nothing to do with the celebration. It was sitting Outside, looking at the mountains, experiencing something that he might never see again that took him down. He needed cheering up.

"City guide," he said.

A holomap of Mile High appeared before him. He racked his brain, trying to remember the name of the rave Marissa told him about. He squinted his eyes and it popped in his head.

"Juke!" he said. "Take me to Juke."

The EV lifted then weaved through the hi-rises, touching down in the Mile-High entertainment district. Antwon heard Juke before he saw the flashing old-fashion neon sign mounted over the rave entrance. A line of people snaked from the entrance and around the building for two blocks. Antwon climbed out of the EV then strolled to the entrance. He usually kept his profile incognito, but tonight he decided to be a celebrity. A quick brush of his forearm and he was exposed. The security drones hovering over the crowd pivoted toward him, their green LEDs flashing. Before the crowd could surge toward him the heavies arrived, forming a circle of muscles and suits around him. One of the guards, a brown-skinned man as wide as he was tall, lowered his shades and he smiled.

"Twon the Don in Mile High? Ice! I'm Bruno Bruiser. Follow me."

The heavies pushed through the throng and into the rave. Antwon was showered with pulsing bass and lights. He was feeling better already. The heavies took him to the DJ booth, where a straw blonde woman wearing a neon orange jumpsuit greeted him with a joyful smile.

"Twon the Don! To what do I owe this privilege?

"Roxy Row!" Twon replied. "I didn't know this was your spot."

They did the Jay dap then hugged.

"Only been here two weeks," Roxy said. "Dooley's got stingy, so I bounced. You bring your shit?"

"Always," Antwon replied.

Antwon punched his code then swiped his forearm. His holoboard appeared next to Roxy's set up.

"Epic!" Roxy shouted. "Let's do a tag team!"

The boards synced and it was on. Roxy and Antwon went beat for beat, mixing into each other's selections and remixing on the breaks. The crowd felt the energy and responded, their dancing more vigorous. It had been a long time since Antwon did a duo session and he was reminded how much he missed it. As they mixed, he captured snippets of beats from each song, familiarizing himself with the Mile-High groove. Every city had a groove, a little something their inhabitants responded to. In the Aytee-El they called it Durty. In Queen City they called it Bop. Antwon didn't know what it was called in Mile High, but he was about to find out.

"You're about to do it, aren't you?" Roxy said.

Antwon answered with a smirk and a wink.

Roxy punched the air. "Shit yeah!" She swiped her holoboard away. "Don't start until I'm on the floor."

Antwon gave Roxy the thumbs up and she hurried out the booth. Antwon continued to harvest the beats until he saw her stepping into the crowd. Antwon turned on the mic.

"Mile High, how you feeling?"

The crowd answered with a roar. Antwon grinned.

"Twon the Don on the boards tonight," he said. "And it's about to go down!"

Twon went freestyle and the crowd exploded. This was his domain, the vibe he was known for. As he layered the beats, he watched the crowd, feeding off their energy. Seconds later they were zoning, deep into the perfect moment of give and take.

"Are you with me!?" he shouted.

"Yeah!" the crowd back.

"Are you with me?"

"Yeah!"

"Then show me!"

Antwon switch into deep bass breakdown and the crowd responded.

"This is brand new, y'all!" he said. "It's called the Mile-High Durty!"

Antwon glanced up, camera drones jostled outside the deejay booth window. He flashed his signature smile, flashed a peace sign, then went back to work. Antwon lost track of time. When the lights flickered for last call it caught him by surprise.

Roxy entered the booth, her eyes wide with wonder.

"That was hot as fleek!"

She swiped her forearm and her holoboard reappeared. Antwon closed out his board.

"Thanks for letting me spin," he said. "I needed it."

Roxy tapped her board. Fifteen hundred crypts downloaded into his account.

"Hey, you didn't need to do that," he said.

"You know how much I'm going to make on residual feeds?" she said. "This set has 2mil views already."

"What time is it?" Antwon asked.

"Six a.m."

"Fleek! Gotta go. My Bullet leaves at 7:30."

Antwon gave Roxy dap then hurried away.

"Let me know when you come to the A," he shouted. "We can do this again."

"Will do!" Roxy shouted back.

"If I'm not in prison," Antwon whispered.

The crowd had dispersed when he went outside. A few folks asked for his autograph which he obliged before calling a Rideout. He hopped in and the EV whisked him to the Tube terminal. Antwon used extra crypts to upgrade his seat to private on the way to the station. He worked his way to his Bullet and to the VIP cubes. Once inside the plush compartment he jumped on the bed, closed his eyes and fell asleep.

* * *

"Welcome to Aytee-El."

Antwon sat up and rubbed his eyes. His cabin pulsed with baby blue light while the local news played on the vid. First level riders got the privilege to disembark first, but Antwon decided to grab a few extra minutes of sleep by waiting until the bullet was empty.

"Mr. Pierce?"

Antwon woke up a second time to the pleasant face of a bullet steward on his screen.

"We have to ask you to leave the bullet. We can't board new passengers until the train is empty.

"My bad," Antwon said. He gathered his things then hurried off the train. He walked with the throng to the Metro, and then hopped on for the twenty-minute ride into the Pit. As he rode the Peachtree Station escalator to the surface, the details of his trip to Mile-High rolled around in his head. Spending that short time Outside affected him more than he realized. The more he thought about it, the more it worried him. He was so immersed he didn't realize he'd reached the top of the escalator.

"Sir?"

Antwon turned to see an attractive woman smiling at him. "Yes?"

"You're blocking the escalator."

"What . . . oh, I'm sorry."

He stepped aside, freeing the others to go about their daily business. He shook his head clear then called up Marissa. Her bright face filled his view.

"Morning, love," she said. "Back from Mile High?"

"Yep."

"Saw your set last night on the wave. Ice!"

"Thanks. How's the prep going?"

"Great, but Kye and Dame are still bitching. They want to know what you got planned. Krak, I want to know what you got planned."

"All in good time," Antwon replied.

Marissa gave him that special smile. "Can I come over?"

Antwon chuckled. "I got to get to the crib and get some sleep. I'll meet y'all at the center around fourteen hundred. After that, we'll see. Ice?"

"Ice."

Antwon was only a few blocks from his condo, so he decided to walk the rest of the way. He was walking up to the entrance when his phone buzzed.

"Speak."

Kadisha's face appeared.

"Change of plans," she said. "I'll be in Aytee-El tomorrow morning."

"What's the matter?"

"I need to get into the ADOT."

Antwon ran his hand over his head. "Really? The code was written to work externally."

"It won't," Kadisha replied. "And don't ask me if I'm sure. I am."

"I don't know," Antwon replied. "The ADOT? That's heavy security."

"Don't worry about that," Kadisha said. "Meet me at the station at oh seven hundred."

Antwon scratched his head. "Wow, Kadisha. I don't know."

"You want your Carnival?" she asked.

"Of course, I do."

"Then meet me at seven," Kadisha said. "Otherwise it's not happening."

Kadisha cut him off. Antwon continued to stare where her face had been, his mind tumbling. This was serious shit. Breaking into a government facility? That was serious.

Antwon was so preoccupied he walked by his condo. He wandered the streets for an hour, going over the code. Hunger pangs hit him, and he worked his way to Piedmont Park then bought a loaded sausage dog from the Weiner King food truck. He sat on a nearby bench, absently eating as code filled his head. Then he saw it.

"Fleek!"

He threw away the rest of the sausage dog and jogged to his condo. He spent the rest of the day and most of the night trying to fix the code, but by the time the sun rose over the city he gave up. Kadisha was right. They had to go in.

His cell buzzed and he sighed. He punched his forearm and Kadisha's face filled the screen.

"I'm here," she said.

"I'm on my way," he replied.

"Don't bother. I'll be there in a few."

"Wait! What?"

The screen went blank. Antwon scrambled to clean up his condo before her arrival, not wanting to appear the slob he was. Fifteen minutes later the door buzzed, and he let Kadisha in.

"Hey! What's . . ."

Kadisha handed him a clothes box.

"Get dressed. Where's your bathroom?"

"Down the hall," he said as he took the box. Kadisha nodded then marched to the bathroom. Antwon went to his bedroom and opened the box. Inside was an Aytee-EL DOT uniform.

"Oh shit," he said.

"You dressed yet?" Kadisha called out from the bathroom.

"Almost," Antwon called out. He undressed and put on the uniform. When he turned around Kadisha stood in his bedroom door, her hand extended. In it was an ADOT employee badge.

"Um, did you see me in my . . ."

'Boy please. Let's go," she said.

She turned then strode for the door. Antwon ran behind her.

"Why such a hurry? Can't we talk about this?"

"We have a small window of opportunity," Kadisha replied. "We can talk on the way."

Antwon followed Kadisha to the street. A Rideout appeared and they climbed in.

"I assume you found the error?" Kadisha asked.

"Yeah," Antwon said. "I tried . . ."

"I could kick myself for missing it," Kadisha said, cutting him off. "If I'd seen it sooner, I would have turned you down."

Antwon's eyes widened. "Is it that bad?"

"Look at us," she answered. "It's that bad."

Antwon and Kadisha hurried from the condo to the streets. Antwon summoned a Rideout.

"Aytee . . ."

"No," Kadisha interjected. "Rising Star Restaurant."

Antwon gave Kadisha a questioning look.

"It's a popular restaurant for ADOT employees," she said. "We'll walk from there."

"How do you know all this?" Antwon asked.

Kadisha smirked. "You really have to ask?"

The Rideout whisked them to Rising Star, a small breakfast spot on the corner of Ellis and Vine. Antwon's stomach rumbled as they entered. He didn't have breakfast. He was eyeing a delicious looking sausage sandwich when Kadisha turned him about.

"No time for that," she said. "Let's go."

They walked with a group of ADOT workers to the building. The workers chatted with each other while glancing at Kadisha and Antwon. A few shared smiles, some looked at them suspiciously. One woman in particular kept staring at Antwon, her face scrunched up in that way people do when trying to remember someone. Her eyes went wide and a big grin appeared on her face.

"Twon the Don!" she exclaimed.

"Sheeit!" Antwon said under his breath.

The woman made her way to him.

"You look just like him," she said.

"Who?" Antwon said.

"Twon the Don. I was just rocking off one of his vids yesterday. He's so cool."

Kadisha came and stood between him and the woman.

"He gets that a lot," she said. "And who are you?"

The woman frowned. "My bad. I didn't know y'all were together."

"You do now," Kadisha said.

The woman gave Antwon a side eye. "You need to check your woman."

The woman walked away. Antwon did his best to keep from laughing. Kadisha was not amused. They reached the ADOT entrance, passing through security without a hitch.

"You sure we're ice?" Antwon asked.

"We have employment records in their system dating back five years," she said.

"But what if no one recognizes us?"

"The system is always right," Kadisha said. "That's what makes my job so easy. This way."

Antwon followed Kadisha through the building. They took the elevator down to the IT department. The entire area was empty.

"Where is everybody?" Antwon asked.

"They were given the day off," Kadisha replied. "Come on, we only have a few minutes."

Kadisha walked up to one of the consoles and began typing.

"What do you need me to do?" Antwon asked.

"Nothing yet. Just keep an eye on the elevator."

Antwon's attention vacillated between the door and Kadisha. After ten minutes she stood then marched to the hardware. She took out a tool kit and Antwon's eyes bucked. He ran over to and grabbed her hand. Kadisha snarled as she jerked her hand free then punched him hard in the chest, knocking wind out of him. Antwon fell on his ass, gasping.

"Don't touch me!" she spat. "Don't ever touch me!"

Antwon rubbed his chest. "You're installing hardware. Can't do that."

"I have to if you want your plan to work," Kadisha said. "Do you?"

Antwon stood on shaky legs. "Of course, I do."

"Then make up your mind. I put this in and you're a go. I don't, you're fleeked."

Antwon chewed his nails. Hardware was traceable. There was no way he would be able to retrieve it, which meant he was certain to go to jail after Carnival. Was it really worth it?

Antwon lowered his hand.

"Do it," he said.

Kadisha nodded then went to work, opening the console with her tools and installing the chip.

"Let's go," she said.

They took the elevator to the main floor then fast-walked to the exit.

"Hey!"

Antwon and Kadisha turned to see a tall muscular man wearing the maroon blazer and gray slacks of ADOT security, his badge on his pocket. He walked to them then folded his thick arms across his broad chest.

"Who are you, and what were you doing in IT?"

Antwon froze; Kadisha extended her hand.

"Caroline Brooks," she said. "This is Tom Clay. We're from DDOT."

The man's eyes narrowed, and he rubbed his chin.

"I don't see you on my schedule," he said.

"We shouldn't be," Kadisha said. "We received a personal invite from John."

"John Chu?" the security agent asked.

"Is there another John?" Kadisha retorted.

Not only is she lying, she's arrogant about it, Antwon thought. *I like her.*

"I need a few minutes to check this all out," the security guard said.

"We don't have a few minutes," Kadisha replied. "We traveled all the way from Mile High for this meeting and nobody's here. A waste of our time."

The guard reached inside his pocket and pulled out a pair of vidspecs. He put them on then tapped the right side.

"That's unusual. There's been a schedule mix up. Everyone is off today."

"Like I said, a waste of our time." Kadisha nodded at Antwon. "Come on, Tom. Let's go."

Kadisha strode toward the door, Antwon running to catch up.

"Wait!" the guard called out. "We're not finished!"

"Yes, we are," Kadisha called back. "Tell John he owes me."

Kadisha summoned a Rideout before they were out the door. The vehicle landed as they reached the curb; they climbed inside and they were on their way before the security guard reached the door. Kadisha took a deep breath then exhaled. She looked at Antwon, sharing a wide smile.

"That was fun."

"No, it wasn't," Antwon replied. "You get to go home. This guard's going to see my face on Carnival and put two and two together."

"You're already screwed," Kadisha said. "The hardware, remember?"

Antwon fell back on his seat, massaging his forehead.

"Hey. Here."

Antwon turned his head to Kadisha. She was holding his flash drive.

"I created you a new identity. I didn't give it to you earlier because I didn't know which way you were going to go. Everything is on this. You can ghost for a few months, maybe a few years to let things cool down. You're breaking the law but you're not killing anybody. You can download it from a library console. I think they still have a few units that take flash drives."

Antwon took the flash drive.

"Thanks."

"No problem. I don't do this for everybody, but I like you. You got balls."

"So that's what you call it?"

The Rideout landed at the ATL Tube. The door lifted and Kadisha climbed out.

"Good luck, Antwon. If you get a craving for the Outside, come visit. It's in your profile."

The Rideout door rose and Kadisha climbed out.

"Enjoy Carnival."

Kadisha smiled then strolled away. Antwon watched her walk away.

"You're a bad ass," he said.

His com buzzed as the Rideout door closed. He swiped his forearm and Marissa's face appeared.

"Hey love. You coming to the rehearsal?"

"I'm on my way."

"Excellent. See you soon."

Marissa's face disappeared and Antwon settled into the Rideout.

"King Center," he said.

Antwon arrived at the center ten minutes later. He worked his way through the throng leaving the center, his head down so no one would recognize him. When he reached the door, Marissa greeted him with her big smile and a bigger hug. Her dreads were loose, which meant she had plans for him later. The thought eased his tension a bit, but not all the way. His days of freedom were coming to an end.

"Are they ready?" he asked.

"Yep," Marissa replied. "The last dress rehearsal before Carnival. Wait until you see it."

"I've seen it a thousand times."

"Not like this."

Antwon followed Marissa to the dance hall. Kye and Dame stood in the middle of the floor in costume. They both smiled at him.

"Y'all ready for this?" Kye said.

"Of course," Antwon replied.

"Dim lights," Kye said. The dance hall went completely dark. Marissa grabbed Antwon's ass and he almost laughed.

"Cue music," Kye said.

The beat dropped and Kye and Dame holo-costumes burst out with brilliant light. Kye and Dame became fluid syncopated motion and Antwon was overwhelmed. No matter how many times he's seen the routine in simulation, nothing compared to what he saw at that moment. Kye had worked her magic when he wasn't looking, adding accents and steps that took the dance to the next level. When the music switched from soca to genuine Aytee-El hyper-trap, tears came to Antwon's eyes. Kye and Dame worked the hometown groove like they were born to it, and they were. He had to be honest; they could win Carnival without his surprise.

The music ended and the light came on. Kye and Dame panted, sweated and smiled.

"So?" Dame said.

Antwon couldn't answer. He was wiping his eyes.

"Damn!" Marissa said. "You done danced the man speechless!"

Antwon walked to Dame and Kye and wrapped his arms around both.

"That was so ice!" he said. "I never imagined it could look so tight."

"Sims ain't got nothing on the real thing," Kye said. "Now what do you have planned that could possibly add to this?"

"Get dressed," Antwon said. "We're going to my crib. We'll order up food and I'll show you."

Dame and Kye trotted off to the dressing rooms. Marissa came up behind him and wrapped her arms around his waist.

"I thought it was going to be you and me tonight," she said.

Antwon turned around in her embrace and hugged her back. He grabbed a handful of her dreads, lifted them to his nose and inhaled. Her hair always smelled so good.

"After they're gone it's going to be you and me until Carnival."

"Hope you took your vits," Marissa whispered.

"Hope you took yours," Antwon replied.

The four of them hopped a Rideout to his crib. Marissa took care of the delivery orders. Ten minutes after they settled in, the drop drones arrived with their feast; Jamaican, Soul, Low

Country, and Trinidadian cuisine from the best restaurants in the city. It was too much to eat in one night, but Antwon didn't care. He was splurging for what probably were his last days of freedom.

After eating their fill, they paired up in the den.

"I wasn't going to show you this," Antwon said. "But I decided I should so you wouldn't be shook when it went down."

"Let's see it already!" Kye said.

The lights dimmed and the simulation began. Antwon watched everyone as they watched the sim. Marissa dropped her fork, spilling oxtails on his Persian rug. Kye covered her mouth with her hands, her eyes glistening. Dame bobbed his head with the music as he laughed.

"This is so ice!" he exclaimed. "So, ice!"

Kye uncovered her mouth then turned to look at him.

"I'm glad you shared this. No way I could have danced through this."

Marissa pressed against him then whispered in his ear.

"You're going to jail for this, aren't you?"

Antwon kissed her cheek.

"Most likely."

Her hand found its way between his legs.

"Then let's get rid of the dancing duo. I don't want to waste a minute."

Marissa shooed Dame and Kye from the condo as Antwon cleaned up. He didn't get far; Marissa was pulling at his clothes as soon as the door closed. They were naked before they reached the floor, ignoring the simulation that bathed the room in powder blue light.

Antwon and Marissa spent the next four days in erotic bliss, taking a break from each other to eat leftovers or go to the bathroom. As they passed the time, Aytee-El prepared for Carnival. Traffic was rerouted from the designated areas and decorations were set up by workbots. Music broke out spontaneously, and people danced at random. On Carnival Day morning Antwon sat up, rubbing his eyes. Marissa lay beside him, her cute snoring making him laugh.

"Don't be laughing at me, bwoi," she said, her eyes still closed.

"Wake up," he said. "It's Carnival."

Marissa grabbed his arm and pulled him down.

"Wake me up."

Antwon pulled away. "Not this morning. This is it."

Marissa sat up and threw the covers aside.

"Okay." She jumped out the bed then trudged to the bathroom like a disappointed child.

Antwon followed her and they showered, made love, then showered again. They emerged into the condo then dressed slowly.

"So, you're going to do this," Marissa said.

"Yep," Antwon replied.

"You don't have to," she said. "The show is good enough as it is."

"But it will be so much better with the rest."

Marissa hugged him. "Fuck the show. Let's get Dame and Kye set up then come back here. They'll be alright."

Antwon stopped buttoning his shirt. He stared at Marissa and she stared back, a pleading look in her eyes. Their relationship had always been casual, but at that moment he sensed they were at the verge of something deeper. Was he ready to give up on a show of the lifetime for it?"

"Come on," he said. "First things first."

They called a Rideout to the Center. Dame and Kye were waiting with the rest of the crew. They all turned toward Antwon and clapped as he entered. Twon the Don was in the house.

"Y'all ready to win this shit?" he shouted.

"Yei yeah!" everyone shouted back.

"Then let's do it!"

The drummers emerged from the crowd and played. Everyone stepped and swayed to the beat before following them out of the building. A crowd waited outside, cheering as they came to the street. Carnival was on. Antwon's crew marched to Peachtree Street and joined the parade, dancing its way to Millennial Park. ATLiens packed the sidewalks, some in costumes, others in casual clothes, all enjoying the music and the celebration. The crews reached the Park and circled the performance area three times, dancing to the same beat. After the third round they took their designated places and the competition began.

The other crews were incredible. Word leaked that Antwon had something spectacular planned and the crews responded. The entire global union was celebrating Carnival, but the net was focused on Aytee-El. Antwon grew more nervous; Marissa held his hand.

"We got this, love," she said.

"Yeah," he replied. "We got this."

It was their turn. The drummers led a procession to the performing platform, which lowered so Dam and Kye could mount it. Antwon went to the mixing station, replacing the mixer for the Trinis. He swiped his program into the console then waited for Dame and Kye to give him the signal. Kye nodded. They were ready.

"Kill the lights, please," Antwon said. His voice reverberated across the field and the crowd shifted nervously in the darkness.

"ATLiens and the world, this is Twon the Don!"

The crowd erupted in claps and cheers. Antwon waited for them to settle down, his finger hovering over the start button. Marissa said he didn't have to do it. She said that Dame and Kye were good on their own. But Marissa was wrong. He had to do it. He had to be his best at all costs, even if it meant going to jail for jacking the grid. He pressed the button.

Dame and Kye appeared in an explosion of light, sound and motion. The crowd was captivated in seconds. Antwon slipped away from the board, seeking a vantage point to see what was about to happen next. As he worked his way back, he saw the lines coming to the performance field. By the time he reached the viewing tower the crowd could see them as well. Every Rideout in the city converged on the field, their lights pulsing in time with the music. Most were empty, but a few held riders who were stunned and confused. The vehicles reached the field and split into separate circles, forming a globe of strobing lights around Dame and Kye. The dancers' colored plumage expanded, enveloping the entire globe. Antwon had reached the top of the viewing tower when something happen that caught him off guard. Every light in the Aytee-El began pulsing with the music.

"By the ancestors!" he whispered.

His cell buzzed and he answered it. Kadisha's smug face greeted him.

"Surprise."

"You're a fleeking genius," Antwon said.

"Every screen on the net is watching right now," Kadisha said. "You're beyond viral. Now the bad news. You have ten minutes before the ADOT shuts it down. You got five minutes to get to the Tube and ghost."

"I'm not going," Antwon said.

"Don't be stupid," Kadisha replied. "Get out of town, get settled then send for Marissa."

"How did you know about Marissa?"

"You keep forgetting who I am. I can scramble the APD GPS and give you another two minutes, but you have to go now!"

"How am I going to get to the station with all the Rideouts . . .?"

A Rideout appeared before him and the door opened.

"Thank you for choosing Rideout."

Antwon jumped inside.

"Destination please?"

"Tube Station Central," Antwon said. He looked and Kadisha smiled.

"You're welcome," she said. "It was good working with you. Good luck with your new life."

His screen went blank.

Antwon looked back as the Rideout took him to Central Station. The entire city . . . no, the entire world, was watching. He felt a twinge of sadness because he wouldn't be able to celebrate with his crew, but that was the price of greatness…and freedom. The time would come, and he would make the best of it.

The Rideout touched down at the station. Antwon hurried inside. He didn't take any time to think about where to go. He boarded the first Bullet he saw with the doors open. The scanner collected his credits and confirmed his papers and he sat down beside a middle-aged man with a gray beard. He was watching Dame and Kye on his cell.

The doors closed and the Bullet streaked from the station. Antwon watched the screen, trying to hold back tears of happiness. The man looked at him and smiled.

"It's amazing, isn't it?" he said.

"Yes, it is."

"That Twon the Don is a genius. I can't imagine him doing that by himself."

"He didn't. He had help."

The man looked at him puzzled.

"At least that's what I heard," Antwon said.

"Oh," the man replied.

"Where is this Bullet going, by the way?" Antwon asked the man.

"Lasgidi," the man replied. "Are you visiting?"

"Relocating, actually," Antwon replied. "I've never been."

"You'll love it," the man said.

"I hope so," Antwon replied. "I'm going to be there for a while."

The viewing screen on the Bullet turned on, broadcasting the performance. Others had joined Dame and Kye on the stage. The party was on.

"You did it, Twon," he whispered. "Yes, you did."

Antwon closed his eyes and let the rhythm lull him to sleep.

* * *

The Mviti Bullet was late. Agitated Naijans glared at their cells, gestured angrily, and yelled as they looked into the dark tunnel for signs of the bullet's arrival. Ten minutes later lights appeared in the distance and the riders released a crescendo of cheers. The bullet from the East African coastal city eased to a stop and crowd monitors rolled into position, clearing a space between the Bullet doors and the expectant passengers.

"Please be patient as passengers disembark," the monitors sang in their generic voice. "Thank you for your cooperation."

The bullet doors slipped open, releasing its passengers. The Naijans foul mood disappeared as they welcomed the arrivals, some returning home, others visiting for the first time. The last person to exit the train was neither. He was a man moving between worlds, at least for the time being.

Antwon was glad to be back in Lasgidi. Although he still didn't consider it home after living there for ten months, it was the most familiar of his haunts. Kadisha warned him not to get too settled and he took her advice to heart. He bounced around the globe, taking low-key deejay jobs and contract sound engineering projects along the way. All the while he kept up with the happenings in Aytee-El. People were still buzzing about Carnival. The ADOT was grilled on how someone could hack their system so completely and the officials had no explanation. Although they new Antwon was involved, they surmised that he did not have the expertise to pull off such a serious breach. He had help, they said. They were right.

Antwon summoned an okada for the ride home. He called up the heavens and checked his accounts as the EV merged into the go-slow.

"Fleek," he said as he looked at his viral account. It was up to 33M cryptos and he couldn't touch it. Carnival feed was making him a wealthy man, but as soon as he touched it, APD would be on his ass. He was taking a chance by even looking at it. He shut the link down. His screen took longer than normal to fade; Antwon sat straight when a word scripted in neon flashed in his face.

"Surprise!"

"What the fleek?"

He reached his flat ten minutes later. The word made him nervous. Maybe he spent too much time looking at his account and the APD were on the bullet now. Or maybe it was a joke some hacker was playing on him. Antwon couldn't take any chances. He would have to move.

He entered his flat and was met with the smell of rice and peas, cabbage and oxtails.

"Hey bwoi."

Marissa stood before his stove, wearing a Naija t-shirt and blue jean shorts, her dreads loose. Antwon dropped his bag and ran to her. They kissed for what seemed like hours.

"How did you find me?" he asked.

"Kadisha is a good friend to you," Marissa replied. "She told me where you were two months ago. I wanted to come then but she made me wait. She said she had to fix things."

"Fix things?"

Marissa led him to his couch. Antwon sat down; Marissa sat on his lap.

"She felt bad about what happened to you."

Antwon kissed Marissa's chin. "It wasn't her fault. It was my idea. I got what I deserved. Besides, I feel bad for doing it. You told me I didn't have to."

"And I'm still pissed about that!" Marissa said in mock anger. She popped his head with her hand. "Anyway, she skimmed your virtual funds and hired a law firm to represent you. They're close to coming to a deal with ADOT. She said you should be able to come home in a few weeks."

Antwon frowned. "What's it going to cost?"

"Your virtual account. Every crypto."

Antwon chuckled. "Well, it was nice while it lasted."

He squeezed Marissa. "Doesn't matter. I have all I need right here."

Marissa put her lips near his ear. "We have a few weeks. I hope you took your vits."

Antwon kissed her earlobe.

"I hope you took yours."

Underground Problems
by
Ashleigh Davenport

Chapter One

"Nothing strange going on here," Zaria said as she combed her fingers through her kinky twists and walked through the ever-busy Underground Atlanta.

The constant foot traffic and loud crowds made for a tedious search-and-neutralize mission. It was a mystery who tipped off the Paranormal Investigation League, but she was stuck within a mass of people, which wasn't very high on her preference list.

Although, it was amazing how they kept the red and black brick floor so clean. Plus, the smell of food was as incredible as Zaria remembered when she frequented the place years ago. Now, it was easier to order everything to be delivered, except for one place.

"Oh, come on, you just got there," Curtis whined over the phone. "All you have to do is walk through the place and use that sixth sense of yours to see if there are any void pockets."

Zaria continued to stroll through the underground, "Uh-huh, what store you tryin' to get me to stop at?"

"I mean, it might be fun for you to pick up some cake and maybe a piece for me too?"

"I knew it," Zaria shook her head.

Curtis was a sucker for Mama Kay's Cake Shop, which was okay since she wanted to pick up a piece of cake anyway. "The Chocolate Assassin, right?"

"Yes, ma'am!"

Zaria had to move the phone away from her ear as she grimaced at his octave.

"Make sure you get some extra sauce on the side."

Zaria laughed, "You're already getting four different kinds of chocolate in that thing. Why do you need so much sauce?"

"You know I like my cake wet." His pronunciation of wet had an 'h' in it, making it extra naughty.

"That is just nasty."

"Oh, I assure you, it most certainly is."

Zaria rolled her reddish-brown eyes, "Man, you're always telling your business." She imagined him sticking out his curled tongue as he laughed and looked at her with a side-eye.

Curtis's mischievous chuckle signaled he was doing precisely that, "You mad?"

Zaria paused in front of a shoe shop, "Nah, maybe a little jealous." Then, she looked up at a group of girls as they laughed and pointed at another one who stood against a wall.

She was quiet, keeping her head down and holding one of her arms as they criticized her outfit. They volleyed superficial insults about how cheap and outdated it was. Her jeans, green T-shirt, and clean tennis shoes didn't seem to be a big issue. Compared to Zaria's own black tennis shoes, dark blue jeans, and an oversized hoodie, they had close to the same style. The little assholes touched on the same crap that made Zaria's early school life a terror. The foolish shit kids used to feel better while making someone else's life a living hell. Honestly, it wasn't very reassuring to see history repeating.

Zaria pushed up her sleeves, exposing her warm brown skin speckled with blooms of pink and white, and pulled out a piece of paper. When she walked between the semi-circle of the obvious bullies and their victim, she kept her head down to read the sheet, "Wait, I don't know where to go," She looked at the brick wall. A map of Underground Atlanta covered in stickers and writing distorted some of the names and landmarks.

"Oh, you gotta be kidding me," Curtis sighed, "just because I'm a little nasty doesn't mean you can't just pick me up some cake and sauce!"

"You're not just nasty," Zaria looked at the scared teen, then back at the paper, "you're a tad freaky, to be honest." Zaria felt a pinprick of pressure at the base of her neck. The quiet girl had a small seed of magic within her.

Someone tapped Zaria on the shoulder, and she looked at the bully who just touched her, "Yes?"

"Um, you're in the way," the short teenage girl in designer everything twisted her neck at her. Her two cronies stood behind her with their arms crossed and stared daggers at Zaria.

"I'm almost done, just a little lost," Zaria said in an upbeat, pleasant tone and smiled at her, then looked back at the map. To her surprise, their victim had slipped away. Good, the best thing the girl could do was avoid them. Soon, the trivial insults wouldn't matter when she started tapping into whatever ability manifesting within her.

"Where the hell did she go?" One of the other girls said behind her.

The short one scoffed, "Whatever, we'll find her later."

When the bullies huffed and walked off, Zaria continued to check the area while Curtis complained and begged on the phone.

"Still stepping in for humans that don't appreciate you?" A familiar, gruff voice said behind Zaria.

Heat rushed to her cheeks as she gritted her teeth, "Stop tripping, Curtis; I'll call you back when I get the cake."

"Oh, bye!"

Zaria hung up the phone and steeled herself before turning to her old friend, "What are you doing here, Acar?"

He grinned at her, his white teeth contrasting his beautiful deep umber skin, "Whatever you want me to do."

She sucked her teeth and started moving again. The demon was always able to get her temperature up without much work. The problem was that it wasn't a bad thing most of the time. A glance at his tan high-neck sweater that clung to his thick arms oh so nicely and gray plaid suit pants with brown leather shoes was enough to sear his image into her brain. Not to mention his waist-length locs styled into a braid atop his undercut fade. Dammit, he always looked so lovely.

Acar took a few large strides and caught up with Zaria, "Wait a sec," he said, "I'm here because of a small portal to the demon realm showing up earlier today."

Zaria paused and turned to him, "Really, P.I.L. got a tip that there was a void pocket here; could it be the same thing?"

"So, now you're interested?"

"What?" Zaria pursed her lips, "Yeah, it might have something to do with the job." A void pocket could lead to a portal and if they weren't careful, something could push through. Knowing it was from Acar's realm meant that whatever it was would be dangerous.

"In that case," he ran his thumb and index finger down the sides of his neat beard, "I would love to tell you more, but I'm a little thirsty. Let's grab a drink." He pointed a thumb at a small bar.

Zaria shook her head and turned to leave, "Not happening." The last time she went out drinking with him, she woke up in his bed. She did her best to avoid being alone with him anytime they met after. She couldn't bring herself to ask how she got there. Now, one of her most cherished friendships had devolved into awkwardness.

Acar grabbed her hand, stopping her retreat, "Don't run again," he pleaded as he pulled her close.

Zaria kept her face stoic as she looked up from his broad chest and said, "I have to work." At the same time, her insides were heating up to the Sahara desert's mid-summer temperatures.

His plump lips were too close, and the memory of them on her own made them tingle with anticipation. Too bad she didn't remember most of that night. But it must have been great since he swore allegiance to Zaria as her familiar. Something unheard of being done by such a high-ranking demon.

"Can we talk after you're done?" He locked his gaze on her eyes, refusing to back down.

Zaria was the first to look away and sighed, "Okay, we-" she was cut off by the pulsating pressure radiating at the base of her neck, "Damn."

Chapter Two

The large shopping area lost power, eliciting small gasps from the bustling crowd and making everyone and everything grind to a halt. Zaria moved towards the feel of magic and retrieved her phone from her pocket. Then, a vacuum of air lurched her forward and out of Acar's grasp.

Screams erupted around them as people lost their balance and slid forward. The force reversed, throwing Zaria back into Acar's chest, and they both tumbled to the floor. Her phone flew out of her hand and skidded under a small kiosk. Zaria rolled off him and stood to conjure a wall-to-wall shield that warbled from the next push and pull of the unstable portal far ahead of them.

"Whoever it is, they're too weak to control the portal," Acar stood up, and the tingle of his magic flowed down Zaria's spine.

Zaria retrieved a small, blue stone from her hoodie's kangaroo pocket and threw it toward the pool of the magic. It exploded upon impact, sending a shockwave of protective magic out and enclosing the area in a dome.

"Everybody, get back!" She yelled at the scrambling patrons. Behind her shield, they were protected from the warping portal and able to right themselves and run away.

Zaria pushed forward as more people began to retreat behind her shield. In front, the pressure became stronger as she moved. The push and pull of the people mimicked plants ebbing and flowing at the bottom of the ocean. As if a swirling current was tossing them.

The pressure of the invisible current became more volatile, and Zaria strained to hold her shields. More people felt the relief of normal pressure and got up to run, just in time for the portal to stabilize and create a swirling black hole in midair.

Zaria was close enough to see the bullied teen sitting cross-legged on the floor just behind and off to the right of the portal. Her eyes were white, and her crown of corkscrew coils whipped in the wind. She was hiding her magic earlier, but she wasn't strong enough to handle whatever she'd summoned.

Some people behind the portal watched and filmed the events with their cell phones while others were smart and kept running.

Zaria made it about 15 feet away from the doorway, and all the pressure, pushing, and pulling stopped. Everyone gasped, waiting for the next one to rattle them even more, but none came. Disoriented and disheveled, people began to take long breaths and try to reorient themselves. Their belongings were scattered, and some even were injured.

The girls who were bullying the other were splayed out on the floor in front of Zaria. Having suffered the brunt of the portal's faltering magic, they looked worse for wear. Zaria took a few more steps and said, "Y'all need to get up and get out."

"No!" their victim yelled, and Zaria snapped her attention back to her.

The girl's eyes rolled down from her eyelids, and her face scrunched with rage, "This is all for them. They can't leave."

The salty and slightly sweet smell of the ocean wafted from the portal. The black swirls stabilized and became a solid transparent wall with dark blue water on the other side.

"They're not worth all this." Zaria's voice was low and pleading, "You can learn to use your powers with people who aren't so immature."

The short bully staggered to her feet and cried, "I'm sorry, Nora."

"Oh no, you're sorry?" Nora sneered, "I should stop then, right?" She grinned, "Like you did when I kept apologizing for nothing?"

"We got a big one coming," Acar said as he moved forward, just past her shield.

His body shifted and popped as black feathers grew out of his head and back. The girls scrambled and screamed at the sight, but Nora watched in awe, matching Zaria. His clothes melted away as he added inches to his height. Silver-tipped wings sprouted from his arms and spread as his back arched. Then, a 7-foot blackbird stood in his place and settled its wings at its sides. A crown of thin silver and white feathers grew from his head to match his elongated beak.

It had to be bad if he was shifting into his demon form, yet Zaria had to jest, "P.I.L. is gonna be pissed."

"Oh, well." Acar's telepathic voice sounded in her head, "I don't work for them."

An unworldly large and muscular ochre-colored tentacle shot out from the portal and slammed into Acar.

Chapter Three

Acar flew back and tumbled head over talons across the floor while the prehensile appendage smashed against Zaria's shield. It flickered under pressure, and the tentacle slid to the ground.

"They're getting away!" Nora yelled.

Two more tentacles squeezed through and gripped the ground with the third.

"You okay back there!" Zaria called back to Acar, who was righting himself with a flutter of his wings.

"Not in the slightest."

Zaria braced herself as the glistening arms pulled another set into the space, shooting straight for her. They smashed into the invisible wall, and the force made her drop to a knee. She panted and strained to hold up the blockade. All the training in the world couldn't have prepared Zaria for the brute strength of this demon. Then, all the tentacles pulled back and hit it simultaneously.

The wall shattered, and Zaria conjured another one, but she knew it would be too weak to withstand the same type of hit the appendages were preparing again. People were still trying to get away, while others stood frozen in fear. She had to try.

The scent of ozone washed over her as the tentacles cut through Zaria's shields. The air crackled, and a bright white rod of lightning slammed down in front of her, burning through one of the limbs.

"Move!" Acar's voice screamed in her head, and she did. Zaria had to get to Nora.

One arm lashed at her, and Acar latched onto it with his talons, and another lightning strike burned through it. The creature shrieked and thrashed, but Acar held on until it receded into the portal. He flapped his wings to help him hop back and landed on another one.

Zaria made a shield rise from under it, slicing it in half. It shriveled back into the abyss with another cry of pain. Then, the tentacles pulled back into the portal, but it didn't close.

"No, come back!" Nora screamed at the watery abyss.

Zaria made it to the teen and yelled, "Are you going to be worse than those assholes?"

Nora turned her burning eyes to Zaria, "What are you talking about?" She screamed, "They deserve worse for the years of tormenting me every chance they got!"

"Let's throw her into the portal." Acar's gruff voice growled in her head.

Zaria ignored him and asked, "What about the other people you're hurting?"

Nora's face scrunched in confusion, "I'm not," she looked behind Zaria and saw a woman trying to help a battered and bleeding young man. Her face fell at the sight of their pain, "I- I didn't mean to."

"Just close the portal, and we can work on fixing this."

Tears filled Nora's eyes, "I...I don't know how. The book didn't say."

Zaria understood the kid's feelings. Trying to get back at someone with something that would destroy them for life is a tempting thing. But magic without knowing how to use it could take it too far. And, who's grimoire did she have?

"It's okay," Zaria said calmly, "Take a deep breath." Nora did as instructed, and Zaria put her hands on the teen's shoulders, closed her eyes, and matched her breathing.

Zaria would have to help Nora find the link to the portal within her and sever it. An advanced technique practiced at the end of portal training is easier with a connected guide.

A garbled roar exploded from the portal, and Zaria felt her connection to Nora snap. When she opened her eyes, Nora's eyes had rolled back into her head.

"Shit!" Zaria turned to Acar as he flared out his wings and screeched at the opening, prepared for an attack, "It's controlling her!"

A mass of tentacles burst through, and Acar's lightning couldn't stop them from slamming into him.

Chapter Four

Acar crashed through a line of kiosks and skid to a stop hundreds of feet away. He shook his head, stumbled to his feet, and fell back down.

Zaria gasped and shook Nora, "Wake up!"

The portal expanded, allowing more of the beast to squeeze through. Some of the tentacles slammed against the floor, latching down their suction cups. Then, they pulled the bulk of the body through the opening. Wet flesh squelched against the sides of the opening, and a low pop sounded as a black eye came through and locked onto Zaria.

"Oh, hell," Zaria exclaimed and let go of Nora. She conjured a shield to throw at its face, but the thickest part of one of its limbs blocked it. Another was quick to ensnare and yank her away from its link to the human realm.

Air rushed out of Zaria's lungs as it squeezed her enough to make a crack reverberate through her body, then slung her away from it and Nora. Acar staggered up to his feet and looked up in time for Zaria to slam into him, forcing a short shriek from his beak. He tucked and rolled backward, folding his wings to keep her tight against his chest.

A sharp pain seared through Zaria as she took a gasping breath and curled over to cradle her ribs. She craned her head to look up, rubbing her cheek against the soft feathers of Acar's underbelly.

"Zaria," Acar's voice was gentle, "Are you hurt?"

"Possibly mortally wounded," she chuckled then groaned. She didn't want to move and hoped that the people had finally made it out of the containment field.

"Take me as your familiar," he lifted his head to peer at her, "You'll be able to heal."

Zaria shook her head, "I can't make you a servant," she coughed and stiffened, "and it would be like you had sex with your boss."

Acar chirped and cocked his head to the side, "I'm asking to be your partner, and there's no way we did anything after you got drunk enough to throw up all over me."

"What!" Zaria's head swiveled back up, "Oww, shit!"

"It was rancid," Acar laughed, "but at least you finally admitted you loved me."

Acar jerked from under Zaria and yelped as a tentacle dragged him by the leg along the floor. Zaria strained to get up, using a toppled kiosk to help her stand. The Kraken had pulled itself fully through the portal. It splayed open its arms to reveal its massive beak and the sound of it chopping together reverberated through the hall.

Zaria's heart raced, and panic set in as she stumbled forward. The pain in her ribs kept her from gaining speed. Acar squawked and made bolt after bolt crash into the Kraken's body, but its tensed bulk ate each hit. She swiped her hand through the air but couldn't reach it with her weaponized shields. She wouldn't make it.

"I accept!" She screamed.

Acar turned and shrieked an arch of lightning at Zaria. She jerked to a stop and felt the healing bolt course through her. The feel of Acar's magic wrapped around her spine in waves of heat. Then it was over with a loud, pain-filled cry from Acar.

The Kraken had crushed Acar's leg as he beat against it with his wings and pierced it with his beak. Zaria ran and slammed a shield down on several of the creature's tentacles, forcing it to let go of Acar with a roar. He rolled out of the way as she surrounded the octopus with an invisible wall. It tried to force the walls apart, and Zaria struggled to keep it in place.

The air sizzled around her, and Acar yelled, "Hit 'em hard!"

Acar's innate knowledge of using his lightning rushed Zaria's mind. She took the warm tingle of the bolt down her spine and laced it through her shields. The Kraken seized from wave after wave of shocks, hitting it from every direction.

When Zaria finally dropped her shields, the Kraken splayed across the floor in a twitching mass of steaming muscles. Nora blinked, free of its control, and jumped back. Acar put out a wing to stop her retreat.

"Oh, no, honey," Zaria said in a harsh tone, "You got a mess to clean up."

Epilogue

P.I.L. agents overran the shopping center, rounding up all the people they could find. It was lucky that Curtis quickly called in reinforcements when she threw down the containment spell. He saved the day, and Zaria was confident he would make sure she remembered it.

Nora had a personal P.I.L. agent interviewing her. It was a given they would try recruiting the little witch with so much potential. It was that, or they would lock her powers away as punishment for almost causing a tragedy.

The healing team set up a medic station and treated the injured. Relief washed over Zaria when she found out no one had died. It was good that the Kraken didn't catch Nora's bullies. Since they were the target, they wouldn't have made it out alive. The only reason it went after Zaria and Acar was because they stood in the way.

The girls huddled together beside the medic station, taking glances at Nora and the team handling the disoriented Kraken. The portal was now stable and a liaison was speaking with the creature's disgruntled mother on the other side. To think so much trouble was caused by a duo of teens.

The other people who weren't too hurt chattered and laughed in disbelief. Magic was real, and they were going to tell everyone. That was a nice thought. Once all the nonmagical people passed the perimeter of the containment shield, they wouldn't remember a thing. Zaria always thought it was a shame that magic users still had to stay hidden. But fear of the unknown pushed people to kill it with fire. Plus, they were in the U.S., and there was no way they would survive another witch-burning season.

"You alright?" Acar asked, pulling Zaria from her thoughts.

He was back in his human form and holding out his hand to her. Zaria took it, letting him help her stand.

"Yeah," she blushed, "You're ready for that talk, huh?"

Acar lifted her hand and kissed the back of it, "I'm ready whenever you're ready."

Zaria smiled and knew it was goofy, "Okay, but first I have to grab something."

She led him to Mama Kay's Cake Shop, which had missed the extent of the battle. Two young women were chattering about not getting reception to post the videos they had taken. Their eyes went wide when they saw Zaria and Acar step to the counter.

"Hey, can I get two orders of the Chocolate Assassin with extra sauce on the side for both?"

Green Treacheries
By
Edward Austin Hall

Overhead, an oak tree dangles its murderer from a stout branch in the still February air. The cluster of mistletoe shows stolen verdure in a brazen inversion of its gray-barked host; fulsome leaves, ready to sever themselves and drop to earth with the least of breezes, form something like a baby tree just yanked from a green womb.

Standing near the foot of the oak, Heygee points at the pendant growth but says nothing as he meets Mikhi's gaze. The two men nod as if yoked.

Heygee turns again and lifts the double barrels of his shotgun to his still-pointing hand, aims, and fires once. The wood above the hanging plant scatters into a splintery cloud, and the mistletoe plummets.

Mikhi, gripping the bottom corners of a dark apron looped over his neck but uncinched at the waist, races to intercept the falling greenery.

Apart from the mistletoe, everything around the two men bears that drained forest-in-winter palette: their coats, the bare branches, the lichen-crusted trunks, the spent leaves and dead grasses, all beneath a steely sky. With the apron's black cotton stretched before him, Mikhi overlooks an oak root in his path. He trips and falls onto his extended arms. Breath leaves him in a sound somewhere between bark and cough. The unloaded shotgun slung across Mikhi's back slides forward, and its butt conks the rear of his skull.

The younger man groans as he rolls onto his left side.

Heygee squats beside him. "You okay?"

Mikhi nods as he stares, not at Heygee but at the mistletoe on the ground, ten feet away from them. "Shit."

"No worries. We got enough time to find another one."

Scowling, Mikhi rubs the back of his head. "Tell me again why it can't touch ground."

"You tell me. Druids started that b'iness. Anybody who knows what the stuff's good for knows windfall mistletoe ain't worth shit."

"You make it fall, not wind."

Heygee looks up to examine the network of branches. "Same difference. Once it touches the ground, the shit don' work. Tha's how I learned it, and I got no interest in testin' that rule."

As Heygee stands, Mikhi sits up. The older man extends a hand to the younger one.

As Mikhi regains his feet, he says, "Too many god-damned rules." His accent is most obvious around the strand of emphatic *D*s, at the slightly rolled *R*, in the clipped trailing *S*. "Which way?"

Heygee retrieves a shotgun shell from his right coat pocket and reloads as he stares at the darkened remains of another fallen mistletoe cluster, which lies like a burnt offering at the base of an adjacent oak. "You pick. I been out here too much. In fact, remind me never to come out here again for supplies."

He looks down at his feet. "By the way, I brought somethin' in case we need to make an emergency exit, but … I don' want to use it if we don' have to. So, choose a direction and le's hope it doe'n't take us too much deeper into the woods. If possible, I wan' to stick wit' the plan and leave by boat."

His breath visible in the cold, Mikhi faces right, then left, then right again. He upnods in that direction.

Heygee recognizes the gesture and smiles. Like so much else, it's something Mikhi assuredly learned at Heygee's side. In lockstep, they head that way, frozen stuff crackling beneath their feet.

The two men examine the canopies of many more trees before they speak again.

"How you find out about all this stuff, Gee?"

"From my dad. A lot from him, anyway."

"The va—"

Even before Mikhi can complete the word, Heygee holds his upturned palm toward the other man. Mikhi fishes forth his wallet, extracts a five-dollar bill, and places it in Heygee's hand.

Heygee stuffs the cash inside his coat's breast pocket. "What do we say, Mikhi?"

"''lifer.' Sorry."

"You should be. Loose lips sink shit." Heygee gazes right, left, focuses again on the forest floor. Ahead, the leaf litter supports or partly conceals many more dead limbs than does their path to this spot. The flesh around Heygee's right eye twitches.

"Your father taught you about 'lifers? I thought—"

Heygee raises an open hand for quiet. "There's something wrong out here."

Mikhi jerks his head at the ground they've already crossed. "Sure. In trunk of Wriggle's car. At edge of lake, where we leave it."

"Yeah, not the fresh kind of wrong. Up ahead? Tha's a dead zone."

"Left alone, mistletoe kills tree, da?"

"Da. But …."

Mikhi scowls. "But what?"

"I spent the last decade takin' mistletoe from this stretch of woods. You'd think that would'e saved some of these trees."

They stare along a corridor of ghostly, rotting trunks and fungus-riddled logs. "Looks like forest is not grateful for help, Gee."

"Yeah, no lie."

* * *

Thanks to a phone call Heygee overheard just after New Year's, he knew Mikhi had been lying to him. As soon as the noisy exchange ended, Mikhi identified the caller as his landlord, unhappy about late rent. Heygee, however, felt sure that Mikhi spoke to some mafiya asshole who'd promised to slide an icepick into tender parts of the younger man. The precise details didn't matter, as Heygee couldn't untell all the secrets he'd already shared with Mikhi. His bigger problem was a reluctance to do anything. Heygee, not much given to introspection, recognized the difficulty he had in getting people to stick around. Mikhi, so far, had outlasted all the others. Before his arrival, a lot of the time Heygee spent at the garage, he spent there alone.

When the opportunity arose to rob the local mortician of a luxury car, with the dangerous cargo of a 'lifer in its trunk, a plan budded in Heygee's bent-on-get-back brain. If the plan worked, he could untangle this betrayal, fuck over his unfavorite neighbor, and perform what he saw as a civic duty undreamt of by other petty criminals.

* * *

This time, Heygee picks their path. They head south—away from the dead zone, from the car and the boat hidden near it, from the lake itself, and back toward home, toward Atlanta, half a day's walk from the forest they search. In patchwork form, those woods stretch all the way back to Georgia's capital, still an urban forest, despite builders' decades-long efforts to the contrary.

Mikhi adjusts his muffler against the cold. "Gee, I see mistletoe all over town when I'm driving tow truck. Why not use some of that?"

"And harvest it how? You been keepin' secrets? You can levitate forty feet, hover in the air? Saw through four inches o' live wood while you' at it?"

"No! But you. You can do ... strange things with little bits of junk."

"Not fly."

"No, but you have ... pal ... with tree service—"

"—an' he don't know shit about 'lifers. I plan to keep it that way. You can't tell, just ... anybody about these things. Most folks would think I'm batshit crazy if I tol' 'em 'bout half the stuff I seen in Atlanta over the years. E'body else would pack a bag and unass the area before sundown." Heygee lets his gaze drift from denuded limbs to the sky behind them. "Which might be the best thing for some people I know." Purposely, he does not look at Mikhi.

Mikhi barrels onward, seemingly oblivious to the message Heygee is sending. "What about fire? Do evil things not burn?"

Heygee snorts twin plumes into the chill. "Hm. What I hear is, they get all burnt-lookin', but that might be ... I don't know, some kin' o' shell? They come back from that extra-pissed. Pop told me about—wait, when did you grow a bump o' curiosity? When the shotgun hit your head?" He barks out a mirthless laugh.

"Always you call me terrible student. I try to be better."

"Well, keep trying. We'll see where that lands you."

*   *   *

Trust being the rarest thing ever to possess Heygee, he lent it accordingly. One of his early assistant mechanics complimented him for working "magic" on a car; when she arrived for work the next day, Heygee fired her and gave no cause, as allowed by Georgia law. Indeed, he had used magic on the vehicle to make it run again … after he used magic to disable it on the street alongside his garage. That car's owner drove it away three days later, grateful for the "brand-new transmission" he believed Heygee had, providentially, installed.

Seven assistant mechanics later, Mikhi walked into the garage to ask about the HELP WANTED sign in one of the front windows.

*   *   *

Mikhi speaks after a silence long enough to qualify as a reminder of Heygee's self-interrupted story, rather than a test by tongue of Heygee's barb: "What did your father tell you?"

"He told me Atlanta cops have a special unit that covers up 'lifer stuff."

"How could he know this?"

Heygee turns to look Mikhi in the face but says nothing.

"Your dad was police, Gee? He protected 'lifers?"

Heygee nods. "Not firsthand. Cops on that squad don't get to quit. Pop quit his beat, but nobody on the force knew what all 'e knew by then."

Mikhi frowns. "Your father knew how you make living?"

"He knew a long time before I ever opened the garage that he and I didn' see eye to eye on the law. But hey, he was a German

POW who got to live here after the war, so his idea of the States was …."

"Was what?"

"Narrow. Like most white folks I know, he lacked enough experience of black people to see Ma was one."

"You mean like me with you on day we meet?"

"You caught on quick enough. Dude who asked for the job that same week talked himself out of it just as fast. Asked me if 'Clancy' ever worked for me, in response to which I equivocated. Not only did he not get hired, I wanded his car as he was leavin'."

"Killed it dead?"

"Yep."

"But who is Clancy, Gee? What did he do to you?"

Both men fall silent as they navigate the baroque roots of a squat oak whose girth is twice that of its neighbors. Heygee pauses every few steps to glance up in search of mistletoe, to no avail.

"Tha's white-supremacist code speak, man: 'Klan, see'? Thought he was talkin' to another member of his tribe. Dumb motherfucker. After I used the wand, he asked me to tow his shit. I tol' him I was too backed up, an' he'd have to wait till the end o' business. An' he did! So I hooked up his car, drove him to his bank, had him pull out cash, then I told him what I charge per mile. You should'e seen his face. Seein' as he couldn' afford me takin' 'im much farther, he paid me, an' I dropped him an' his big ol' American piece o' shit at Torkel's shop."

Mikhi erupts in laughter, and Heygee joins him. They laugh till all their breath is gone.

Once Mikhi recovers to breakthrough chortling, he says, "Torkel is worse crook than you'll ever be, Gee!"

"Who you tellin'?"

They stand atop a ragged knot of tree roots and dissolve further into mirth.

Heygee sobers up sooner than Mikhi does. He stares toward the ground, his eyes focused on nothing. Without a word, he looks up and clomps away from the enormous oak, and from Mikhi. "Come on. Le's get it done."

Terminus[2]

* * *

That summer's day when Heygee met Mikhi, the lot beside the garage looked like pre-Internet–pre-Christmas parking someplace shoppers didn't give a shit whether anyone else could ever squeeze back into a car—or if somebody starved to death on the wait to get out of one. Homicidal Georgia sun shone down on Heygee, who wore his coverall peeled to the waist and a sweat-soaked anti-nuke tank-top that read NO in blocky Russian.

Mikhi walked up wearing a gray coverall that complemented Heygee's half-shucked blue one. He stammered a bit as he asked whether the mechanic position the sign advertised was filled yet. As the question hung in the air, he looked away from Heygee's bare arms and barely covered, message-heavy chest.

With a glance at the wear and laundry-defying grime of the gray coverall to assure himself of its authenticity, Heygee asked whether things looked as if the position were filled. He bent to give attention to a gaping engine compartment. "Want the job? Help out. Give you eighteen bucks an hour. Do good work, you keep gettin' the eighteen bucks."

Mikhi asked where to begin, and Heygee pointed out cars that wore tiny cones of red, yellow, or green plastic, the be-greened ones of which needed moving into the clotted lot. The younger mechanic opened his mouth to ask another question, saw Heygee's focus on recalcitrant spark plugs, closed his mouth, and entered the garage to find the key rack.

Hours later, the two exhausted men sat opposite each other and drank bottled water. Mikhi angled the mouth of his bottle toward Heygee's chest and said, "You feel strongly about this?"

Ever cautious, Heygee glanced down at the stylized incoming missiles and the accompanying three letters that appeared to read HET, looked up again at Mikhi, and lied, "I got this thing used. Liked the design. Is it Russian?" For years thereafter, he chose how and when to undo the manifold illusions these words cast, each time to his advantage. And elsewise.

* * *

They find the largest cluster of the day so far, a plump, pre-
mortem tumbleweed of a mistletoe plant, just as winds stir
around them. At a spot directly beneath the clump, the two men
part. Mikhi eyes the path he takes to a place near the tree's trunk
as Heygee turns to head at a right angle toward the limits of the
parasitized oak's canopy.

Heygee wheels to face his target, looks up, and sees the mistletoe tugged off vertical by the swelling wind. "Ah, shit."

"Give it minute, Gee."

They wait. Breeze becomes bluster.

As if the earth beneath Heygee's feet draws desperate breath,
the ground he stands on swells into a hill. Heygee's eyes widen,
and he scrambles away from what appears to be some infernal
birthing.

Mikhi stands still for a moment as the tree behind him leans
closer. He looks over one shoulder, then the other. Then he
laughs.

"Wha's funny?"

"Is wind, Gee. Not afterlifer sneak attack." Mikhi points
across the crest of the surprise hillock, which aligns with the targeted tree and several of its neighbors. "Roots are dead there.
Trees will fall soon."

Even more alarmed, Heygee yells, "Why the hell are you still
standin' there, man? Move!"

As Mikhi smiles and eases out of the tree's shadow, wood
crackles, roots rip, soil geysers—and the massive oak topples his
way. Ground crumbles beneath him, and Mikhi loses his footing.

"Mikhail!" Heygee drops his shotgun and races toward the
other man.

With a sound like an angry god slamming heaven's door, the
tree's tonnage strikes the ground. The shock wave tosses
Heygee off his feet.

Terminus[2]

* * *

Most folks stepped over the fallen things that Heygee claimed for magical use. Many people never noticed them at all, given their chaotic origins in car crashes or amid the routine wear of operating any vehicle on Atlanta's uneven and ill-maintained streets. Heygee himself first saw perhaps the most potent of these seemingly mundane tools the day he first witnessed one at work.

That day, for his lunchtime walk, Heygee pocketed an extra bottle of water, left the garage, and headed north on Lowery. As he approached the far side of the Interstate 20 overpass, he saw Alvin—a veteran who lived atop the slanting eastern support wall for the highway overhead—standing at the curb and staring up the exit ramp at oncoming traffic. Heygee called the other man's name, but Alvin showed no sign of having heard him. Instead, despite the DON'T WALK sign being lit, Alvin stepped off the curb, into the crosswalk—and into the path of a speeding BMW. Heygee yelled and ran toward the intersection, but several dozen feet and too little time separated the two men. The BMW's driver held down the horn but, to Heygee's ears, never braked. Alvin, at the center of the crosswalk, stopped moving—except for his right hand, which gripped a slender rod of some kind and swiveled to point it at the hurtling car. As he did, the car's horn fell silent, as did the roar of its engine. Alvin sprung back into motion and narrowly eluded the BMW as it rolled into the intersection. A slack-jawed Heygee watched the bearded driver wrestle the powerless car to a slowly curving stop beneath the highway. Heygee thought for a moment that the driver was somehow hurt, only to realize that what he'd mistaken for a wound was a large strawberry birthmark on the balding man's scalp. As the driver looked his way, Heygee turned away and startled a bit to find Alvin standing beside him.

The two pedestrians swapped empty niceties until Heygee asked, quietly, if he'd just seen Alvin slap some mojo on the stilled automobile. Heygee never forgot the care with which Alvin whispered his reply: "I 'on't know nothin' 'bout no hoodoo."

With a snorting smirk at this transparent fib, Heygee unpocketed the extra water from his Afghanistan camouflage pants and handed it to Alvin, who slipped it into a wide pocket of his own, far less recently washed pair.

Months passed before Heygee first found a wand of his own.

* * *

Heygee rolls sideways over leaves and far harder things hidden by them. He slaps the ground, regains his footing, and runs to Mikhi's side. Pulverized leaf dust clouds the air near the collapsed oak. Both men cough as Heygee takes a knee next to Mikhi.

"Sor—sorry, Gee. You're right." Mikhi coughs, then winces in pain. "I am terrible student."

"Can you stand?"

Mikhi tries to put weight on his right hand, cries out, settles again into the leaf litter. "Ground gives way, and I go ass under teakettle."

"Your ass could be under that oak tree. Damn near was."

"I think things are broken, Gee. Wrist, maybe. Ankle for sure."

"One thing at a—shit. Hold tight. I'll be back. Yell if you need me." Heygee springs to his feet, retraces his steps, looks for the shotgun. The leaves here, he realizes, are deeper than they are elsewhere, and the shotgun lies, concealed, somewhere beneath them. *Looks like forest is* not *grateful for help.*

Heygee glances at the spoiled mistletoe, crushed by the branch that must have nurtured it for years. He surveys the area near the tree for saplings and limbs to scavenge, unsheaths a knife, and chops at skinny trunks until he gathers a suitably lengthy set of five. Heygee darts his gaze at the sky and doffs his coat. He rejoins Mikhi. As he squats to gently remove Mikhi's boot laces, Heygee stares into his eyes.

"What's your name?"

"Seriously? Tree does not land on my head, Gee. I fall wrong."

"Yeah, you sound like you. Okay, can you raise your arm? I'll carry your shotgun." Heygee lifts the weapon clear and slings it over his own shoulder.

"How can we get mistletoe now, Gee?"

"Le's get you mobile first. Worry about the rest after that." Heygee lays out his two longer wood cuttings in an uneven X and places the three shorter ones as crossbars to the X's largest section. He notches and bevels lengths of wood, then lashes them together—first with boot laces, later with snaky roots he slices off the oak's freshly revealed nethers.

By the time Heygee wrestles Mikhi onto the travois cross-bars, the once-gunmetal sky is the shade of slate. With his back to Mikhi—whose head rests on Heygee's coat, tied with its sleeves to the crossbar just behind the crux of the travois— Heygee stands between the bars of the X's smallest section, squats to grasp them, then stands again to tug his cargo into motion.

They travel this way for less than a mile until Heygee, flushed and huffing, halts. "Son of a bitch," Heygee says. He pulls the travois in a brief arc to his left and tells Mikhi, "Look north. To your left."

A few hundred feet away from them sprawls a lowish, octo-poidal oak. Many of its branches hover mere yards above the ground.

The tree teems with mistletoe.

"Forest has change of heart." Mikhi looks back and forth, from oak to Heygee to oak again.

Heygee wags his head in disbelief. "Like magic."

* * *

Whether he thought of it as *hoodoo* or *sympathetic transfer-ence* or whichever of the many names he gave it over time, magic consumed Heygee once he replicated Alvin's feat. He found it an ideal toolbox for dealing with Atlanta's countless willfully ignorant and inattentive drivers. Wands—lengths of wire made baroque by the compressing passage of numerous tires—exerted the broadest effect. All that torque, imparted on the anvil of Georgia asphalt, let a wand control any sort of machine, as if the contorted bit of metal were a remote and universal on/off switch.

One day Heygee glimpsed an intact plastic signal cover, ejected from the bumper of a car in some collision, lying in the gutter along Lowery Boulevard. Except for the absence of the vehicle that carried it to that spot, this translucent orange plate was perfect, as if it might have skipped integration into an automobile altogether and come to this place directly from its manufacturer. As Heygee retrieved it from the concrete, a car passed behind the chromatic little window. Heygee stood upright and blinked. He held the thing at arm's length and looked through it, again, at the same car, which waited at the Oglethorpe intersection for the traffic light to change. Etched in varying shades of orange, Heygee saw a backward-facing toddler, strapped into a safety seat. He lowered the gleaming piece of plastic and saw only the car's rear-end exterior; raised it again to see spectral drivers traverse the intersection. *Yes.* He hadn't imagined it: the signal cover let him see through the skin of that car, of every car in sight, like some hand-held X-ray.

At that stage, Heygee wondered whether these powers were inherent to the objects or if he and Alvin might be … different in some way. But Heygee trusted no one enough to ask and, thus, to put such uncertainties to the test.

The day he plucked a shiny-because-road-rashed wheel weight—one of the adhesive rectangular kind used to reduce tire wear through balancing—from an inch-deep crack on Ralph David Abernathy Boulevard, he stopped caring about the earlier mystery. For whatever reason, at a touch he knew, without needing to see its power demonstrated, exactly what that drossy little ingot would do, and how he could activate its arcane energies.

Mostly, Heygee used these things, and others like them, to do what he saw as good. His crooked heart stretched Heygee's definition of *good* to limits that would appall a genuinely decent Atlanta resident—could such a person have been found.

Terminus[2]

* * *

As Mikhi lies on the travois nine feet below him, Heygee clings to a stout oak branch. Beneath Heygee, a sleek mistletoe specimen points suggestively from the branch's underside at the immobilized mechanic.

"Is bit of role reversal, eh, Gee?"

"Heavens, young man! You kiss your mother with that mouth?"

"I kiss only you with this mouth."

Heygee tests an upward-sprouting stub of a branch as hand-hold and finds it firm. He unsheathes his knife, leans into the air beside the branch, looks up at dimming sky, then down at Mikhi. "Listen, we ain' got much time, but you need to know some things. I know about Icepick Ivan." He pronounces the name the long-*I* American way.

Mikhi's features freeze.

"What I don't know is what you're s'posed to give 'im so you can stay unperforated."

"No, Gee, you—"

"I what? I don't understand?" In perfectly accented Russian, Heygee says, "I understand more than you can ever know."

"Is not about me staying unperfor—"

"Please stop lying to me, Mikhail."

"No." Mikhi blinks back tears. "You misunderstand. This man, this mobster, he is killer—"

"Comes with the job, I imagi—"

"No! Gee, he does not threaten me with icepick. He threatens you."

"Mikhail, I heard what you said to him. I heard you tell me he was your landlord. After he promised to icepick you in your gulliboy asshole—"

"That is what you mishear, Gee! He promises me he will put icepick in his—'yevó'—gulliboy asshole. Meaning yours. I think that you think you hear 'tvoî'—your—meaning mine, da?" For a moment, Mikhi does not blink as he holds Heygee's gaze. As tears flood Mikhi's cheeks, he closes his eyes and turns away from Heygee's looming visage. "If mafiyoski kill me, I am dead, Gee. If they kill you, I do not wish to live."

Silence hovers between the two men.

Heygee breaks it: "Mikhail, why didn't you tell me? We do everything together. We can fix this. Together."

Mikhi opens his eyes. "Do you still mishear? I fear for your life!"

After another lengthy silence, Heygee exhales audibly. "Okay. Okay. Get your apron set. I'm 'o'n' cut this loose, we goin' back to the car, we kill the 'lifer, and we take the boat the hell away from here. You ready?"

Mikhi meets Heygee's gaze and nods.

Heygee saws through the mistletoe's stem and watches it drop into Mikhi's lap. He sheathes his knife.

"Hold on," Heygee says. "I'm comin'." He inches backward, along the moss-coated branch, toward the trunk of the oak.

Once he makes his way down the trunk, he strides across the crackling detritus to Mikhi. As he had earlier, he looks down at his leather-shod feet. "These boots I'm wearin' are paratrooper issue. If anything happens to me, you peel 'em off me, put 'em on your own feet. You can leap miles in these things. But leave e'rything else behin', you hear? Includin' me. They work for one person. Not for two."

Mikhi, his gaze lowered, his eyes unfocused, nods.

"Now, tell me all about Vlad the icepicker, or whatever 'is fuckin' name is."

* * *

If Heygee's first encounter with Riley Wriggle had bred only one of its terrible sequels, and not both, the mechanic might never have recognized their connections with Atlanta's Undertaker to the Famed. Heygee was driving a car to determine whether he'd fixed its strange tendency to stall. Driving his own car and homeward bound as soon as Heygee's test drive looped them back to the garage, Oscar—Mikhi's immediate predecessor—followed his boss. As they threaded the parked car's bracketing the street alongside the Wriggle Funeral Parlour, Heygee found his path blocked by a tall, graying man who stood mid-road, with his back to traffic. Heygee's hand stopped before touching the center of the steering wheel. A tiny interior voice told him, *No, don't*. No matter: Oscar, seemingly impatient to get home, loosed a sustained note. As if the sound of the car horn were thawing him free of a glacial burial, the man looked up slowly from his phone but, elsewise, did not move. Even given that over-the-shoulder posture, though, there could be no mistaking the mummified-crocodile visage of Riley Wriggle, which Heygee knew from far too many Atlanta billboards. Heygee's hand still hovered in position to make the sound, but he lowered it before Oscar's second peal. Only then did Wriggle step between two parked cars to let them pass.

Because neither he nor Oscar was driving a stolen car at the time, Heygee was, at first, just annoyed to see in the side mirror that Wriggle photographed both their license plates, and not in a furtive way. Once the owner of the repaired car went missing—from home, according to neighbors, and without ever reclaiming from the garage his "only way to get around"—Heygee's annoyance mutated to suspicion. Once Oscar failed ever to show up again at work, or anywhere else, that suspicion curdled into something far worse. Heygee felt no surprise at the utter lack of any inquiry by the police. The choice not to report Oscar's vanishing struck Heygee as his best way to not find himself likewise disappeared.

* * *

Heygee pauses for breath atop a low hill. "So, you never seen this guy face to face, even once?"

"He is voice on phone. One night I come home, find door ajar—"

"When was this?"

"Week after you first spend night with me. All is normal except in bedroom …."

Heygee resumes dragging the travois. "Yeah?"

"Is photograph of us … together. In bed. Stuck to pillow with icepick."

Heygee mutters undifferentiated obscenities. "All o' this … for a wand?"

"He never says 'wand' to me. He says he wants 'car stopper.'"

"So, he's seen it work … but he doe'n't know what it i—"

A distant sound of metal on metal silences Heygee mid-word. He halts and slowly lowers the travois to the ground.

Mikhi whispers, "Is coming from—"

"—the car," Heygee says, also hushed.

The noise repeats, then worsens.

"Is 'lifer … escaping?"

"It's not nightfall yet. That thing's still asleep. This sounds like … a hydraulic spreader?"

"Jaws of life?"

"Mm hmm. You know what that means."

"Cops," Mikhi says. He looks up at Heygee, who nods. "Leave me, Gee. Use boots and go—"

"Nope. No chance o' that. But also—" Heygee reaches inside his shirt to peel something noisily free of his chest and extracts a wand covered with transparent strapping tape. "—unless they cut the car into pieces, and prob'ly the 'lifer wit' it, they got no chance of openin' that trunk till I use this. Again."

"Okay. Then what?"

"Hang on. I feel a plan comin' together."

* * *

Heygee's plan for stealing Wriggle's Lexus unfolded over almost two weeks. Because Heygee thought that the mortician might recognize him, Mikhi surveilled Wriggle's place.

For the first few days, while Heygee resumed his solo act at the garage, Mikhi rendered himself invisible with an unshaved face, unwashed clothes, and an unsound suitcase on wheels. He spent daytime hours on well-sunned benches in the public park opposite the funeral home. Whenever a hearse left the premises, Mikhi called Heygee and spoke into the phone inside his coat, via the earbuds concealed by his upturned collar and grimy watch cap. The seeming nonsense he uttered, which made other park visitors within earshot veer even farther from him than they'd already intended, always included a direction and a street name.

At the garage, Heygee worked with the front doors rolled down, the high side windows open, and a virtual assistant screening calls. He despised these devices, which he called canned spies, but he couldn't handle a smart phone in the midst of the Wriggle campaign. Whenever Mikhi's calls came through, he dropped whatever he was doing, exited the garage by the side door, into the lot, and borrowed one of several privacy glass–clad cars parked there. From the garage, he'd take a route to put him at the likelier neighborhood gas station near the funeral home, given Mikhi's coded cues. There, he parked rudely, to render two pumps useless at the same time. Then, he waited in hopes of a hearse's arrival.

This stratagem paid off after five days. Heygee was cleaning his borrowed car's spotless windshield when one of Wriggle's three newest hearses queued behind him. He hustled to pump a paid-for gallon of gasoline into his Trojan sedan. As he finished, he sleight-of-handed an ingot into the pump spout before racking it. He was climbing into the car as a second Wriggle hearse arrived and stopped at a just-vacated island. He cursed at the missed opportunity but could do nothing else.

That night, the result of Heygee's sabotage made national news.

Legacy media coverage characterized the event as a costly mechanical failure. On social media, it sparked the #POSSESSEDHEARSE hashtag. Just after the vehicle, dosed in its fuel tank with Heygee's magical wheel weight, returned home, and as its driver was only steps away from the not-running meat wagon, it roared to life in Wriggle's parking lot. Despite its lack of a driver, the hearse performed destruction-derby wheelies amid Wriggle's fleet of limousines and other funereal conveyances. This inexplicable malfunction went on for hours—even after police shot out the hearse's tires and repeatedly targeted its engine compartment.

In his bed that night, a slack-jawed Mikhi looked up from his laptop, even as video of the hearse-as-dervish continued in a YouTube tab. "Oh. My. Fucking. God."

Seated against the headboard next to Mikhi, Heygee smiled. "And guess who made it possible: my fucking god. Come 'ere, you."

"But what is next part of plan?"

"First things first."

The next part of the plan entailed tactical wanding of Wriggle's surviving vehicles. As Heygee predicted, Wriggle's drivers shied from the gas station where the sabotage occurred. Each driver avoided all the neighborhood outlets, as if they might draw gasoline from a lone, contaminated tank. No matter. Mikhi's undercover op entered a new phase that involved gazing through casements—Heygee's name for ensorcelled signal covers—in search of arriving afterlifers.

Mikhi told Heygee that he worried about distinguishing between regular corpses and the bloodthirsty animated variety.

On the morning of day thirteen, Heygee heard the spy can announce Mikhi's incoming call. "Shira: Answer," Heygee said. "What y' got?"

"Weird shit. Know how dead people look like silhouettes in casement?"

"Mm hmm."

"One that just got wheeled inside … glows."

"Tha's it. Be right there. Shira: Hang up!"

As Heygee eyed the key rack, he realized he had no working privacy-glassed cars on the premises. "Fuck it," he said. He grabbed a baseball cap that languished in his lost-and-found box, donned it, and lowered the bill as far as he could. His hand hovered beside keys to the most recently arrived car that moved—but on a whim, Heygee unhooked the key to an already-fixed cream-colored Lexus, whose owner he'd been lying to for days in regard to its status. He pulled on his coat, whose interior pocket held a plastic pencil box with two wands inside, and left.

Heygee's cell rang as he was en route. "Da?"

"Worm is turning—" This phrase indicated that Wriggle was outside the funeral home, so Heygee needed to proceed with care. "—Mister President, you hear? Worm is turning." Mikhi ended the call.

"Fuck." Heygee pulled over and texted a reply. The moment he pressed send, he put the Lexus back into gear, made a U-turn, and took a different route toward Mikhi.

Heygee sat parked behind a commercial building that faced the park near Wriggle's. He saw Mikhi appear from the side street. Heygee rolled down his window and beckoned him.

As Mikhi approached the driver's door, Heygee opened it, scooted over the center console, exited by the front passenger-side door, removed his coat, and got in back. There, he lay on the floor and covered himself with his coat. "You drive," he said. "And switch hats with me."

As they rolled onto the side street to view the funeral home from a safe distance, Mikhi described the meltdown Wriggle had been undergoing for the last quarter hour. "He fires every-one, Gee. Loudly. Says they put his ass in worst possible sling— Gee, Wriggle leaves in Lexus!"

"Use the casement."

Mikhi fumbled audibly in a pocket. "Bingo. Afterlifer on board. He heads north."

"Go, go! Follow 'im."

Heygee felt Mikhi accelerate onto Abernathy, heard a truck horn sound that seemed uncomfortably close, felt Mikhi turn again to trace the other Lexus's path. "If he takes the interstate," Heygee said, "that's our best chance. We wand his car, pretend to help, knock out 'is phone. Cool?" He slid the pencil box onto the center console.

"Cool."

Heygee got tossed about through three more turns before he felt the car race up a mild incline. "I-20?"

Mikhi said, "Da."

"Try to get him right before the 75/85 exit. I have an idea."

Heygee was again pressed against the back seat as the Lexus accelerated once more. A swift lane change and sudden laughter, followed by sudden braking, told Heygee what he had been waiting to hear, even before Mikhi said it: "We have him."

"Hurry! He'll be on his phone soon as he sees 'e can't call through the car!"

Cold air rushed briefly beneath the cover of Heygee's coat as Mikhi exited and closed his door. Heygee sat up, found the pencil box, and fetched the remaining wand from it. He reached across the car to open the rear passenger-side door, unfolded himself from the Lexus, and stood beside it. He turned to face Wriggle's car, a twin of their vehicle, and saw its driver standing at its trunk, trying to make his phone work. Mikhi stood calmly behind their car and faced oncoming traffic, his hands peaceably folded.

Wriggle saw Heygee. The elderly man raised a shaking hand and pointed at the older of the two mechanics. "You. You, you, you're dead."

Pinching the wand between thumb and forefinger, Heygee casually flattened both his hands on the roof of the borrowed Lexus. "Sir," he said, "have we met?"

Wriggle made panicked swivelhead moves, fixed upon the concrete barriers that lined the safety lane. As he climbed across one of them, he dropped his phone on the asphalt and rent his thousand-dollar suit, then stumbled down a steep slope to cross a dry concrete ditch.

"Sir," Heygee repeated. "Is something wrong?"

"Carjackers," Wriggle yelled. "Help!" He saw a tent and staggered toward it.

The tent moved a bit, its flap opened, and Alvin came out of the little structure.

"'Ey, Nhombre," Heygee yelled. "How you been, man?"

"Gunga Din! Wha's up? Wha's this Negro talkin' 'bout?"

"If I had to guess," Heygee said, "I'd say 'e had a friend o' mine killed, an' 'e thought 'e got me, too."

Alvin said, "Oh, hell no," balled a fist, and charged Wriggle.

Wriggle raised empty hands and backpedaled. He toppled into the ditch, where Alvin joined him. Harsh, meaty sounds of impact ensued.

"Le's go," Heygee said, as late-morning traffic sped indifferently past. "Unwand the Wrigglemobile. I'll drive that." He scooped up the mortician's phone.

After a brief stop at the garage to replace Wriggle's tag with that of the other Lexus, change clothes, arm themselves, and attach Heygee's outboard boat to the stolen car's trailer hitch, they made for Lake Sidney Lanier with all dispatch.

*   *   *

In the diminishing distance, Heygee sees the stolen Lexus. A car-length or two away rests an Atlanta Police Department cruiser, albeit one bearing nonstandard colors. On its front driver-side door is emblazoned the word BULLBAT. Heygee again wears his coat and their remaining shotgun, which the coat conceals. On the travois, Mikhi's coat drapes him and the mistletoe—which he hugs, with one arm, gently against his chest.

The door of the police car opens. A uniformed officer steps forth.

To the west, a faint bright patch teases the trees as the sun prepares to sneak below the horizon.

"Officer," Heygee yells. He halts his hauling and waves. "We need help!"

The policeman, who wears sunglasses despite the gloom, sidles toward them.

Heygee resumes sledging his way toward the Lexus. Encumbered as he is, he still makes better time than the cop does. They meet a few hundred feet from the cars. Heygee lets the travois settle to the ground behind him.

"Man," Heygee says, sounding extra-Southern, "are we glad to see you." At this distance, Heygee sees that every visible glass surface of the Lexus is spiderwebbed with cracks, and flanges of metal betray several efforts to prise open the vehicle at its seams. The lip of the trunk resembles a preschooler's rendering of a monstrous smile, complete with protuberant fangs.

The cop hooks a thumb over his shoulder. "That your car?"

"That? No, sir. I wish! Well, maybe not now—"

"Who you draggin' there?"

"Tha's my friend Mike. He took a tumble in the woods. I had to rig up this whole—"

"You wouldn't mind givin' me a look at 'im, would you," says the cop. He does not move closer, though.

"Well, yeah, I was hopin' you could get us to a hosp—"

"No," the cop says. "I mean, turn 'im so's I can get a looky-look at 'im. Please."

Heygee murmurs apologetic nonwords and squats to pull Mikhi and the travois into a side-view for the cop. Mikhi's eyes are half-lidded, as if he is drugged. His chin droops, and he drools a bit on himself.

The cop visibly relaxes. He moseys toward them … until he notices the bulge beneath Mikhi's coat. "What you boys huntin' out here?"

As he faces the cop, Heygee shakes his head, slowly opens his hands, and shows his palms—and the very tip of the wand he bears, taped to his forearm, under several layers of sleeve, and pointed at the policeman. "We ain' hun'ers, off'cer."

The cop audibly unsnaps the holster guard for his sidearm, which he leaves his hand atop. "Real slow, now. You show me what's under that coat."

Heygee, really slowly indeed, inverts his hands in a gesture of appeasement. Painstakingly, he reaches for Mikhi's coat—which he whips aside in a blur to reveal a wide-eyed Mikhi aiming the other wand at the cop.

The cop squeezes the trigger of his semi-automatic, to no avail. In a blur of his own, he unholsters and aims a TASER, which likewise fails.

Heygee levels the shotgun at the cop. In a voice far less nasal than the one he'd directed previously at the policeman, he says, "Drop it, motherfucker."

The policeman obeys.

"Now drop everything. Except your handcuffs."

Again, the policeman complies. His truncheon rings dully as it strikes the gravel underfoot. "You boys are makin' a big mistake. False imprisonment—"

"Shut the fuck up. And cuff yourself."

His breath growing audible, the policeman looks from Heygee to Mikhi, then toward the fast-setting sun. "Okay, listen. Somethin's about to happen here. I don't know how to explain it—"

"Should I just shoot 'im, Mike?"

Mikhi says nothing, but he nods as if agreeing to another beer.

"Wait! Don't shoot! See? I—I'm doin' what you said." Steel teeth rasp as the officer closes one bracelet around his left wrist.

"Put that hand between your legs."

The officer's mouth opens.

Heygee cocks the shotgun. "Say one more fuckin' syllable and you're a dead man."

A rasp different from that of the handcuffs issues from the trunk of the Lexus.

"If I stay out here, I'm a dead man either way." The officer turns to run.

Heygee drops the barrel and fires. The slug takes off the officer's right foot at the ankle. "God damn it," Heygee says. He sheds his coat, unslings the shotgun, marches over, and slams its butt against the screaming cop's head.

When the officer comes to, Heygee faces him from ten feet away, where he cradles the mistletoe. The bleeding man tries to raise his left hand to his face, but the handcuffs click against the Lexus's trailer hitch. His hand stops short. Clawing noises come nonstop from the trunk.

"If you hadn't shown up," Heygee says, "this last part would've been way riskier for us."

"Please," says the officer, "my soul'll be swimmin' around inside that thing for who knows how long. Maybe forever. You can't—"

"And tha's how I know you done this t' somebody else. And that is why I got nothin' for you. Not a god-damn thing." Heygee looks down at Mikhi, who lies at his side, on the travois. "Ready?"

Mikhi nods. He aims the wand at the trunk.

The trunk lid bursts open. Standing in the trunk is what looks like a perfect, if hollow, wax effigy of a man in a ten-thousand-

131

dollar suit. The being's translucent eyes swivel toward the offering within reach. More like quicksilver than like wax, the thing's see-through head morphs into that of a human-sized lamprey. It lunges onto the bleeding man. Radial bands of teeth—so, so many teeth—engulf the squirming offering's face, muffle his screams. Blood gushes into the freshly morphed head, fills the uncanny effigy, imbrues its sharp, glassy hands as they grip the dying man. Sated, the thing looks up at Heygee—at the instant he hurls the mistletoe onto it.

In a flash, the sloshing red inside the thing changes to the tint of guilloched shadows. Without any shift to its posture or shape, it sprouts instant leaves. Mistletoe leaves. It becomes a crouching green man. In a ten-thousand-dollar suit.

Heygee exhales. "That," he says, "never gets old." He takes up the handles of the travois. "Le's get to the boat."

Mikhi shakes his head. "Can you not hear them, Gee?"

Even as Heygee's mouth forms the question, the sound of sirens crosses the threshold between Mikhi's younger ears and his own.

"We can use the boots—"

"Gee, no. Is over. As you say, boots work for one, not for two. And I cannot stand."

Heygee's jaw works mutely for a moment.

"Gee, shoot me. That way I cannot betray you again."

"Wha—what is wrong with you?" Heygee bats his hands against his own torso as he struggles to unburden himself of the weapon. He opens it, ascertains that both barrels are empty, slings it against his back once more. Then he kneels, scoops Mikhi into his arms, and vaults into the sky.

Heygee soars through the air upright, as if he rides some vast, unseen escalator. Lake Lanier passes beneath them. The higher they go, the more the cold increases its bite. Heygee sees a string of police cars—all limned by winking red, all dressed in the bruise hues of the Bullbat Squad—headed to the place he and Mikhi just fled.

And still the two men rise.

"You tell truth about chances of two surviving leap with boots?"

"Mm hmm."

Mikhi inhales raggedly. "I lie to you."

"What? When?"

"Mafiyoski come to my home. Months ago. Boss sees you outside garage, sees me, they follow. They call me weak link. Gulliboy. They … hurt me. Tonight they wait for you at garage. Their boss, they call him Otmechennyy—"

"Like … Gorbachev?"

"Da. He has—" Mikhi gestures with his good hand at his left brow.

"—a strawberry birthmark."

"Yes. I hope someday you can forgive me, Gee." With unexpected force, Mikhi shoves both his hands against Heygee's chest. What makes Heygee flinch, though—what makes his grip fail—is Mikhi's agonized mewl that accompanies this act.

Heygee screams as his lover is swallowed by the night. He reaches as if he might save Mikhi from the darkness below, but the magic of the boots does not allow it. Already past the zenith of his leap, Heygee descends as if borne by some invisible parachute.

All the way down, he weeps.

The Crossing: Moonlit Skies
By
Robert Jeffrey II

International Crossing Governing Body/ Classified Audio File
Transcript of Crossing Entry 29876, Professor Jun Patton, Audio Diary

[Audio begins]
We've hit another world. Another lead, time spent scouring yet another place for any sign of this psycho and the abductee.

I think Dad might've been right. Maybe I bit off a bit more than I can possibly even swallow at this point. Maybe my place is just in the classroom, and research libraries, nose plastered into vid-logs of others' cross dimensional journeys.

No, that's that stupid self-doubt creeping in. The same self-doubt that crept in on the Zombie world, Utopia World, Neo-Fascist Pumpkin world.

The less said there the better.

It's just.... we keep coming so close to getting this guy. FBI Agent Ms. Kayla "Tight Pants" Cooke says this is all a part of the investigation, the chase. She's had investigations that have lasted months, years even.

"You have to be patient" is her constant refrain. And that's when she talks. This woman has the whole "stoic warrior" down to a tee. I can't even get a laugh out of her.

And hey, this is me we're talking about! The life of the party. The "funny professor" that all the kids love.

But when you've seen some of the stuff we've come across, maybe laughing isn't an option. For every world we've hit where strife and worry are an afterthought, there have been just

*as many worlds that will always leave me tossing and turning in
bed for years to come.*

We've done some good, helped some people.

[Pause in recording, audible sigh]

Couldn't help everyone.

[Another pause in recording. Silence]

Dammit Dad.

[Audible movement, shuffling.]

*We've done good so far with the surviving. We're still
breathing. But she knows, and I sure as hell know, that the further this guy gets with Crossing from world to world, our
chances get slimmer to catching them.*

*So, as I get a first look at the double moons on this new
Earth, I have to believe that we still have a chance.*

*A little girl's life depends on me tackling this creeping self-
doubt.*

End of entry. Jun Patton out.

[Audio entry ends]

Earth 2418, 18:42:13

The duo ran towards the departing grav train, arms' fire
punctuating the air. Shots meant for them hit the gleaming alloy
of the train's shell above their heads. The open door of the supply car beckoned further ahead.

Jun dropped lower to the ground, ducking the shots, as Kayla
turned and fired several rounds from her RH-80, one slug finding a snug home in another pursuer.

"Get on the train!" Kayla shifted into a more stable shooter's
stance. Jun reached for her sidearm. "No! You're running! I'm
shooting! Do it!"

Jun responded with a frustrated nod and sprinted towards the
open supply car door.

Another set of rounds fired by the special agent, the bright-
ened colors of her tracer fire becoming lost in the neon blue tint
of the sleek looking train's bottom carriage.

Their followers wildly discharged their own technologically
modified weapons, shots scattering across the double moon
drenched train yard. Even with the perpetual night of this world,

both otherworldly bodies managed to bathe the landscape in an eerie cream-colored glow.

It was one of the things Jun loved about this place, and that she hated leaving behind.

Unfortunately, if they stayed, they'd both wind up sacrificed to the Lunar Deities of Earth 2418. Flayed and begging for death, like the other cursed souls they'd left behind.

Long story. Not enough time to tell. Gunfire and what not.

As several rounds continued to strike the ground in front of her, one even coming shockingly close to her head, Kayla never lost her nerve. She kept faith that her experienced marksmanship trumped the inexperienced grandstand shooting of the cult foot soldiers.

She pulled the trigger, two more went down, cloaked bodies tumbling to the tracks.

Gotta make sure I get enough space between them, and Jun. Kayla felt the updraft of the departing cargo gravity train.

This world had introduced numerous wonders to the world's' trotting duo, the grav train being one of many things that had kept Jun blabbering endlessly about "science" this and "techno-logical advancements unheard of" that.

Jun. Where the hell is she?

"Up here!" Jun's voice carried over the rising noise of the train.

Kayla looked up to see her young companion looking out the open door, as the grav train picked up speed.

"Now, you run! I shoot!" Jun yelled, holding her gun out.

Kayla understood, realizing she couldn't continue to lay down cover fire and jump on a semi-speeding train. There was only so much she was capable of.

And besides, Jun apparently had a little bit of weapons train-ing in her dossier.

Gunfire erupted above her head as Jun trained her sights on the pursuing cult members, not flinching with every shot she let loose.

The good thing about these trains was they were low to the ground. As she leaped onto the now accelerating vehicle, Kayla caught a glimpse of a round race near where she'd just been, whizzing off into the distance.

Kayla rolled to a crouch bringing her gun up in a fluid movement.

But as they sped into the Wastelands of Georgia (formerly known as Outside the Perimeter/ OTP), there was no need for more gunfire as their attackers receded into the distance.

Jun turned with a huge grin on her face, the smile accenting her mocha skin tone. With her small afro pulled back in a puff, her youth was even more on display, relishing in the small bit of action they'd just been a part of.

"I think I probably got a couple of them!" She walked towards a palm sized panel. Slapping her hand down, a force field shimmered to life leaving an open view to the blighted landscape that whizzed by. Kayla ran her hand through her hair, feeling the adrenaline of the chase finally wearing off.

Mark would've suggested I leave the running and shooting to the younger agents. She smiled.

The familiar pang struck as the agent thought of him, the laugh he would've followed up with as he walked away. The abruptness of the oncoming flood of memories began to trickle through, interrupted by her companion's voice.

"You ok?" Jun asked, looking at her with concern. "I mean, that's like the first time you've smiled since we've first met. It's weird."

"You screwed up back there in a major way. We have an assignment," Kayla said ignoring the professor's concern.

Jun held the agent's stare, not giving an inch in the argument that was soon to come. "We're doing this? Now? After we barely escape with our lives from the Jonestown cult with laser guns?"

Kayla continued to stare out the shimmering force field at the remains of I-285, where rusted out hulks of vehicles pockmarked the once mighty Spaghetti Junction. They'd had variations of the same discussion before, and it was wearing thin.

"We could've done something."

"Instead of just running, like we keep doing."

"I've said this before. We can't save everyone," Kayla calmly replied.

Jun stood silent for a moment, lost in thought.

"Zhè shì yuè lái yuè jíqí gǔlǎo," Jun mumbled in an angry tone, breaking the quiet.

"Wǒ qīngxiàng yú tóngyì," Kayla said.

With an arched eyebrow Jun said, "They teach you that at Quantico?"

"Taught myself," she replied. "Some of us didn't have the luxury of learning from their parents."

Kayla watched as she reached inside the book bag slung across her shoulders, shaking her head with a terse smile.

"I don't get you. At all. And I'm usually a pretty good judge of character. Comes from the teaching," Jun said still digging. "One minute you're smiling as you watch Crappy Moonlit Homicidal Land whizz by, and the next you're jumping down my throat."

Kayla motioned for her to sit down. "I'm a complicated lady."

"I guess you can call it that." She sat on the floor next to Kayla, now watching the depressing scenery continue to go by.

"I understand where you're coming from. I get it," Kayla said. "We've seen some crappy stuff as we've hit these worlds. Things that I'd normally wade waist deep into. But we can't deal with any of that today. Later, maybe."

"The further he gets away with the kid, the less of a chance we have of getting her back home. You know this better than me. Hell, you're the brains of the operation."

Jun opened her book bag, reaching inside for the Crossing device, anticipating the obligatory—

"What's our window?" Kayla asked watching her fiddle with the device's touchscreen.

"You never miss a beat," Jun replied with a grin. "We're looking at 5 minutes and counting. So just sit back—"

A blaring siren in the train car cut her off, punctuated by a red flashing light. Kayla instinctively went for her weapon, as Jun started to search for the source of the alarm.

"Lunar grav transport launch will commence in 5:00 minutes," a monotone voice said over the train car's loud-speaker.

"Jun," Kayla said.

"I'm on it," her companion replied, fingers flying on the wall keypad from earlier.

The furrow on Jun's brow deepened a bit more as she continued to pound at the keys.

"Jun," Kayla said again, voice rising a little, the flashing lights and alarm continuing to blare in the train car.

"This is a grav transport bound for space," Jun said not looking up from the panel.

"Wait- what?!" Kayla holstered her weapon. "You mean "Space space?!"

Jun stepped away from the wall panel, which showed a trajectory from central Georgia to the lower atmosphere of Earth. The dotted line showed a destination of the second moon, where a glowing orb flashed green.

"How?" Kayla stared at Jun, who focused on the Crossing device.

"I think we got sidetracked with the "being shot at" portion of our trip," Jun replied, bottom lip bit as her mind raced. "Got on the wrong grav train."

"How much time?

"Lunar grav transport launch will commence in three minutes and counting," chimed the car's loudspeaker as if responding to the law woman.

"How the hell did we just lose a minute?" Kayla scanned the cabin for an exit.

"Actually, remember, and it's kind of awesome, time here has a 'differential' loss between what we see as linear and this may not be the time for a science lesson," Jun replied.

The car shook with a sudden force, hurling the duo to the back of the car, while the nearby cargo remained stationary. Kayla tried to grab Jun, as the car started to rattle, creating a loud din of noise as the train prepared for its stellar bound ascent.

The rocket propulsion system blared from the rear of the train, shooting the formerly grounded vehicle into the nighttime skies above.

Kayla watched as the blighted Georgia landscape was replaced by the nighttime sky. Littered by white clouds, the skies bathed the interior of the car with a milky color, creating an ethereal mood.

"We're not going to space!" Kayla yelled over the blaring alarms, and fierce rattling of the space bound vehicle.

Motioning towards the Crossing device that she held with a death like grip, Jun said, "We have to get outside! We can't cross from in here!"

Kayla, disbelief etched on her face, yelled back, "Wait- outside how?"

"Do you want a science lesson, or do you want to live?!"

With that, Jun hitched her backpack, the Crossing device now secure in her hand, and began the tilted ascent to the panel that controlled the force field.

Kayla followed suit behind the professor and watched warily as she began to type the needed sequence to bring down the force field.

"Grab onto me and hold on tight!" Jun yelled. "Only a few seconds left. We jump on three!"

Kayla wrapped her arms around his companion's waist and said a silent prayer.

"Three!" Jun smacked the panel with such force that Kayla knew they might have to have a doctor look at her hand on the next world.

Or that's what she almost thought, as her mind became extremely preoccupied with being snatched into the nighttime sky, the whipping winds playing havoc with her ears.

Jun was yelling something, frantically typing at the Crossing device.

And oh yeah, they were tumbling head over heel the entire time. Made it somewhat difficult to get their bearings.

Jun's right. The agent gripped her companion even harder, teeth chattering.

The sky on this world was beautiful.

Kayla then chose this opportunity to black out.

TO BE CONTINUED IN THE CROSSING

Now and Then
By
Alan Jones

Part 1: Smoke & Ashes - Blerd

From beneath his top hat, Grimes offered, "… That's why I like broke girls, they work harder."

"You mean broken girls, don't you?" my lady responded.

"Tomato, *tomato*, whatever. MG, you gonna finish that?" the ubiquitous and unashamed Grimes asked, after tilting back his hat, either missing completely the irony of his request given his own financial struggles or exhibiting a level of comic genius beyond most mortals. He made his request just as Marketing Girl was examining the birthmark on my right shoulder blade, which had become inflamed overnight. Voodoo Priestess told us years ago that the mark resembled Igbo symbols which translated into the word "Amaechi" or "who knows tomorrow?". Voodoo Priestess and Cousin Kisha were stamped with similar birthmarks, which could be interpreted as Igbo symbols. And though interpretations of such things are, to a degree, in the eye of the beholder, I trusted Voodoo Priestess in her assessment. Oddly, mine was mad itching that morning, so much so that I kept squirming in my chair to scratch that itch. I marked it up to staying in the shower too long.

After Marketing Girl ceased rubbing my back, she at last responded to Grimes' request, "I might and I might not. What does it matter to you?"

"I'm just saying…"

Marketing Girl leaned forward just a bit, flashing the little bit of *street* she had within her, "And I'm just saying that, I'll let you know… So, don't be asking me no more. Blerd, get your boy, before I do!" The three of us sat at a table for four, in the outdoor seating of the first-floor café outside of our high-rise condo. We'd received a message from Nia via a homing pigeon (which was the only way we communicated regarding Nia's movements when she was stateside), that she'd meet us for brunch downstairs this morning. And thus, we'd held an open seat for our gifted protégé, that morning. Grimes had crashed the party, as was his way. But for the moment it didn't matter, since Nia was running late.

Grimes, a well-known hacker in the digital streets, was just a guy in real life, a guy living well beyond his means. He joined us for breakfast largely because, living in our same building, he was indeed rent-poor. That and the fact that he liked to front when in the company of the ladies on Friday and Saturday nights, meant that at least once or twice a month he'd not so randomly show up at our brunch table on Sunday mornings. Leaning his chair back against the building's marble slate exterior, Grimes blew a funnel of smoke off to the side away from MG and me. "My bad MG, but…"

"Yes, I know." A moment later, MG acquiesced to her inner compass, removing her coffee cup from its saucer before sliding half of her omelet onto it for the man-child.

Grimes smiled, "Thanks, MG…!"

After seeing Grimes take his first bite, MG turned to me and asked, "So, in actually feeding this fool, am I contributing to the collapse of modern civilization?"

"Most likely, yes. But the Universe knows your heart…" Then, after plopping one of the two turkey sausage patties from my own meal atop of Grimes' newly found breakfast plate, I asked him, "So, no honey this morning for you to boo up with?"

"Naw, but I got one coming through tonight."

"And what are you going to feed her?" MG asked.

Grimes shrugged his shoulders, giving Marketing Girl a knowing look.

Marketing Girl nearly growled at him, "I'm talking about food, fool!"

"Oh…, I told her to pick up some Five Guys for the two of us. I might be broke until the first, but my liquor cabinet is still on point. We'll eat and drink out on the balcony. She'll trip on the view and that, will be that." Mind you, while he was indeed a very talented hacker, he didn't play well with others, such as employers or paying clients. Thus, through his many self-inflicted wounds, his pockets held little more than lint, and the lint was making plans that didn't include him.

MG shook her head, before asking, "Do have any money whatsoever saved up?"

"On the real? Honestly, I have just one bank account, a checking account at Spirit bank, and it's overdrawn." To which MG covered her face with the palms of her hand, as Grimes steadily marched towards that enviable cliff, "You know, y'all could let me post up in that room y'all keep open for Nia when she's in town? And on the days she's in town, I could just sleep on your couch. I'm just saying…"

My boy is so full of foolishness, that sometimes, despite his best efforts, it just spills over. I looked off into the distance, not wanting to be swept away by the coming storm, but instead, Marketing Girl simply gave him the death stare that every woman has in her arsenal. It was a look which let Grimes know that she thought him to be the most trifling man she'd ever met.

Grimes, feeling compelled to respond to my wife's silence, carried on only as he could, "MG, I've told you a hundred times. *We're all gonna die someday*, and since we can't take it with us, the only way to win is to make sure that we're tapped out every single day. Let tomorrow take care of tomorrow. So, no I don't have a savings or a retirement account. Because, since all of us will die sooner than we expect, what's the point of it?"

My wife leaned in again to ask, "But what if you live?"

Then, as on cue, the Universe weighed in as we heard a not-so-distant boom down the street. The three of us raced out onto the sidewalk to witness plumes of smoke billowing out of a high-rise three blocks down. "What the…" I uttered. But in that moment of asking the question, my gift of knowing kicked in, and I knew that this was the work of our eternal enemy, Entropy, a shadowy online collective of nihilists bent on bringing about the end of the world. Their motive operandi to this point had been to radicalize useful idiots online and then equip them to do their treacherous will. But my gift told me right off that this time was different. Whatever this was, it wasn't a bunch of radicalized fanboys playing dress up.

Through the debris and smoke, I could see our opponent take shape. At first, it appeared to be a densely populated swarm of bees or locust moving as one. But upon closer inspection, as it

144

passed from the darkness into the light, I could see that these weren't mortal creatures at all, but instead, a swarm of drones moving as one giant body. Then, I saw something else descending from the rooftop. This other thing moved quickly towards the ground, but not so much so that it was free falling. Then, upon reaching the ground, it became apparent that it too was not a single being, but rather a cluster of beings ferrying a larger one to the ground. Then in doing so, I saw that this passenger was Nia, the youngest of our team, and she was engaged in a battle to the death with this electronic abomination from the sky.

"Nia...!" I cried out, even though given the distance and the roar of the ongoing destruction, I was too far away from our spiritual daughter for her to hear me. Grimes, MG and I ran towards the commotion, even as waves of human beings raced against and past us.

One man frantically pushing past us, dropped a couple of fresh slices of Blaze pizza after bumping into Grimes. So, of course my boy picked them up and took a bite. Marketing Girl gave him a look of disgust, to which he responded, "Hey, this here is damn good pizza!"

Through her panting, MG quipped, "I try not to eat food with bite marks on it. Not judging, just not my thing."

The assortment of winged escorts, which had carefully clenched Nia with their talons to transport the princess to the ground, released her. Then the birds began to swirl around her at a furious pace, as if to protect her. Nia the powerful mute, through the magic of spooky quantum action, could communicate with many creatures and forces of the earth. I knew that with birds her pathway into their consciousness was the same one that allowed migratory birds to read the magnetic bands of the earth and flawlessly navigate thousands of miles each year. So, when Nia spoke, the earth and her many creatures who we often considered as lesser, heard her voice loud and clear.

As we closed in on Nia's location, I motioned for Marketing Girl to hang back. Though Grimes wasn't much of a shot, he never left home without his strap. Thus, so long as we were close in, he could be effective (note that his weapon of choice was a shotgun; but even in Atlanta it's frowned upon to openly carry one around in the streets). Then just as we stepped upon Nia's block, I saw the nature queen lift an arm towards the flowing assembly of drones, and in doing so, her servant protectors flew off towards the swarm of armed drones.

In response, the flowing drone assembly lifted an arm composed of micro drones towards Nia and fired what were extremely small caliber metal armaments at her. Each round fired equated to a sewing needle, which wouldn't be very effective against hard targets, but in large quantity against flesh and blood, could cause significant damage. Thus, against Nia's winged protectors, it was very effective.

Angered at the sight of her winged friends falling from the heavens to the unforgiving concrete below, Nia cried aloud, as she lifted her arms towards the sky. As she did so, every fire hydrant and facet within a two-block radius gave up the precious conduit of life, liquid water. In concert with the movement of Nia's arms, the waters moved like a living torrent, crashing into the high-tech abomination, to good effect.

"Blerd!" I heard off to my right as I saw Cousin Kisha stroll up. Living only two blocks north of us, she too had heard the commotion. But before I could respond to her greeting, I saw the abomination's abdomen open up, forming a hole through which Nia's torrent passed right through. A moment later, once the waters dispersed into sky beyond, the creature returned to its original form. Seeing this, the three of us could only respond with a collective "damn…"

"Let me try…" Kisha offered. Having by this time come into her gift of being able to generate portals into the underworld, she lifted her hands towards the side of the building next to and above Nia at the end of the block. Instantly, what was once solid, appeared to liquify and then began to slowly swirl beside the behemoth as it stood menacingly above Nia.

Once the portal was fully formed, we stood for a moment awaiting the effect of Kisha's work. But all we saw, surprising as it was, was that several folks hiding on the opposite side of the street from the battle with tarnished souls were snatched up, and taken into the Pit. Some would say long before their time. Kisha exclaimed, "It's not working. Whatever AI is operating that thing, it's not self-aware." Kisha's portals only work against beings who possess an awareness of self, and thus a soul, as we now call it. Kisha lamented, "I could create a hundred of these portals on every building and street in Atlanta, but that thing would have to intentionally walk into one…"

Seeing our latest tactic fail, Nia called the clouds floating high above us to the ground with an unimaginable quickness. Then she knelt down, placing her hand on the sidewalk. I'd seen her do this several times before, and yet it still amazed me. As the clouds enveloped the beast, Nia created such an imbalance between the earth and sky that lightening erupted from the ground. Such was the effect that in the darkness of the clouds, we saw the charges erupting from the ground into and through the target.

As I and the others closed to within twenty yards of her position, Nia threw up a hand, warning us to stand back. The four of us went motionless and silent as we listened in the relative quiet. Then, in that peace, we heard the very soft sound of metal striking concrete. And for a moment, we were hopeful. But when what should have built into a crescendo subsided into silence, we sighed collectively. Leveraging my gift of knowing, I yelled out to Nia, "Move to your right, now…!!!" as half a second later a high intensity energy beam struck where Nia had been kneeling. I rushed in grabbing her and pulled her back to the group. In that moment, I didn't even need my gift to realize that this *thing* was well beyond what Entropy was capable of creating. In that same moment, I realized who was behind this assault.

An exasperated and winded Nia gasped and signed, "Shit…" at seeing the beast absorb the lightning she'd sent through it, rather than the fact that she was nearly vaporized by a new age ray beam. This young woman was fearless.

"I know…" I said, as I tried to comfort her, knowing much of what she would say, had her voice been something that men could hear.

Nia signed back to me frantically, "If there weren't a transit line right below us, maybe I could open up the ground beneath it and somehow bury it, but how would we stop it from flying off?"

I said to her, "No, that would be hard to pull off, and there would likely be a lot of collateral damage, even if you did."

Nia nodded silent agreement.

But then a thought exploded into my consciousness, leading me to look our protégé in the eye and state to her over the chaos, "…but if you open up the ground one street over, where they've cleared the block for that new high-rise, I have a plan."

The young prodigy tilted her head towards me in puzzlement as the words departed my mouth.

I went on speaking confidently to Nia, "Look, I know what I'm doing," even as I prepared my soul to jump into the abyss. Nia was clearly our most powerful member, especially when assessing an asset by its value on a battlefield. And yet, there I was claiming what could not be seen by any rational being. As Nia ran to the other side of the street so that she had a clear line of sight to the lot I referenced, I added, "No matter what you see, don't follow me in. No matter what…!"

For a moment her lips moved, as she mouthed a single silent word "Blerd..???"

As I began peeling off the prosthetics I wore when out and about in the streets of Atlanta to hide my identity, I shouted to my team "The Engineer; he's behind this thing. This is the branch in the timeline we've been waiting for. That means that project Omega is a go, regardless of how today ends." As their stunned faces took me and my words in, I removed my last bit of protection, the baseball cap I wore pulled down low whenever I left the crib. I did all of this to allow Entropy's monstrosity to see me clearly. Then seeing parts of the drone assembly light up, I intuitively knew that it recognized me as a high value target. At that moment of recognition, I turned and began running full out towards the empty lot, zigging and zagging all along the way. Though, I must say that it was my gift of knowing that instructed me on when to zig and when to zag.

Arriving at the site, as per Nia's gift, streams of dirt poured upwards towards the sky, so much so that it would have appeared to the casual observer that time must have been running backwards. As I entered the depths, my eyes were of little use, as the dust from Nia's excavation was thicker than gumbo. I relied my ability of knowing. Covering my nose as best I could, I jumped from safe spot to safe spot. And as I am not omniscient, I only come to know as I seek. Thus, as I sought footing, my feet landed everywhere they needed to for me to reach my destination, though I never actually saw a single stony footstool. Not one.

Upon reaching my destination, I glanced back for the first time. There my eyes fell upon them, and they appeared as some new-age curse, blotting out the midmorning sun completely, moving as one, as they followed me into the pit, and descended upon me. Opening its mouth, the beast swallowed me whole.

There in the darkness, for a fraction of a moment, I was at peace. At peace with all that was, is and would ever be. That is until the next moment, when I realized that I could not breathe. And not being able to breathe caused a tsunami of fear and panic to wash over me which would not be quelled. And just like in the previous handful of times when I feared for my life, something erupted within me that was not of me. It was something that raged so I seemed to have no hope of controlling it… which was just as I had planned. Allowing the fear of being buried alive within the belly of that beast shook me as I struggled to be free. But in not being able to save myself, I became frantic, and in that moment I transformed. I felt myself moving from flesh to fluid to spirit. No longer in the flesh, there seemed to be no limit on what I could do, not in time or space. For being free of life, I was also free from death. The brightness of me overwhelmed all, and yet did not blind me, at least not to those things which must be seen. I felt myself moving to and from, enveloping every bit of the darkness which had swallowed me whole, the darkness of that hole, and the darkness of any being which dared to look upon me in that moment. For I knew that even the masters which held the strings to this puppet were also consumed in that insatiable fire. All these parties connected together, moving through time at the speed of light, until the moment when I whispered, "*Stop…*"

And then, silence.

I returned to myself, standing naked and alone at the bottom of the excavation. In that moment, I realized the truth in Voodoo

Priestess' words spoken to me years before of who I was. For in my distress, when I had no other choice, I'd become one with the universe and with a word, halted the flow of time within my opponents, causing them to instantly disintegrate as the walls of the pit crystalized. Even the fillings within my own mouth failed to survive the instant when time stood still.

Seven steps into my ascent from the pit, through the haze, I caught sight of four hazy figures standing along its rim. From the mist one of them called out, "Okay, now I'm officially triggered…"

"Negro, please…" I heard Marketing Girl answer Grimes.

But Grimes, being Grimes, he continued unabated, yelling "Dude, put some damn clothes on…!!!" as he tossed down his high hat into the pit, as I'd already moved to where I knew it would land. Only in reaching for Grimes' hat to cover myself and tasting the salty tears in my own mouth as I ascended, did the transformation fully leave me. But what remained was the sweet breeze of unencumbered Black Joy, as an unquenchable smile beamed from me to my loved ones. I let that joy rest upon me for as long as I could.

As I neared my crew, I chuckled at their attempt to each shed an article of clothing to provide me some sense of modesty. But as they did so, I glanced once more towards the pit behind me, and thought, that in spite of everything that the enemy sent against us, all that remained of their efforts were the same as all who live, smoke and ashes.

Part 2: A Matter of Time - Kisha

The illusion of time, distorted and stretched out, is a funhouse from which none in the flesh can escape. And yet, I have done this thing, that all that should be, will be, in every branch of time which flows from this particular well to this sea.

I entered this host while she was sleeping. And while I am wholly her, surprisingly, I am still wholly me. Two consciousnesses within a single body. Entanglement is real y'all.

My host has been augmented, such that when she wakes from slumber, the current date and time appear in the foreground of her vision. Thus, I knew right away that I was in the year 4224, an age of starships, terraforming and Time Lords. And despite it all, these advancements, as always, it was also still a time of assholes.

I marveled at the fact that Voodoo Priestess had done for me what she'd done for my cousin Blerd. But this time, rather than sending his consciousness into one of our ancestors, she'd sent my consciousness into one of my descendants, more than two thousand years in the future. In sharing this host, I instantly became aware of certain realities of life in this future time. On Earth at least, the total impact of every person was tracked to make sure that no one exceeded the allocated limit, be it our carbon footprint, social equity, or whatever. Thus, one could at any given moment examine their societal value and course correct as needed. My host was different from most in that she'd opted for a real shower in her personal living quarters. Also, she only consumed eco-positive foods such as grain derivatives like oat milk. And being a healthcare worker, she also got eco points each period for her fulltime service to the common good.

Even as we readied for work, I came to know what this shared consciousness truly meant. Certainly, I expected to know all that she knew, but instantly she became aware of all that I knew as well, including why I'd crossed this middle passage. Interestingly, where I expected conflict between us, there was only unity. I also noticed in the mirror a birthmark on my right shoulder blade very similar to the one I had over two thousand years ago. Despite the defect, my birth mother had chosen not to have my gestation terminated. Moved by the Spirit, she often told me that I was marked for a purpose. Thus, I assumed that perhaps, that's why I chose healthcare as my profession.

As we entered the thoroughfare, a map popped up in the foreground of our vision, noting the fastest path to the care facility in which I worked—my hometown of what was once known as Atlanta. In fact, the only remnants of the Atlanta we knew were Peachtree Street and Piedmont Park. Almost everything else from before was either gone or had a new name. The names of new heroes and villains supplanted almost all of what was before, with the interesting exception of several private institutions of higher learning. In this life, my name was Binta, and in my three hundred plus years of circling the sun, I'd done nothing which would give cause for anything to be named after me. My friends teased me regarding my lack of a legacy, because I was the only one in our little squad who'd never been anywhere beyond the terraformed moons of Planet X. All the while, my friends journeyed across the known universe, claiming planets, continents and settlements after themselves. But being an old soul, as my mother would often say, I knew all their claims and deeds were temporal. Granted, that since humankind had overcome aging and all terrestrial disease, the only real risk to life, were to be found in the stars. And yet, more than ninety nine percent of earthlings leave Earth for new settlements across the universe before their hundredth birthday. Since settlers fly to and fro cost free in this cosmic government land grant venture, virtually everyone eventually succumbed not just to the lure of personal wealth, but most likely the generational wealth that these land grabs would bring; everyone, except me, so it seemed. And now that we were one, perhaps we would too. But we had work to do before any such considerations held any ground in our own mind.

Before I left the age into which I was born, Blerd, the one who knows, told me that the target was placed under house arrest by the Time Lords, right here in what was once known as Atlanta. Once I reached the main thoroughfare, I noticed right off, that after two thousand years, we were indeed one people. But my host knew all too well that colorism was still a thing. And thus, as I was before, we were still, unapologetically black.

I've always been direct to a fault, thus the passage of a couple millennia hadn't changed that, nor did merging with this host. We were of one mind, to never compromise. However, in this future state the relationship deal breaker over the last three hundred years had been my refusal to leave the solar system. Hell, I only left the planet once a decade, if that. Everyone believed that it was an irrational fear of interstellar travel which held me so close to home. But it was never that. It was simply this overwhelming sense that my destiny in this life was to be fulfilled on Earth.

Atlanta, from its founding had always been a transportation hub. And so it was two thousand years later, with The Time Lords choosing it for their headquarters. And as such, it was also the location where they interned the most dangerous offenders of the timeline, one of which was our target. And though his location was not public knowledge, Blerd had given me his exact location.

Arriving at the Time Lord compound, I first had to check in with security. But randomly, but not so randomly, their security verification system went down, right as they were looking up old boy's authorized visitation list. After showing them my massage therapist license and much back and forth (massage therapy was my side hustle that I did not so much for the money, but for the community around our solar system which still appreciated the art of touch and scent; plus I got flown out to some very plush locales for my services), I convinced them to search me old school style on my way in and to do the same coming out. Searching me and finding nothing odd on me, in my bag or the mat I was carrying, they sent me on my way. When I reached the spot, I saw that it was a ranch quadplex, but there was no doubt as to which unit belonged to the target. This arrogant asshole had glued a golden crown above his front doorway. Clueless to the end, he was.

As he opened the door, I spoke first while resisting the urge to call him Asshole Number One, as I had so often thousands of years ago, literally in another life, "Sir, you ordered a massage treatment. I'm your therapist for today." I saw, but ignored the look of confusion he initially flashed in response to my words.

"Oh, yes, come right in." he offered.

"Is it okay if I set up my table right here?"

"Sure, that's fine," he grinned, as he assumed that he was getting over with a free massage.

After lighting my candles and making sure that he was on the table and settled, I began to stroke his back slowly for a minute or so before breaking the silence, "So, how did you wind up here, if you don't mind my asking?"

"Oh, no worries. Basically, I got put in timeout for some bullshit."

"Really?"

"Yeah, I got locked up for trying to make things better for people who look like us."

"For real…?"

"Yeah, I traveled back in time to get us our forty acres and a mule, so to speak."

"Really…"

"Actually, it was a plan to establish a homeland for African-Americans in the southeastern United States."

"Wow, so what was the problem?"

"Well, these assholes here are obsessed with preserving the timeline. They're afraid that folks like me will do something to alter this reality. They claim, that they do this to preserve the lives of those born into the existing timeline."

"Is that true?"

"Well, technically, yes. But if you or I had never been born, and the world was a better place, Isn't that worth it?"

"If it were just a couple people, sure. But how many people are we talking about?"

I felt him tense up just a bit beneath my hands before offering, "Oh, it's hard to say."

"Just a guess then…"

"Millions…for sure, but more likely billions. There are so many variables to account for. I mean no great migration from the south. No brothers or sisters drafted into their foreign wars. And when one considers just the randomness of human pairings, who knows. But pairings in small towns in the rural south, isolated as they were, would have most likely played out much the same. But yeah, tons of folks, too many to count. Though…"

I interrupted, "…Not to mention the fact, that with Florida and all of Georgia south of Macon being completely underwater when the oceans rose, where would all of those people have gone?"

"Yeah, but you're missing the point. With our own nation and self-determination, we would have found a way."

"No doubt. We always do. But if I may ask, who gave you the right to decide for all of us?"

Just then, even as he was still lying face down on the massage table, I felt him freeze completely. "Who are you, again?"

"I'm Binta, your therapist. Did you not catch that when I arrived?"

"No, but who are you really?"

We offered the Engineer a sly smile, as we lifted our left hand towards the far wall. As we did so, the wall appeared to liquify. Tilting our head towards him, we gave him a knowing look. "Bruh, you of all people should have seen this coming."

Dude dropped his head and then raised it again, "So, you're here because of what I did in eighteen seventy-eight? Because you didn't like my plan for saving our people from our oppressor?"

"Nah…and you know better. We come to you today with full knowledge of your misdeeds, even the ones the Time Lords know nothing of." We turned towards his dining area, lifting our right hand towards the table therein. "But we know mischief and the source of it. Blerd has spoken of its existence, and my hand reveals it now." Our gift of truth, illuminated what was hidden within a temporal fold that the Time Lords could not see. The device allowed him to transmit energy through time to do his bidding, and even allowed him to project images, though typically, expectedly, they were images of himself.

The Engineer sat up, only in his skivvies and looking pensive, as the liquified wall began to twirl.

"But here's the good news, if your deeds were indeed righteous, you have nothing to worry about." We paused for a moment, "…but, do you recall the time you reached back through the years to boil a young boy alive?"

"I only did that to reveal the sins of our government, to rally the people to revolt against them. Nothing sparks a revolution like the death of an innocent."

We interrupted again, "…and not to mention, when you sent future tech to our enemies, that they might kill us on your behalf."

The Engineer sighed, and then posed, "Kisha, right?"

We nodded our head.

The Engineer dropped his own head once more, realizing at last that this line of objection was barren. "But if your test does not draw me down into the pit, will you leave me be?"

"Yes. That is our way in these affairs. We are not after all, murderers. For it's not our right to judge you, we merely bring you before the eternal court. The outcome is not up to us."

The Engineer laughed mockingly, "So, you gave up your life two thousand years ago, just on the chance that you might be able to level some sort of justice upon me?"

"Yes…"

"Really?"

"Yes, for the innocents, those I love in my own time, and most importantly the consequences of your wanton lack of respect for the lives of others, from this point forward." We paused for a second, caught up in a moment of reflection of the cost paid, the daunting bill still to be paid and the callousness of this one soul's lack of humanity and the resulting carnage. We were swept with a sense to read aloud all the names of those who suffered to that date from his actions. But due to the circumstances, there was literally no *time* for that…lest the Time Lords become suspicious of us.

As the swirling of the wall before us picked up speed, the Engineer began to laugh as nothing appeared to be happening, "Huh, looks like you gave up your life for nothing."

But then as on que, one by one, every version of The Engineer, which found itself in that room, on that day, prompted by his most recent attempt to kill us all, was pulled into the abyss. At last, we spoke the final words he would hear on this side of existence, "Your heart has been weighed, and has been found lacking." As each image, from every timeline which converged in that moment, each one in which he had sent technology back in time to our opponent, that they might construct the abomination in our time to slay us all, departed the table, each instance becoming like vapor as they streamed past us into the eternal.

Once the process was done, I closed the portal. Just as Time Lord security rushed in, I turned to see that all that remained of The Engineer were his white undies and the tracking implant they'd imbedded within him.

The security team questioned me for three hours before releasing me. My story to them, that he just simply disappeared, was met with the great skepticism it deserved. But their evidence gathering bots could find nothing, for there was nothing in this level of existence, to be found. That was in part, why I had to be the one to make this journey. My cleanup game was tight, in that exercising my gift left no trace.

See, unlike when Blerd's consciousness was sent back in time into the soul of one of our common ancestors to prevent The Engineer from altering history, this time my consciousness was sent two thousand years forward in time, into each version of the timeline where The Engineer attempted to kill us all on that day two thousand years prior.

The consequences for Blerd, were that he didn't know what would happen when his host body died. I know that both he and Voodoo Priestess expected it to be a one-way trip. But with the lives of millions, if not billions, depending on him stepping up to the challenge, he did what had to be done, without hesitation. As it turned out, after living many years of a shared existence in the flesh of our common ancestor, upon his death, Blerd's consciousness returned to his own flesh, in his own time, mere moments after he'd initially departed. But having to endure the brutality of reconstruction, and the rise of the horror, which was the Klan during that time, was a burden none should bare.

But by me going to the future rather than the past, my consequences were different than Blerd's. For his gift had informed him, that every timeline going forward, in which this more malevolent version of The Engineer existed, was also a timeline in which he tried to kill us all. Without fail, that was the branching within the timeline which identified where we needed to inject ourselves. Blerd had the ability to collapse probability waves in such a way that he knew exactly where we needed to intervene to change an outcome. He would often laugh that he could see inside the box, so to speak, though he thought it wise to only share with me what I needed to know to complete my mission. And though I'm no quantum physicist, and much less a Blerd, I knew enough that my consciousness was being replicated across every possible future where the Engineer had taken this darker turn. Causality, they call it. Far too simple a word and far too simple a concept for all that it conveys. Suffice it to say, though it was typically Binta with whom I merged, I knew that across the various relevant timelines, my consciousness, was actually imposed upon four of my daughters in this future age to cover every possibility that flowed from that single event too long ago. And consequently, each future me would eventually converge upon me in the age of my birth, two thousand years prior. At that time, I will have the memories of each and every future version of myself, from the Earth, to everywhere across the universe my future selves traveled. And consequently, every morning in which I awoke with new memories was a sign of another convergence, another of my future self, returning home to me.

And though others like the Engineer would have seen this as sacrificing my own life to live an eternal life in that new age, I did not. For even though I'd been reborn into an age that has conquered aging and overcome death on all tier one worlds, I knew better. For I knew that whether I remained in the relative safety of Earth and her sister worlds, or should I take to the stars like so many others had, I knew that one day I would die, because I knew without a doubt, that all who are born, will someday die. And though it might be thousands of years, but my future selves walked in the confidence, that each us would someday return home, to see those I loved once more in the flesh, now that this thing was done. It was this hope that kept me warm on the coldest of worlds. For now that I'd done this thing, it's only a matter of time.

Hunted
By
Kyoko M

Someone was stalking me.

And anyone stalking a werewolf was either batshit crazy or had balls of titanium.

Don't get me wrong—I've been stalked before, for serious and for playtime. The latter, I honestly found a bit of a turn on if done properly by a fellow wolf of the opposite sex. Still, the few times it had happened had been playful, flirtatious, and reciprocated. A game of wits.

This was an entirely different game.

To his credit, the stalker was quite good. He stayed downwind of me so I couldn't smell him. He kept out of my peripherals. He moved slowly, gradually, his paws light on the grass and the leaves of the forest. It was late, past any good girl's bedtime, but I hadn't been a good girl since I was probably about fourteen years old. Bad girls stayed out late and played in the moonlight. I'd been a bit restless lately, so I'd gone out for a midnight run through Fernbank Forest to clear my head. Sometimes I'd play tag with any local wildlife I could find. Deer were excellent sport, but rabbits were even better—they were faster and harder to catch. Still, in the city of Atlanta, deer weren't exactly in massive supply, especially the closer you got to downtown. You had to go to the peripheral suburbs for proper fauna.

"Well," you ask. "If you didn't see him and didn't smell him, Cassandra, how did you know he was there in the first place?"

Instinct.

Werewolves are sort of odd. A lot of folks think we're wolves in human form or humans in wolf form, but it's honestly both. When I changed into my wolf form, part of my human brain rested, and the wolf stepped into the control room. All animals had a sense of when they were being watched. It was a survival tactic. Humans have it too, but it's just not as acute as animals, and especially apex predators. Wolves were at the top of their food chains wherever they were that didn't have men with guns. Wolves knew their surroundings as if it was a part of them, and in some ways, it was. Nature breathed life into us, supernatural as it was, and so we always knew on a subconscious level what was around us, in the wind, in the trees, in the sky.

So, what did my stalker want?

I had a few theories as I merrily strolled through the woods, pretending like I didn't know better. I was trotting down a hill with a sharp decline, and I'd done it on purpose. He couldn't stay low if he had to cross the hill at some point to keep tailing me.

Theories formed in my head. I was third in line for pack leadership here in the southeast. My father was the original Wolfman. My mother was the lupa, his mate. We had a pack of seventy or so raggedy miscreants who took care of each other and made nice with other packs who came through town for a good time. Every so often, I'd get some admirer trying to suck up to me with the scheme to be next in line for the throne. If he married me, he'd become royalty, effectively. Not that my family flaunted anything. We were well off, not rich, and most of what we made went back into the pack anyhow. Foolish men had tried and failed one by one over the last decade. If they stepped up, I swatted them down. However, none of them ever stalked me beforehand. Typically, they'd show up to pack meetings and introduce themselves, flirt with me, butter up my folks, only to be told a very firm no. So theory one was out the window.

I reached about ten yards from the top of the hill and then dug myself a nice shallow ditch before flumping down into it. My fur was a rich medium brown with black streaks over my spine and at the tuft of my tail, which effectively made me invisible in the dark of the forest. I shut my eyes and considered Theory Two: a rogue werewolf. They were rare, but they happened sometimes. Every so often, someone who had never had a pack, usually the survivor of an attack, traveled around making trouble for others to prove themselves. That wouldn't go well for him. I'd killed before in self-defense, and as much as I didn't like it, I could do it again.

I concentrated. A few minutes into my wait, I felt him. I waited until clouds slid over the full moon and took a peek.

He was all black. Rare. He kept as low to the ground as possible, but I could see him from here since I'd forced him over the hill. The forest cast shadows over him. He was a big fella, bigger than me, probably a good bit stronger too. He sniffed the air, hoping to catch my scent, but I was downwind this time. The clouds shifted again and just before I shut my eyes, I saw the color of his: bright, arctic blue, like a sparkling iceberg floating through the ocean at night. Interesting. Where had I seen eyes like that before?

The stalker determined that I was nowhere in the vicinity and eased his way down the hill, still soundless as a shadow. He was an impressive predator. He'd done this before. Maybe he was just curious. Theory Number Three was simple enough: some wolves were simply lonely and looking for connection, even if they knew they could have that if they joined the pack. I could sympathize. I was basically an introvert who could fake being an extrovert when needed. I valued my time alone. But even I got lonely.

The black wolf still hadn't spotted me. By the time he did, it was too late.

I pounced up from my hidden spot and slammed all four of my paws into his side. Not hard enough to crack any ribs, but he'd damn well know he was in a fight. He yelped and hit the bottom of a thick oak tree beside us, landing in a heap at the roots. I planted my paws as I landed neatly in front of him and bared my fangs in my meanest, scariest growl.

"Why are you following me?"

The wolf shook his mane and then glanced up at me in surprise. He didn't snap at me. He didn't try to fight me.

Then I heard a familiar deep, baritone voice with just a hint of a Transylvanian accent in my head.

"My, my, Cassandra, dear. Are you always so rough on old men?"

I didn't hesitate. I shifted back into my human form.

It always felt a little odd—not painful, but disorienting as the world shrank away from my ears and nose and my sense of sight and taste became the most prominent. I was tall for a girl, about 5'9'', and I was built like a heavyweight female boxer—long, sturdy legs, wide hips, strong biceps. I'd let my hair get longer than I usually kept it simply because being a werewolf meant I was getting weekly cuts and I'd gotten tired of it. My bouncy brown curls hit the middle of my back and frankly, I sort of liked it. It reminded me of having fur.

"Fangface!" I cried, and I flung myself at him in the mother of all bear hugs.

Vladmir Tepes, the father of all vampires, Dracula, He Who Conquers, wrapped his own now-human arms around me as well and squeezed me to him just as tightly. "I've missed you, my dear."

I pulled away and smacked his bare chest with my palm. It didn't give much, mind you. Vlad was a shapeshifter, and changed his appearance based on whatever mood he was in. For the sake of nostalgia, he'd chosen a form he liked to wear around me; that of a Swedish male model, as I jokingly considered it to be. He was around 6'4'' and pale as alabaster, with a slender but still appropriately muscular build. His hair was black like his fur had been and a few forelocks hung over his brow as he grinned down at me.

"What is wrong with you?" I said after I hit him, glaring despite how much I wanted to smile. "I could have ripped your throat out."

He waggled his dark eyebrows at me. "Kinky."

I sucked my teeth. "God, you're still an insufferable flirt."

"Shush," he scoffed. "You love it. Tell me the truth, sweet. You missed me."

I pursed my lips. "Not even slightly."

Vlad pouted. Dracula actually pouted at me. Oh, Lord. I burst into giggles and hugged him again. Who was I kidding? It was nigh impossible to stay mad at him. "Why didn't you tell me you were going to be stateside?"

"I wanted to surprise you," he said once I'd drawn away. "Your parents thought it would be amusing. They were right."

"Of course they're in on this," I said, shaking my head.

He touched my hair, brushing it back from my forehead, his smile deepening enough to reveal dimples. "You let it grow. It suits you."

I was dark-skinned enough that he couldn't see me blush, but I still did anyway. "Thanks. What brings you to town?"

"I needed to get out of Europe," he said, taking my hand and tugging me to walk with him. His hand was cool and his fingers were soft but strong. I liked holding his hand. "Get some fresh air and see some friends."

"Oh, so I'm your friend now, huh?" I asked, arching an eyebrow. "I haven't seen you in person for almost five years, you know. That's not awfully friendly."

"I called you."

"Yes, you called me. And I appreciate that. But it's not the same and you know it."

He sighed. "True enough. I may or may not also have made this trip with the intention of repairing the damage I've done to our friendship. I've wanted to see you, sweet. I promise. But things have gotten a bit hairy since the war started."

"I know," I said softly. "I'm only teasing, Vlad. It's been rough for you lately, hasn't it?"

"Nothing I can't handle," he assured me, squeezing my fingers a bit. "But it's devoured what little free time I've had since the last time I saw you."

He cast a sidelong glance at me, and just a touch of vulnerability shone in his baby blues. "I have missed you, you know."

Again, I thanked the Lord for my dark brown skin. Not that he couldn't sense the hot blood rushing up towards my cheeks. "You really want me to say it, don't you?"

He batted his eyelashes. "Pretty please?"

I rolled my eyes. "Fine. I missed you too, Fangface."

Vlad clucked his tongue. "You are the only living being allowed to call me that without inciting dire consequences."

"Such as?"

"Oh, I don't know," he said casually, slipping his arms around my back and pulling me close, those arctic eyes suddenly warming with lust. "I can think of a thing or two."

A few years ago, our current entanglement would have made me very nervous. But I was older, stronger, wiser, and far more experienced in matters of sex. I relaxed in his grip and sent him a challenging smirk. "Just a thing or two? Are you losing your touch, old man? I thought there were entire libraries filled with all the depraved things you've done to unsuspecting women."

Vlad grinned. "I've missed that sharp tongue of yours as well."

"Spent a lot of nights thinking about my tongue, have you?"

Vlad laughed softly. "I confess that I have, my dear."

The wind rustled the trees and swept over my naked skin. I pretended that was why I was shivering instead of the handsome, naked vampire with his arms around me. I hadn't forgotten The Kiss. Yes, one that had been so good it warranted capitalization in my memory bank. Five years ago, he and I had fought off a rogue pack of wolves together. He kissed me not long afterward, and it had seared itself into my memory as the best kiss I'd ever been given, wolf or human or vampire alike. There was a reason one of his titles was He Who Conquers, and it had nothing to do with killing.

My pulse throbbed in my neck. I wanted him to kiss me. Badly. And do other stuff to me. Fun stuff. Stuff that would get the both of us in serious trouble with my parents. Vlad was essentially best friends with my father, and I was, oh, you know, a few *centuries* too young to even be thinking about kissing him. We both knew damn well we were playing with fire.

But oh, what a lovely way to burn.

His fingers stroked up and down my spine. If I'd been a cat, I'd be purring right now. Damn him. He was super good at this shit. I was dangerously close to throwing him down on that pile of leaves over there and going to town on the guy, regardless of the consequences.

Luckily, just then, I smelled trouble. Literally.

Vlad's head lifted the same time I cocked mine towards the left. We were no longer alone. I sniffed the air and then my eyes widened as I recognized the scent on it.

Gun powder.

A second later, my ears popped and then Vlad's hand lashed out an inch away from the back of my neck. When he opened his fist, there was a silver bullet, still hot from being fired out of a barrel, resting on his palm.

Vlad tightened his arms around me and yanked me behind the nearest, thickest tree, his eyes narrowed as he glanced in the direction the shot had been fired from. "Damn it. I've been followed."

"Hand."

"Must be hunters," he muttered, mostly to himself. "Someone tipped them off that I arrived in Georgia, I suspect."

"Hand."

"They must be rather good. It's not easy to tail me--"

"Vlad," I said, my voice strained. "Your *hand*."

He blinked at me and then glanced down. He turned beet red and removed his hand from where he'd accidentally been copping a feel of my backside when he moved us behind the tree. "My apologies, sweet."

"Thank you," I said in relief, and then angled my face towards the wind again. I shut my eyes and breathed in. "Male. Late forties. Maybe five hundred feet due west of us. He's up in a tree."

"Is he alone?"

I listened closely and sampled the night air again. "I think so. That or backup is outside of my range of smell."

"Foolish," Vlad growled. "To come for Dracula himself alone."

"Well, male ego and all that," I said.

He scowled at me. "I find that offensive."

"I'm sure you'll get over it." I wiggled. Vlad groaned lustfully, and it did Things to me in Places.

"Merciful heavens, don't do that," the vampire pleaded.

"Let go," I said. "We're not going to get out of this by hiding.

We need to take him out."

"We have cover. It's safer here."

"All we need to do is find him," I said. "Between the two of us, we can flush him out."

Vlad's eyes hardened to ice. "I will not let any harm come to you, Cassandra. This happened because of me. If we head in the other direction, he won't have a clear shot—"

"—and he'll just come after you some other time," I countered. "And I'm not a little girl anymore, Vlad. I can take care of myself."

He held me closer still. "Cassandra, I have never doubted your capabilities."

His voice softened and there was something worried and desperate in his gaze. "But if you got hurt, I would never forgive myself."

I let that sink in for a moment. Something in my stomach churned. Damn it all. "You vampires. You're big softies under all the glamor."

"Perhaps we are."

"I'll be fine, Vlad." After a moment, I smiled. "I'm with you, after all."

His shoulders straightened a bit. It was the smallest of change in his posture that let me know I'd said the right words to reassure him. Vlad let out a long breath and then unwound his arms from around my waist. "Very well. What's the plan?"

"He can't shoot us both at the same time. I'll shift and draw his attention. You go all dark and creepy and sniff him out. If he's a hunter, he'll know your weaknesses. I wouldn't try to kill him up close. I'd honestly just knock him out of the tree and let gravity do the work."

Vlad nodded. "On three?"

"Yeah. One...two...th—"

Vlad stooped enough to kiss me. It was brief, but luscious and affectionate and it warmed me right down to my toes. He pulled away and winked before whispering, "For luck, sweet."

I grinned. "Three."

I shifted and took off in the direction of west. Almost immediately, the gun shots barked in the cool night air. I darted between the trees as I heard them. One was close enough to singe the fur on my rear left leg. Whoever he was, he was good, but not perfect. It was extremely hard to hit a ridiculously fast dark-colored wolf, even with a night-vision scope. After four shots, I managed to get a general idea of where he was based on the trajectory; there was a huge, gnarled tree at the top of the hill we'd gone over earlier. No way I could climb it in full wolf form. Maybe turning into my hybrid form would do the trick, but that wasn't my objective.

After all, I was the distraction.

The seventh shot from the hunter's rifle punched a hole in the ground directly in front of me.

I darted behind a thick tree and stayed low near the trunk. Shit. I'd been careless. He'd almost gotten me that time, which meant he'd had the skill to adjust and lead the target. I was about ten yards out from his perch. From this close, I could hear him loading the rifle again.

But that wasn't the only thing I could hear.

"Fe-fi-fo-fum," Vlad purred in his most disturbingly calm voice that somehow was everywhere and nowhere at once. "I smell the blood of an Englishman."

The hunter made a choking sound. I peeked around the tree to see an enormous mass of writhing shadows and tentacles blotting out the moonlight right above the tree. I shuddered a little as I spotted Vlad's glowing silvery-blue eyes in the middle of that mass, narrowed and staring hungrily at the hunter.

The hunter snapped the rifle's barrel shut and aimed, but he was too slow. One of Vlad's tendrils formed a wickedly sharp machete and sliced the tree right in half. The tree snapped, cracked, and then went crashing to the ground forty feet below, taking the hunter with it. The man got out a short scream before he hit the ground and got buried beneath heavy limbs and branches.

I exhaled in relief and returned to my human form. Vlad shrunk back into his human body as well, except for that long, black machete-shaped limb. He kicked a few tree limbs aside until he uncovered the badly injured hunter. Both of the man's legs were broken, as was his left arm, and the rifle had landed right below his head. His brown eyes were wide with terror as the two of us closed in on him.

"Tell me," Vlad said, his tone still serene and placid as the surface of a lake. "Who sent you?"

The man wheezed a couple times—probably thanks to some broken ribs—and tried his best to glare. "No one sent me, monster. I've come for you on my own."

Vlad lifted a dark eyebrow. "And you've performed magnificently."

The man lobbed spit at Vlad, but it fell a bit short. "Mocking me only proves my point, you venomous serpent. Your kind is a plague upon this world. How many people have you drained in your time, Count? How vacuous is that hole in your chest where your heart should be? You are nothing. You are a void. My death is not in vain. For every one of us that you strike down, two more take their place. One day, we will rid the world of you and your wretched fledglings."

"Goodness me," Vlad deadpanned. "I'm shaking in my boots, hunter."

"You're not wearing boots, Vlad," I reminded him.

"Ah. Fair point, sweet."

The hunter glared at me. "Filthy beast. You're no better."

Vlad narrowed his eyes. "Make your final words a prayer, not an insult, mortal, or I'll revoke the mercy I intend by keeping you alive."

A cruel smirk found his lips, wide and terrible enough to expose his sharp canines. "Or would you rather become that which you hate?"

The hunter struggled for a moment in vain, far more scared than before. "Don't touch me!"

Vlad stroked his chin. "You know, I am looking for new recruits. Perhaps you'd like to spend eternity at my side making me Bloody Mary's in my castle. Do you have any cooking experience? I quite like having a crumpet with mine in the morning."

"You wouldn't dare!"

"Try me, human. Apologize to the lady and I'll end it quickly."

"Go to hell, monster!"

"Would you care to join me, insect?"

"Vlad," I said softly.

He glanced at me. I nodded to one side and he followed me until we were out of earshot.

"This isn't what we discussed," I continued. "It was supposed to be quick and painless. Why are you tormenting him?"

"He just tried to kill the both of us."

"So have a lot of people."

"He insulted you."

"I've got a thick pelt. I'll live. What's up with you? You've never been the kind for cruelty."

Vlad winced. I touched his wrist gently. "Do the right thing. Let him have a little honor."

He exhaled. "Very well, sweet."

He strode to the hunter's side again. I didn't watch him, but I heard his voice, this time absent of the mocking arrogance and black humor I'd heard before. "May you find peace in the next life."

He swung and then the night fell deathly silent for a moment. Even the crickets quieted. Then, Vlad took a breath and the forest breathed with him. Life began anew.

He joined me once more and we continued through the forest. Someone would find the man eventually; the people who ran Fernbank Forest first, then the local police, and they'd get word back to his kin if he had any, or more likely, fellow hunters.

"This war," Vlad said quietly. "It has changed me. You were right. I try not to be what they think of me, but sometimes I can't resist becoming the monster they fear. Wearing the mask that keeps their babes awake at night and their women clutching their throats in fear of me. I feed on the fear as much as the blood sometimes."

I didn't say anything at first. I just held his hand again. He didn't pull away.

"We're both monsters," I said. "But that doesn't mean we have to be monsters to them. That's the difference. Be what you want to be, not what they fear you are."

"He wasn't wrong, you know. About how many of their kind

I've killed."

"You are what you are. You have a code, and you try to stick by it. I've always admired that about you."

He made a bitter chuckle in his throat. "You should find a better role model."

I rolled my eyes. "I said I admired it. It's not the same as being my role model.

"Who *is* your role model?"

I thought about it. "Michelle Obama."

Vlad laughed. It was free of the pain he'd been carrying in his words moments ago, and I felt better. "Excellent choice, my dear."

He stopped. I did too and turned to face him. "I…"

He bit his lower lip, hesitating. "Might I see you again tomorrow night?"

I nearly frowned at him in confusion. "Of course. You don't have to ask, Vlad."

"Forgive me. I thought…what happened just now might have changed your mind about me."

"Bullshit," I said. "You can be a monster and a good man, you know. And I'm not as pure as the driven snow either. My hands have plenty of blood on them as well."

I pushed his hair off of his forehead. He sighed a little and caught my wrist, keeping my palm pressed to the side of his face. "Like you said. We're friends. Always, Vlad."

He kissed my palm gently, his voice tender and almost…afraid. "I hope you know I care for more than just your body. You are my light, Cassandra. You burn so brightly it's nearly blinding."

I smiled. "Sap."

I nodded towards the forest. "Come on. Race you to the car."

Vlad grinned at me. "Do you need a head start?"

"Yeah right, old man." I started to go, but he caught me around the waist, scooping me up easily, and kissed me. It stole my breath. It made up for pretty much every bad thing that had happened to me in the five years we'd been apart.

He drew back enough to send me a playful grin. "Don't get cocky, my little honey wolf. No woman's outrun me so far."

Terminus[2]

I grinned right back at him. "Yeah, well. Things change."

He chuckled as I leaned in for another kiss. "They certainly do."

We ran.

But this time, we ran together.

Panola Mountain
By
Violette L. Meier

"Summers in Atlanta are hot and muggy. The heat probably feels like a wool straitjacket, better yet, a cheap polyester catsuit," Joshua quipped as he walked up the dirt path with his date Imani whom he had met a few nights ago in a bar in East Atlanta Village.

He had noticed her across the room dancing with a group of girls like she had never been anywhere in her life. Arms flailing, hips pumping, neck rolling, her awkward dance moves reminded him of an exotic mating ritual he saw two birds do on the Animal Channel. Her unbashful self-confidence made him smile. It was refreshing to see a woman so comfortable in her skin. He loved her medium brown skin tone and wild natural hair that was cropped on the sides and spiraled high on the top of her head like a bouquet of sandy brown curly fries. Minimal makeup, and a free-flowing sundress that highlighted just enough of her body to let him know that her figure was full in all the right places seduced him from his corner of the room into hers.

Joshua approached her with a friendly hello followed by a round of drinks and eats for her and her friends. The connection was instant. Conversation flowed as if they had been friends for years, so he asked her out on a date. He decided on a hiking adventure because he had heard her tell her friends how much she loved the summer sun. Growing up in the coastal area of Alaska denied her of all the hot summer fun she had witnessed on her television set. Immediately after asking her on a date, he decided to take her to Panola Mountain State Park in Stockbridge, a suburban area in metro Atlanta. A week later, here they were panting and sweating up the heavily forested path.

Joshua regretted taking her hiking the moment that he realized his underarm sweat had made giant circles on the armpits of his t-shirt. He pushed the straps of his backpack deep into his pits to camouflage the widening wetness. Being an Atlanta native, he should have known better than sweating and panting up the side of a mountain in the middle of July; especially while entertaining an interesting woman. He prayed that the smell of his sweat was an aphrodisiac instead of a repellent.

Imani laughed. She wiped the pooling perspiration from her forehead with the back of her hand and smiled. She felt like Supergirl, drawing energy from the sun, and becoming more invigorated by the minute. Her red, yellow, and blue spandex outfit helped with her superhero vibe.

"I'd rather have a hot and muggy summer than one drenched in ice," Imani replied as she stepped over a twisting tree branch laying across the grassy path. "I don't ever want to live in the cold again. Black people are tropical people!" she laughed. "I don't know what possessed my father to house me and my mother in the arctic."

"Probably the money," Joshua replied blinking rapidly trying to propel salty sweat from his dark brown eyes.

"True," Imani agreed. "My father was able to stack a lot of money while living in that ice cold hell."

"I take it that an Alaskan cruise is out of the question," Joshua joked. "Well, you won't have to worry about freezing to death in Atlanta. It gets cold, but it never stays cold for long. You can pretty much wear the same clothes year around. Just add a coat. We have all four seasons. I appreciate that about this place."

"Were you born here?" she asked while plucking a yellow flower and placing it behind her ear. The smell of it permeated her nostrils and faded.

"Beautiful," he sighed as he looked at the floral accent in her hair.

She smiled. He smiled too revealing deep dimples in each cheek.

"Yes, I was born here and grew up here. Can't you tell by the t-shirt?" he pointed to his t-shirt which read *ATL HOE.*

Imani shook her head and laughed at the two words printed in giant bold letters. She wasn't offended by the popular phrase used by locals to punctuate their city patriotism.

"But I moved to California after college and stayed there for about five years. Then I moved to Mississippi for two years, and Florida for a year and a half. After working and saving, I was able to leave my job and start a successful data consulting firm. I moved back home to Atlanta about three years ago. There's no place like home," he said as he stopped and clicked his heels three times.

Imani immediately picked up on the reference and laughed aloud.

"Were you born in Alaska?" Joshua asked.

Imani replied, "Yep. Born and raised. I escaped to New York during college and lived there for a decade until recently. I let my cousin talk me into moving to *The Black Mecca*." Imani used air quotes when saying *The Black Mecca*. She continued, "I'm single with no children, and between jobs, so I figured it was worth a shot."

"What do you do?" he asked as he picked up a large stick and began to use it as a staff.

"You look like Gandalf the Gray," she laughed.

He held up the stick and yelled, "You shall not pass!"

Their echoing laughs were answered with the sound of whispering insects, singing birds, and conspiring squirrels. Animal noises filled the space around them as they walked slowly up the incline.

Panola Mountain was a strange kind of mountain. It did not visually stand high like most imposing mountainous structures. It couldn't really be seen from the street nor from inside the park. One only became aware of its height when they reached the top and looked down upon the vast landscape beneath or spied the full glory of the city of Atlanta skyline shining in the distance.

"Are you sure that this is a mountain instead of a big hill?" Imani asked as she picked up an acorn and threw it at a huge neon green grasshopper clinging to a tree a couple of yards in front of them. The grasshopper jumped away and vanished into a nearby bush.

"Leave that bug alone," Joshua laughed. "It ain't bothering you!"

"It was bothering me!" she replied chuckling. "The thought of that giant thing landing in my hair is horrific!"

Joshua shook his head and laughed at her once again. He understood her concern because he was secretly afraid of huge hopping bugs too. There was something about things that jumped that made him want to run home screaming, but he couldn't share that. He was a man, and he was sure that no woman wanted a man who would run from bugs faster than she would. Men were predestined to be brave against six legged monsters whether they feared them or not.

"Let's go this way," Joshua suggested when they came to a fork in the path. The park sign told him to go in the opposite direction, but he felt a bit rebellious. It seemed as if the foliage was greener, and the sunlight sparkled against the leaves sprinkling everything in splendor in the direction that he chose.

"Are you sure?" Imani asked. "You're not going to lead me off the edge of this invisible mountain, are you?"

"Never," he replied and winked. Joshua held out his midnight black hand, interlocking his fingers with hers, and she hesitantly followed him down the unknown path.

"Useless fact," Imani stated randomly. "Did you know that panola is the Choctaw word for cotton?"

"I did not know that," Joshua confessed with a grin on his clean shaven face. "Why do you know that?"

"I enjoy trivia and I read an absorbent amount," said Imani. "My head is filled with useless information."

"You seem to have a lot of leisure time," Joshua replied with one eyebrow raised. "What did you say you did again?"

"I didn't say," Imani retorted and raised her eyebrow in reply. "At the moment, I am enjoying my life until I find something that brings me joy. I taught elementary school for a while then became burned out. Then I tried on a few professions trying to find a good fit. I've worked as a life coach, an herbalist, a dance teacher, owned a bakery, and also a self-proclaimed anthropologist and folklorist. Now, I'm here in Atlanta trying to find something new to do."

"Very interesting," Joshua replied sincerely. He admired her free spirit and willingness to explore new things. He wished that he had the luxury to change jobs on a whim. He hoped that she could truly afford to live her life on a whim and that he was not courting an unemployed sofa surfer. It was not that he cared about how much money she made. He made enough for the both of them and a couple people more, but it was important that he dated a woman with her own purpose and passion.

"Living in Alaska made my father very wealthy and being his only child, in turn made me very wealthy as well. Wealth gives me the freedom to explore different options," Imani said.

"That's pretty cool, but what are you passionate about?" he asked, his tone a bit more serious than it had been all day.

"I'm passionate about life," she answered. "I'm passionate about exploring the world and discovering the miracles hidden in the depths of it. Work is not passion. Work is a way to earn. I am rich and I'm smart. My money makes money while I sleep. I don't want to work. I want to learn. I want to help people. I want to witness the holy and the profane so I can be sure of the difference. I want to truly experience life with all five of my senses. That's what I am passionate about."

Joshua nodded and smiled. Imani was unlike anyone he had ever encountered. Her zest for life made him want to journey with her.

The couple walked for about ten minutes until they came to a large clearing under a tightly intertwined canopy of trees. A circle of misshapen rocks surrounded a patch of glowing purple flowers. What appeared to be a trillion lightening bugs hovered over the gleaming blossoms—the smell of them was like honey cakes.

Imani gasped. She said, "I've never seen fireflies glow like this in the daytime. This is amazing!"

Joshua nodded in agreement as he stared at the glittering swarm.

"Do you hear that?" he inquired.

"Hear what?" Imani replied.

"Shhhh. Listen closely," he said sweetly.

Imani leaned her head to the side and listened intensely.

Instead of buzzing, there was music. A strange music that brought to mind the sound of stringed instruments and wooden flutes. Strange music that defied human ability to play in such a whimsical and low pitch descant. Music that floated from the glowing patch on melodic wings into

"Wow," Imani whispered. "I've never heard anything like this."

"Me either," Joshua replied as he stepped closer to the levitating luminous orchestra.

As he approached, the swarm divided into two clouds of light and out of the middle of the flower patch stepped two identical, save for their skin tones, female creatures. One was Carolina blue and the other sapphire blue. Golden eyes stared out from valentine shaped faces. Clouds of big black hair bounced off their shoulders as if a tiny wind blew just for them. Leaves and flowers were their garments draping them in robes of fragrant color. Fluttering amethyst metallic wings protruded from their backs. Standing about four feet tall, the creatures said in unison, "Welcome to our mountain."

Imani blinked her eyes. She asked, "What did you put in those brownies you gave me in the car?"

"Milk chocolate and walnuts," Joshua answered blinking slowly himself.

"Do you see what I see?" Imani asked; her eyes glued to the blue fairies standing right in front of them.

Joshua nodded.

"I think we should leave," Imani urged as she squeezed his hand as tight as she could.

Joshua said nothing. His unblinking eyes locked with the fairies. He shook his hand loose from Imani's.

"Come with us," the fairies implored; their fingers beckoning the couple to come forward. "Joshua, we have been waiting for you."

Joshua walked slowly towards the flower patch, still unblinking.

"Joshua, I think we should go," Imani spat through her teeth, not taking her eyes off the fairies who was now circling Joshua like technicolored vultures and pulling him towards the flower patch.

"Joshua!" Imani screamed as Joshua's feet touched the flower patch and he and the fairies vanished.

* * *

"Where am I?" Joshua asked as he looked around.

Mushrooms the size of cars and flowers the size of buses were everywhere. The strong floral aroma almost made him gag. Blades of grass as thick as tree trunks surrounded him like a jail cell.

"Where am I?" Joshua screamed aloud. There was no answer. There was no sound. No sound at all. Silence. Dead silence.

Days went by, maybe weeks, maybe months, maybe years in the silence. There was no way he could possibly know. The sun never set in the mysterious realm he found himself trapped in. Joshua sat behind the grass bars thinking of ways to escape to no avail. His mind threatened to spiral into chaos. He filled his stomach with berries that grew next to a crystal-clear pond inside the grassy cage. He passed time counting leaves and making rock formations out of pebbles.

"Let me go!" Joshua yelled as loud as his voice could elevate. "I want to go home!"

The fairies appeared, startling him so badly that he fell backwards.

"Where am I?" he asked as he got back on his feet.

"Panola Mountain," they replied.

"I want to leave," he said, his brows furrowing, his fists balled, and his teeth clenched.

"Not yet," they replied. "We have a gift for you."

The fairies revealed hands full of silver mushrooms.

"Eat," they demanded. "Eat and see what we see."

"What is it?" he asked leery of their intentions.

"It will open your eyes," they replied.

"My eyes are already open," he said.

"No, they aren't. We want you to truly see. You are a good man. Your great great grandfather Tom left this gift for you. He knew you would come one day. Take it!" they urged.

"I never knew my great great grandfather Tom. He disappeared years before my great grandfather was born. Family legend said that because Tom was a powerful preacher who educated and liberated a lot of black people, he was probably caught and hanged by the Klan," said Joshua.

"No such thing happened," the fairies laughed. "He climbed this mountain, and he chose to stay here with us. He was weary of fighting an uphill battle. Tom told us that it was easier to light a fire with two wet sticks than to change the hearts of evil people," they said hovering over Joshua like mystical birds. "You can choose to stay here too."

"No thank you," Joshua replied. "Let me out of this cage."

"It's only grass. You can leave at any time. Your imprisonment is in your mind," they said.

Joshua walked over to one of the blades and touched it. It bent easily under the weight of his hand. He whispered a profanity. He felt like an idiot for not even trying before.

"Where is Tom now?" Joshua inquired as he walked through the grass circle that he thought was his cage, onto a pebbled path.

"With your ancestors," they said.

"You mean dead!" Joshua snapped. Anxiety swelled in his chest. There was a chance that the fairies meant to force him to join his ancestors as well.

"Death does not exist," they replied. "We only want you to see."

"See what?" he asked as he walked. He stopped at a pond and watched winged toads hop and fly across crystal-like lily pads.

"See things as they actually are," they answered as they whirred around him.

"If I eat, will you take me back?" Joshua asked, his voice cracking and a bit high pitched. He hated to admit it to himself, but he was scared. He didn't want to die in Never Never Land or whatever this Godforsaken place was.

"Yes," they replied. "We will take you back."

"Promise?" he asked, his voice quaking as he extended his hand. The fairies dropped the metallic mushrooms into his palm.

"We promise," they replied, eyes turning like spinning wheels of flame.

Joshua took a deep breath and ingested the mushrooms. His eyes shot open.

* * *

"Joshua!" Imani screamed. "Where are you?"

"I'm right here," Joshua replied as he sat up in the middle of the no longer luminescent flower patch, violet petals stark against his dark skin. The flickering musical lights were gone. The honey cake smell was gone. The fairies were gone.

Imani ran over to him and caressed his face with her hand. His smooth-shaven face was now adorned with a silver and ebony beard, thick and curly. His tight young skin showed a tinge of age by way of crow's feet and tiny creases around his mouth.

"How long was I gone?" Joshua asked confused by Imani wearing the same outfit she had on when he had left ages ago. He was even more confused by the bright blue aura that surrounded her body.

"Only a few minutes," she replied as she helped him get to his feet. "What happened to you?"

"I don't know," he replied as his eyes adjusted to the world around him. Everything was alive. The trees even seemed to breath. Insects swarmed around in logical patterns that he had never noticed before. Sunbeams sparkled like liquid diamonds dripping on the earth. He looked up at the sky and saw that the pollution particles of chemtrails were simply that, jet fuel exhaust and not some sort of mind control spray. He wondered how many other conspiracy theories his new vision would help him debunk or prove. *What if the Queen of England really was a lizard?* He laughed to himself and shook off the absurd thought.

"Are you okay?" Imani asked, dusting clinging petals from his shorts and the back of his t-shirt.

"I don't know. I don't know," he repeated, "but I'm excited to find out. I want you to see what I see."

"What do you see?" she asked, while watching him stare off into the sky like it was a brand-new thing to behold.

Joshua opened one of his hands and revealed a few silver mushrooms.

"Here," he said. "Eat it."

Imani took the mushrooms and rolled them around in her palm for a while. She looked up into his eyes and decided to trust him. After all, life was about taking chances. Imani placed the metallic fungi upon her tongue and swallowed. She swooned. Unknown colors streamed into her eyes. She gasped at the beauty of the world around her. A bright yellow aura enveloped Joshua. Her eyes were opened.

"Let's go live that life you were telling me about," he said as he grabbed her hand and quickly descended Panola Mountain.

First in the Family
By
Balogun Ojetade

One

"Dang, Shawty! That hurts!" I complain to the school nurse taking my blood.

"I'm sorry, but you have to relax," she says. "It's difficult to get a sample when you tense up like that. If your veins collapse, I can't do anything."

She's been trying to take my blood for the past ten minutes, talkin' 'bout she's gotta do this to fulfill some random health assessment for college. Shawtay. She keeps on jabbin' me and I'm starting to get dizzier than a mug.

"Oh my God," I blurt out. "I think I'm gonna be sick."

"Maybe you should lie down," the nurse suggests as she helps me out of my chair. "Maybe we can get you to an exam table."

"Uh… aight." I say with a nod. Then I stand up. And the room starts to spin. Seconds later, I feel something cold on my back. I think it's the floor. Completely disoriented, I can't move.

"Ricky? Ricky! Can you hear me?" the nurse shouts from above me.

I hear her, but she sounds like she's over at Spelman and I'm at the 'House. That's Morehouse for y'all from Russia or something. Anyway, the nurse's mouth is moving, but the words coming out of it are muffled. I feel like I have *Beats* on my ears.

"Ricky!" The nurse then shouts out into the corridor. "I need some help here. I'm losing him. He's becoming unresponsive. He's too handsome to be unresponsive!"

Well, I added that last part, but I do think she's checking for me, though. Well, she was… until I fainted like a damsel in distress.

Despite the chill on my back, I'm starting to sweat, and my vision is blurry. The room is spinning. Everything's getting darker than a mu—.

Six Months Earlier

"Ricky!" My mama shouts into my room. "You up?"

"Yeah, Ma. Yeah," I reply, still snuggled under the covers.

"You didn't forget, did you?"

"Forget what? Wh-What time is it?"

"It's 6:00 o'clock. And you've got your field trip to the clinic today." She then comes in and steps up to my bed. "You forgot, didn't you?"

"Naw. Uh. No. I didn't."

"Okay, then get up," she says as she rips the covers off me. "Get up! And go make your father and me proud! My baby's gonna be a doctor!"

"Uh-huh," I groan.

"'Uh-huh' nothing. We've always wanted to have a doctor in the family."

I roll to the edge of the bed and plant my feet on the floor. "Isn't Daddy a doctor?"

"He has a PhD… in Manga. A Doctor of Comic Books." She walked off shaking her head.

I think a PhD in Manga is fye.

It's still dark outside, and I want to go back to sleep, but I force myself to get up. First stop, the bathroom.

There I turn on the shower, wait for it to get warm enough, and hop in. The water blasts me straight in the face. Some people drink coffee, but for me, a good shot of water to the face is enough to wake up. That, plus African Black soap from Mama's botanica helps energize me.

After the shower, I brush my teeth, pick my afro, and throw on some skinny Lasheys and a t-shirt. Now I'm definitely awake and ready to start my day. I hop into some kicks and run downstairs to greet my parents.

"Hey son," Dad says. "Big day today?"

"Yeah," I reply. "A few of my classmates and I are spending the day at a clinic. We're going to interact with doctors, nurses, and patients. Get a taste of what a job in medicine is really like."

"Your son is going to be the first doctor in the family," Mama says, beaming with pride.

"Ma, stop. You're embarrassing me."

"That's my job as your Mama, right?"

"Whatever. I gotta go."

"Oh! I almost forgot," she says as she holds out a steaming package wrapped in aluminum foil. "Some hot wings so you can eat on the go. Lemon pepper."

I take the chicken and toss it in my backpack. "Thanks, Ma. Bye, Daddy."

"Bye, son," he says.

My mother hugs me good-bye.

* * *

As I walk to the bus stop, I see everyone else in the neighborhood warming up their cars, grabbing newspapers off their lawns, and generally getting ready to head off to work or school. And no one looks enthusiastic about it, including me.

Getting up this early in the morning is tough. While I'm not really looking forward to going away to college in a few months, I'm never going to schedule any classes before 10:00 AM when I do.

After waiting at the bus stop for a couple of minutes, I hop on the school bus, like I've done for the past three and a half years, and my fellow classmates and I arrive at Carver High fifteen minutes later. Once there, I meet Teniade, Jamal, and Lashey outside of our A.P. Biology class to meet up with our teacher and a handful of other students coming along on the field trip.

The consensus among our group is unanimous. While we're thrilled to get out of class for the day, we're not particularly excited for the field trip to some medical clinic.

"I still can't believe we get to cut an entire day of class for this trip," I say.

"Well, it's not just to get out of class," Teniade says. "It's to see if we really have an interest in biology, premed, and all that medical stuff."

"Whatever. Going from class to boring class is a snooze-fest," Jamal says. "At least today, maybe there'll be some excitement in our lives. Atlanta is boring, shawty!"

"It'll be something different for sure. And we'll have a chance to help people, too," Teniade adds.

"Yeah, that, too. I guess that's a good thing," Jamal says.

Lashey just nods and yawns. It still might be a little too early for her.

As we're talking, Mrs. Vaughan, our AP Biology teacher, comes over to us. She's going to be our chaperone on the field trip.

"How is everyone this morning?" she asks. "I hope you're all looking forward to shadowing the staff at the clinic today. Not many high school students get an opportunity like this, but Carver High School has such a great reputation, they couldn't say no."

I see some of my fellow students nod their heads in sheeplike agreement. I'm not into it either, but I feel like I should at least try to feign some interest. Only a few students were chosen for this experience so I might as well make the most of it. I may want to pursue a career in medicine. I may not. I really don't know. I try to show interest, even if it isn't exactly genuine.

"Are we just shadowing them, or will we be able to help them in some way?"

"Good question, Ricky! I'm not exactly sure to be honest. We'll have to see what they need when we arrive. I'm sure there'll be something for us to sink our teeth into. The main takeaway is to get familiar with the environment and ask lots of questions," Mrs. Vaughan says. "All right everyone, let's go outside and meet the bus. We don't want to be late!"

As we all file out of the school and huddle around one another at the curb, we see another school bus pull up beside us. I saunter up the steps to get into the bus and find a seat. There aren't many of us going on this field trip, so I have a seat to myself and I'm able to sprawl out and chill before our day of medical adventures.

Two

Our bus pulls into the parking lot of the clinic. The building seems pretty plain in design. Granite exterior, lush green grass in need of landscaping, and a sign that simply reads "Eff Cancer." Bold. I kinda like it.

As the school bus doors whoosh open, we all funnel out, walk across the parking lot's blacktop, and open the front glass double doors. Once inside, we congregate in the lobby until a young woman greets us and introduces herself as Olive.

"Hello and welcome to Eff Cancer!" Olive says. "Thank you all so much for taking time away from your studies to learn about what we do here. I think you'll find it'll be a rewarding experience. Why don't we head over to the conference room so you can watch the orientation presentation? Just follow me."

As we fall in line behind Olive, we pass by a larger area with a few tables and chairs, possibly a waiting room, as well as several doctors' offices and nurses' stations. Deep inside the building, we finally reach the conference room. It has a large wooden table and one of the interior walls is made from a clear material—maybe plexiglass—so it's easy to see inside. There's also a big screen TV hanging down from the ceiling and a laptop labeled, "Conference Room," across the top of the monitor screen. It's sitting in front of the first chair closest to the conference room door. We each take a seat as the light in the room dims and the video presentation begins.

The presentation opens by talking about the history of the clinic and how it was founded the previous year by a team of professors and other educators from around the country. Their objective: to tirelessly research, pursue, and one day cure the deadliest forms of cancer so people can live happy and healthy lives.

In the video, they feature interviews with several patients that tug at the heartstrings. They also have clips of doctors and nurses talking about their commitment to this worthy cause. Throughout the video, the name "Toter Corp" pops up several times—a company I've never heard of. Strange name. It was on the introductory screen of the video, and I spotted their logo in various spots around the clinic as we walked through.

After the video comes to an end, Olive moves to stand in front of the screen and asks if we have any questions.

I guess Lashey finally woke up because she's the first to ask a question, "What types of cancers does this clinic specialize in treating?"

"Very good question," Olive says. "We're making progress with some of the most aggressive cancers like pancreatic, prostate, lung, and various blood cancers, such as Non-Hodgkin's lymphoma and leukemia, just to name a few. We still have a lot of work to do and a long way to go."

Silence.

"Any other questions? That's why I'm here." Olive smiles.

I raise my hand.

"Yes, go ahead," she says, looking at me.

"What's Toter Corp?"

"You have a good eye for details," Olive replies. "I love that. To answer your question, Toter Corp is our primary donor. It's the company behind the clinic that keeps the lights on, funds our research, and allows people to seek treatment at no cost."

Another long silence.

"Okay, if there aren't any more questions," she says, "let's get you suited up into scrubs so you can begin the most exciting part of your day. Follow me."

She leads us out of the conference room and down the hall to a couple of changing areas. "Inside each of the stalls, you'll find scrubs just like the doctors and nurses wear on TV. Find your size and get changed. If you have any valuables, you can leave them here with me and we'll store them safely until you're ready to go home."

* * *

After changing into a pair of blue scrubs, I emerge from the dressing room to join the rest of the class. Olive leads us down another hallway and one by one she assigns each of us a doctor or a nurse to shadow. I'm handed off to a Dr. Bohdan Franko. A little nervous, I barely manage a shy, "Hello."

I watch as the rest of the group keeps walking down the hall and I'm left standing in the doorway of Dr. Franko's office.

"What's your name?" he asks.

"My name is Ricky." I can feel my heart beating a million miles an hour. I've never helped a doctor before. The work they do here is so important. I don't want to mess up by doing something stupid.

"Nice to meet you, Ricky." He extends his hand. I quickly do the same and we shake. He's got a serious grip.

"What can I help you with, Dr. Franko ?" I ask.

"For now, we're going to make the rounds to all my patients, get their vitals, and check in on their progress. Basically, get the scoop on what's going on with them. I usually do this first thing in the morning, but I knew you'd be coming, so I delayed it. I thought you might enjoy the experience."

"I appreciate that. Is there anything I can do to help?"

"Of course. You can hold my clipboard for now and just observe. You really want to jump in with both feet, huh?"

"Yes!" I say with a little too much enthusiasm. "Well, I'm considering a major in biology when I go to college and then going pre-med, so the sooner I can get into it, the better."

"I like your energy, but you need to relax. I also have to warn you that being a doctor in the real world may not be as glamorous as you see on TV. I'll do my best to impress, though."

"Okay, Dr. Franko."

"No need to call me Dr. Franko. Franko or just Frank for short—either is fine."

As we leave his office and proceed to the first patient's room, I am beyond nervous. What if I say something dumb? I can feel my stress sweat starting. I can't remember if I put on deodorant this morning. And when I'm nervous, it manifests itself through sweat and a bad habit of pulling at the corners of my eyebrows. Yeah, it's weird, but it helps to diffuse my anxiety... and my eyebrows are always on fleek, too.

Franko enters the first room. The patient is an old man. He seems unresponsive or maybe he's just asleep for now. He's bald and wrinkly. Though the most unusual thing about him is his skin. It looks a light brownish-gray, and you can clearly see his dark veins showing through. It's as if his skin is translucent or some-thin'.

"What's wrong with him?" I ask.

"It's a little bit of a mystery, but we believe he has bone cancer. Basically, we think his blood is sucking the life out of his bones and we don't know why. And the worst part is that it's spreading. We can't seem to stop it no matter what treatment we administer."

"Aw naw," I put my hand over my mouth in shock. I don't know why I didn't realize the patients here would be in such bad condition.

"We're not giving up, though," Franko continues. "He's a fighter and we're not going to let him down."

"Is he in pain?" I ask.

"If he is, he hides it well. We're doing all we can to keep him comfortable."

As Franko reviews his chart and takes his vitals, like blood pressure and such, I just stand there, watching the patient. He seems peaceful until his eyes suddenly pop open.

I'm spooked. I jump, and I take a step back. He sits up quickly and makes a horrible hissing sound, then reaches out, grabs my scrub top, and pulls me close enough I can see the veins pulsing through a gray haze covering his eyeballs.

"Kill me," he mutters.

"Stanton!" Franko shouts. "Stan! What are you doing? Don't frighten him! Stop it!" He unhooks Stan's hand from my top, helps the patient back down onto the bed, and tries talking to him to get him to calm down.

"How are you feeling today, Stan?" Franko asks.

There's no response. Stan's just lying there in bed with his eyes wide open, staring at nothing in particular.

"Stan?" The doctor snaps his fingers in front of his face.

Nothing.

Franko grabs his phone out of his pocket and punches in a few digits. "Nurses' station, please." There's a pause as he waits for an answer. "Yeah. Hi. It's Frank. I'm in room 207. Send up an orderly, all right? Our patient has become a little more unpredict-able. He needs to be restrained."

"Franko…" I say, still recovering from the patient scaring me.

"Yes?"

"Is this guy going to be okay?"

"That's tough to say, Ricky. We're an experimental clinic, so all the hospitals send us their toughest cases. Just know that we're doing everything we can to help him."

Moments later, an orderly rushes through the door with straps. He wraps them around Stan's arms and ties them to the bed frame. He does the same with his legs. He even puts a couple straps over Stan's torso.

"He shouldn't cause any more issues," the orderly says. "He's in there pretty good now."

"Thanks, Tito," Franko says. "We have to continue our rounds. Could you stay here with Stan for a few minutes and just watch him? I want to make sure he's all right."

"Sure thing, Frank," Tito says as he pulls up a chair and sits down. "I'm not gonna complain when the boss wants me to take a break."

As we leave the happy-go-lucky orderly to his babysitting detail, we move to the next room, where Franko and I visit with a young woman who's conscious, but she appears to have some nervous and quite disruptive facial tics.

"How are you doing today, Nina?"

"F-Fine, D-Doctor Frank. H-how are y-you?" she replies. As she speaks, it looks as if her jaw is having trouble following along with her words, like it's moving involuntarily. And it keeps happening over and over again. It's as though she's chewing on something that isn't there.

"I'm doing well, Nina. I want you to meet Ricky. He's shadowing me today. He's from Carver High School and he thinks he wants to be a doctor someday."

"N-Nice to meet-meet y-you." Nina's neck is jerking uncontrollably so she can't keep eye contact for long.

"Nice to meet you as well," I reply, keeping a smile on my face to keep the mood light.

"M-Maybe y-y-you can help-p D-Doctor Frank f-figure o-out w-what's w-wrong w-with meh-me?" She tries to smile, but her face contorts into a creepy smirk instead.

"I'll do my best," I tell her as I watch Franko check her chart. He takes out his stethoscope and walks to the other side of her bed. He gently takes her arm and puts the flat side of the instrument onto the inside of her wrist and listens. He then checks her blood pressure.

"Can you lean forward, Nina?" he asks. "I want to check your breathing." With his help, she scoots forward. "Inhale deeply for me, all right?"

She inhales.

"Go ahead and exhale."

She complies.

"Again."

She inhales again, but this time she coughs a phlegmy, deep bark.

"Exhale."

There's that disturbing cough again.

"Inhale one more time for me," Franko says.

She concurs. Her breathing goes back to normal this time.

"You did good, Nina. Ring the buzzer if you need anything, all right?"

"Okay, D-Doctor."

We take our leave from Nina, exit her room, and begin to walk farther down the corridor. Right before we make it to the third patient room, there's an ear-piercing scream.

Three

"Ahhh! Help! Somebody! Help us!" a woman shouts.

Franko runs down the hallway and I follow close behind. As we arrive on the scene outside of a nearby patient room, we find a flock of frightened employees hiding behind the nurses station and a young woman in a cloth gown on top of a nurse. The woman on top is half naked and biting viciously at the nurse's neck. The nurse on the floor isn't moving. I pray she's just unconscious and not dead. Blood is splattered on their clothing and quickly pooling underneath both of them.

Franko grabs the female patient by the waist and pulls her off the nurse. Her mouth is clamped onto the nurse's neck. She isn't letting go.

"Ricky! Go to the janitor's closet behind the nurses station," he orders. "Grab a broom or a mop. Anything with a long handle and come back. Hurry!"

I take off, run behind the nurses' station, and fumble through the closet. I find a broom, grab it, and run back to Franko . "Here!" I shout.

"Good! Now see if you can slide the broom handle in-between her mouth and the nurse's neck. Don't get too close."

"Okay!" I say as I try to poke the long broom handle in the small open area between this crazy woman's teeth and the nurse's neck. "It won't go!"

"Push harder," Franko replies. "Don't worry about hurting her. We just need to separate them."

I get a better grip on the broom handle, and, with all my strength, I jam it into her jaw. I hear a cracking sound from the wood hitting her teeth. At the same time, the crazy woman looks at me with her wild eyes. She finally releases the nurse and then reaches out for me. Scared, I drop the broom and back up immediately. At the same time, Franko is able to pull her away.

I look at the nurse's neck and see a huge gaping wound. The bite is grotesque and still bleeding profusely. The patient's mouth is plastered with blood. It covers her entire mouth and drips down her chin and neck. I'm overwhelmed and frozen in place watching the scene unfold. I begin to smell her blood wafting over me. I think I'm going to be sick.

"Get her out of here! Now!" Franko commands. Some of the medical staff leave the safety of their station, rush over, and surround their wounded colleague, quickly wheeling her away on a gurney.

The patient is still flailing around in Franko's arms. Her arms and legs feverishly kick and flail as she tries to break free from his grasp. Her jaw is chomping constantly, attempting to lock onto his arm.

"Ricky, grab the broom handle at both ends and push it into her mouth so she bites down on it!" he says.

I do as instructed and grab the broom again.

"Stick it in her mouth, but don't let her bite you."

"Uh-huh," I choke out, fearful of what may happen if she's able to latch onto me. I shove the broom handle into her mouth so she can't bite Franko, me, or anyone else.

In the process of doing it, though, a few of her teeth come loose and fall onto the floor. For a second, I stare at them. I want to help people, and I just failed on my first day.

Tito the orderly rushes in and helps Franko wrestle the woman down to the ground. She's screaming at the top of her lungs, her arms and legs still thrashing about wildly. They try to get her back into her room, but it's a fight because she's got a death grip on the doorframe. Tito holds her as tight as he can while Franko pries back her fingers. Eventually, they drag her back into her room and strap her down. Even secured to her bed, she's still going nuts.

Franko runs out of the patient's room and returns a moment later with a syringe. "I'm going to sedate her," he tells Tito.

As he injects her, Franko asks Tito, "Did she bite you?"

"No, I'm good. You?"

"Just a scratch. Nothing serious."

"Maybe you should get that looked at?"

"I'm a doctor. I think I can handle it."

With the ruckus over for now, I lean against the doorframe and sink down to the floor, shaking. All I can do is stare at the now dark red, almost black, pool of blood coagulating on the hallway floor. When I look the other way, I see the crazy patient, now sedated and unconscious. And the smell—the putrid smell permeates every square inch of the clinic. The odor is foul at best and getting worse.

With so much happening, I didn't even notice Mrs. Vaughan and my friends scattered around the scene watching everything unfold. They look scared and confused, but I don't have the energy to explain what happened, not that I know myself. Teniade has her hand over her mouth like she's going to throw up. Sounds like a good idea.

I get back up on my jelly legs and run to the bathroom, but the rancid smell of blood follows me. I can't get away from it. I check each stall to make sure I'm alone and then lock the door behind me. I open one of the bathroom stalls, drop to my knees, and vomit into the toilet. I see remnants of the lemon pepper my mama made me for breakfast floating in the toilet. I start to cry. That woman almost bit me. I vomit again.

Medicine might not be the path I'm destined to go down. My parents are going to be so disappointed in me. Hell, I'm disappointed in myself, too.

There's a knock at the bathroom door.

"Ricky?" It's Mrs. Vaughan. "Ricky? Are you in there?"

"Yeah," I answer.

"We're going to cut our trip a little short. I think we've all had our fill of this clinic for today. Are you descent? Can you open the door?"

I stand up, rinse my mouth out as best I can, and open the door for her.

"Franko said you did a great job today," she says.

"That's good," I reply.

"Are you all right?"

"I think so. Just a little shaken up, I guess."

"Considering everything that happened today, that's pretty good. Why don't you come along and join us on the bus? We're going to get everyone home."

Four

Back on the bus, I'm sitting alone, still shaking.

Mrs. Vaughan sits down next to me. "Do you want to talk about what happened today?"

"No. Not yet. I think I just want to chill out and forget about it."

"Okay, but if you need to talk, just know I'm here for you."

She gets up and leaves me alone as she tends to other students.

With the seat now empty, I stretch out my legs, lean my upper body against the side of the bus, and close my eyes, which are dry, burning, and have seen some crazy things today. If I close them for just a couple of minutes, it might help me relax.

I clear my mind of everything and consciously try not to think about anything. I feel myself calming down. Then something changes.

I see myself in the hallway at the clinic. The lights are dim and I'm alone. My breathing starts to speed up and my pulse begins to race.

Suddenly, I hear a shrill howl. Which way is it coming from?

I whimper and cover my mouth so whatever is out there doesn't hear me. I quiet down.

The screams are getting louder. They're all around me. I want to run and escape, but I don't know which way to go. I have to do something. I have to get out of here.

I scream and wake myself up. We're still on the bus. Mrs. Vaughan is sitting next to me again, trying to comfort me and find out what's wrong.

"Are you okay?" she asks. "What happened?"

"I'm sorry. I-it was just a dream. I'm sorry."

"It's fine. When we get back to school, I'll call your parents to pick you up. Maybe going home on the bus isn't a good idea today."

"No. No. I'm fine. Really, I am. I promise."

"Are you sure?"

"Yes."

Five

Back at home, it's dinnertime and my folks are asking about my day.

"So? How was the field trip to the clinic?" Mama asks.

"It was…uh, strange."

"How so?"

"So many sick people."

"That sounds about normal. What did you think you'd find in a clinic or a hospital?"

"Honestly? I don't know. Today was just a shock to my system. I didn't expect it."

"Anything you do for the first time is scary. When you go back, you'll be able to cope better."

"Go back?"

"Of course! You're going to be the first doctor in the family. You can't give up after one strange experience, as you call it."

"Ummm. I don't know about that. Listen, I'm finished eating. I'm gonna go upstairs and get some sleep. I'm exhausted."

"Wait, son…" Daddy says.

I rush upstairs to my room. I don't want to hear anything else from them right now.

* * *

I brush my teeth and hop into bed, snuggling up under the covers.

Maybe Mama's right. I can't let one strange day throw me for a loop. Franko looks as though he enjoys his job, and he's trying to help people get better. His job certainly isn't easy. Other doctors and medical professionals transfer the cases they can't solve to him. Every day is a challenge, and my guess is that he's never bored. And if he's part of the team that one day cures cancer, that would be a life-changer for so many people suffering around the world.

I fluff my pillow and turn on my side. With both hands under my pillow for support, I fall asleep.

I'm sitting across from Franko. This time I'm wearing a white doctor's coat just like his.

"Now that you've examined the patient, what's your diagnosis?" he asks me.

I don't know what to say. I don't know what he's talking about. "Uhhh…"

"What's your diagnosis, Doctor?" he asks again. "Without your diagnosis, the patient will die. You don't want that, do you?"

"No. Of course, not."

He's looking at me. I stare into his eyes. Something is wrong.

"Look!" he says.

"Look at what?"

"Here! Where she scratched me!" His face starts to twitch. "What should I do?"

"I thought you took care of that," I say. "Let's get someone to look at it."

"No! They'll only run tests and strap me down. No one can help me now." His jaw starts to make a clicking sound.

"You don't know that." My breathing gets faster. I get up from my seat and start to back out of the room.

"Where are you going?" he asks.

I bolt to the door, but it's closed. I try to open it. No luck. It's locked. I lean my head against the door and close my eyes.

"You're not going anywhere," he says.

He gets up from his seat and slowly saunters his way over to me. Frightened, I turn around. He's an inch from my face. He inhales deeply and then exhales in my face. His breath smells like if shit and pee-pee had a baby on a bed of vomit. I think I'm going to be sick.

His head jerks forward. I try to protect myself by putting my arms in front of my face. His teeth bite into my arm.

I scream myself awake.

* * *

I'm back on the floor in the school infirmary at Morehouse. The nurse is waving smelling salts under my nose. Yuck. The smell of ammonia mixed with a hint of lavender is overpowering, but I guess that's the idea.

"There he is," the nurse says.

"Wha-what happened?" I ask, coming out of my fog.

"I was trying to take your blood for the college health assessment. You passed out. We couldn't wake you up. You scared the hell out of us," she answers.

"How long was I out?"

"Just a couple of minutes. You're okay now. Don't worry."

I sigh, embarrassed I'm so squeamish. "Has anyone else passed out like this?"

"A few people… I guess you're not going pre-med," she jokes, trying to lift my spirits.

"Probably not," I reply.

I look up and see what seems to be the entire staff of the school infirmary looking down at me. What a way to start off my freshman year at the 'House. I'm so embarrassed—mortified is more like it.

"Can you get up?" the nurse asks.

"I think so."

"Don't overdo it," she says, helping me up. Then, to someone else in the crowd of people staring at me, "Someone get him a wheelchair. We want to make sure he doesn't fall again. The last thing we need is him hitting his head on the floor."

Flustered, they lift me into the chair, roll me across the room, and help me onto an exam table. I turn to the nurse, "Did you get the blood sample? Are we done here? I'd like to go now."

"No, hon'. We're just getting started," she says with a warm smile. "Franko will be here soon."

"Aw naw."

The Sleepwalking Dead
By
Glenn Parris

When vampires go to ground, they stay put until dusk—
usually. What to do with a vampire who likes to meander
around in the sun (Zompire)? Quite a challenge for a loyal
Familiar charged with the vampire's safety.

"Check this out!" The high school dropout pointed to a stiff
figure in a woolen suite with suede elbow patches. "Guess this
old Oreo is black enough." The teen's pancake-colored arms
sported a sleeve of tattooed tributes to gothic myth and biker
legend. The object of his amusement, an elderly black man
smeared in a cosmetic mask like muddy guacamole from head to
hands. Behind him trailed another black man in his wake nearly
as old as the first. He carried a black umbrella shading the first
from the midday sun. The man in the obsolete tweed jacket and
mismatched trousers clutched a bundle of books, wore a vacuous smile, and stared forward out of glazed eyes.

Another of the derelicts in the trio said, "Looks like money to
me, bruh. I been watchin' these dudes for a while now." The
bigger man was three shades darker than the tattooed youth.
"They got a real nice ride. That means money. More money than
sense." He buoyed a subtle upward nod. "Look at 'em."

The three men stared like coyotes stalking a sheep. "Easy
money." He pointed at the black Cadillac Escalade. "Get the
plate number. Tell Jackson to tail them home. I think they live
'round here somewhere."

"Hey, lunch breaks over." The beefy white man wore a hard
hat and barked with authority. "Let's get these fellas back to

199

work, Berry. We gotta get this old building cleared out for the contractors coming in next week." He clapped his hands together. "I'm paying you guys by the day not the hour. You get a fair day's pay for a fair day's work." The boss-man eyed the big, black guy named Berry he knew as the ringleader. "All or nothing chief."

All the men got up and languidly got back to work, but not before Berry tipped an imaginary hat and said, "Yassir, Boss."

*　*　*

His brow knitted, Marcus Coke watched his master from the bottom of the staircase. Elmo Hoogle sat there in his attic study, rocking gently in the waning hours of twilight. He was up early, and he had had a snoot full already. Marcus climbed the century old staircase, both he and the wood beneath creaking with each deliberate step.

"Good evening, sir." Marcus intoned. "It's going to be a lovely night, they say. There's a half moon rising and not a cloud in the sky."

Elmo Hoogle looked up with a start. "Oh, it's you Marcus. Sneaky chap, aren't you? Quiet as a mouse!"

"Yes, sir." Marcus frowned. *He should have heard me coming a mile away.*

"May I fix you a cup of tea? I brewed a delicious blend of Earl Grey, owl and rabbit blood. I caught them both an our ago." Marcus raised his eyebrows. "Still fresh."

Marcus cupped his hands and wafted the faint aroma up from the kitchen toward the occupant in the rocking chair. Elmo swayed out of sync with the chair. He gazed absently down through the window overlooking a lightly forested yard and neighboring homes.

"Remarkable. However, did you get them both?" Elmo sipped from his sherry glass. "Humans can't move fast enough to catch a rabbit, much less an owl."

Marcus suppressed a bristle at the formaldehyde on his master's breath as he addressed him. "I used a trap, sir. The rabbit caught his foot in the trap and as he struggled, the owl swooped in for dinner. She dug her claws into the rabbit for the kill and I had them both."

"Hmm. Sounds a bit gamey, don't you think?" Elmo wrapped his lips around the edge of the sherry glass once again.

Marcus sniffed at the comment. *If he goes for his pipe, it might take the whole house up in flames.*

"Why don't we go out for a walk sir? The campus is nearby and nicely wooded for privacy. Love is in the air. There's nothing like young paramours all worked up to whet your appetite."

"Pish posh! Some of those sweet, young people might be my very own students. I can't bring myself to consume them."

"Well, I know you don't like to drink your students, but they may get you in the mood." Marcus wrung his hands. "We might find a nice mugger or two in the seedier part of town later on that might prove tasty."

Neither noticed shadowy figures' furtive movement in the yard below.

"No, for some reason, I'm a little weary tonight. Feels like I've been running a marathon." Elmo placed his glass carefully on the side table and stretched. Before Marcus could scoop it up, Elmo had retrieved the glass and almost reached his lips again.

"Ah, Professor Hoogle, wouldn't you like me to get you a warm bowl of porridge? I made it from calf's blood laden with meaty chunks of marrow. Doesn't that sound delectable?"

"I don't know why you insist on bothering me, Marcus." Elmo shook his fists smartly across his chest in a gesture of contention. "I'm just fine right here, sipping my hot toddy." He wrestled the glass from Marcus again with blinding speed, stirring the aromatic formaldehyde into the intervening air yet spilling nary a drop.

After one hundred fifty years, he found that he didn't seem to need as much sleep as his peers. There were vampires much older than he who slept soundly from dusk 'til dawn.

This troubled Marcus more than his employer. The aging familiar wrung his hands as he watched his employer read a book he'd been paging through since the day of his first hire. Marcus neared the age that Elmo looked, but unlike Marcus, Elmo stopped aging at 72. Horseshoe baldness notwithstanding,

Marcus contended with the fact that he would soon appear to be the elder of the two.

Proffered to him as an easy ward, Elmo was little trouble at night. No voracious prowling the nights hunting street walkers, hobos and ne'er do wells. He contented himself to read with an ever present, vacuous smile on his face.

Page 86. Elmo eventually got to page 86 every few months re-reading *A Tale of Two Cities*. Marcus counted 12 times in the two years of his employment. Dickens had been a contemporary writer through most of Elmo's life. Hoogle never tired of his captivating prose.

In contrast to his easy-going night life. Elmo proved to be the Gild's most challenging ward to day-watch. The Board of Regents wanted an American for this undead transplant from Shropshire, England. Hoogle had been a professor before he was taken. Born in Trinidad, raised in the town of Shrewsbury, east of Whales. The invitation to Shrewsbury castle would last as his proudest moment and his everlasting bane. Elmo never quite overcame the shock of being sucked into the night world of the Vampyre. The Board of Regents added the requirement of Clinical psychology to Marcus's job description to help Elmo Hoogle cope with his transition.

"Marcus," Elmo droned, "Did I ever tell you about my appointment to oversee the education of the 5th Duke of Cleveland?"

"No sir, you've never mentioned it." Marcus lied automatically as he had at least a dozen times over.

"The Duke of Cleveland invited me to see to the proper education of his first and only son. William was a sickly child, but he had a voracious appetite for literature." Elmo smiled in his reverie. "And quite an aptitude for history. He could remember dates and events as if he lived them himself." He laughed softly to himself.

"What a joy it must have been to have such an apt student, sir." Marcus encouraged the distraction as he knew how it soothed the Professor.

"Towards the end, the duke dismissed all the staff but me. Tears welled in his eyes when he told me, 'My son has little time left with us, Elmo. There is a darkness about him. Even the rooms in that isolated wing of the house have grown dim. He calls for you. Says he'll see no one else. You were his favorite teacher. A mentor to him.' He told me." Elmo effected a sad smile. "The duke bowed his head and touched his forehead to mine."

"'Go to him Elmo.' he said, 'You may be the last light that he sees.'" Elmo broke his reverie and looked up at Marcus. "I made the duke a promise that night. I told him, 'I'll not sleep until the lad recovers. I'll keep Death away if I must use my very soul as a shield.' I swore. It was so gloomy, yet the boy seemed to glow with a soft ghastly halo. He closed his eyes and lolled his head to the side. In desperation, I reached for him as if to snatch him from the very jaws of the Devil himself." Elmo crinkled his brow as if straining to recall the next moment, almost fumbling his fingers to grasp it.

"Then what happened?" Marcus prodded. This was the crucial hurdle of memory Elmo never could quite surmount.

"Too sad. For all of us who loved the lad. We blocked it out." Elmo opened a pocket watch and check the time and relaxed. "The next thing I remember I embarked on a steamer to America."

"When was that, sir?" Marcus tried something new.

"Well after the Great War, of course. The Duke of Cleveland rewarded me richly for the loving care of his son." His eyes glazed again, "Yes, William was his name. With Duke Harry's patronage, I purchased this Avelon Estates Mansion."

"Do you recall when that was, sir?"

"Of course, Marcus. Are you daft? It was…" Elmo faltered.

"Yes, Sir?"

"Well, it was nineteen hundred and twenty-four. I selected it for its quaint olde English style as well as its proximity to Oglethorpe University. I held the distinguished Philip Weltner Chair of the Philosophy and Ethics department. Remember the words of Thornwell Jacobs." Elmo recited the school motto, 'Nescit cedere.' We who never give up!"

Marcus wrestled with Elmo Hoogle's tenacious confabulation of tenure at the college. For years, the Board of Regents struggled to obscure Elmo's wanderings on campus as myth and fraternity boys' legend for frightened young freshmen's rite of passage during pledge week. Now after 85 years of haunting the campus and protecting the conservative spirit from the urbanization and progress of the Atlanta outside, Elmo Hoogle was actually inducted into the English department faculty.

Marcus could not fathom how a kookie old man with an obsolete British accent could get hired at Oglethorpe until Elmo told him he would be teaching night classes in classical literature and 19th century fiction.

The 21st century found the English department lacking in diversity, especially when it came to African American faculty. The chair had unrealistically high standards when it came to associate professor candidates' knowledge base of classical, English, and American literature. Most African Americans in this day and age wanted to teach African or African American history, not the classics. Hoogle could talk about nothing else. From Milton to Shakespeare, Hoogle's knowledge of English literature and history surpassed even the chairman's expertise.

"But sir, what about the boy? There was quite some time between the last time you saw young William and when you sailed for America. What happened? That leaves 30 years unaccounted for that you've never told me about." *If I can just get him to realize what he did.*

Leaves rustled along the back wall with the south wind. The often-familiar hoot of the owl ostensibly absent.

"Let's take that walk you've been nagging me about, Marcus. Suddenly, I feel—animated tonight."

That's as close as we've ever come. Marcus sighed. *Well, there's always tomorrow.*

Marcus retrieved Elmo's cloak and umbrella. He carried that antique umbrella everywhere, rain or shine. Once dressed for the streets, the pair met in the garage. Marcus talked the professor into trading in the old Bentley for a Cadillac Escalade. More modern with room for a coffin that could accommodate his daytime escapades if needed for a discrete and hasty exit. At night though, Elmo abhorred driving. He'd rather walk or as familiars called that mode of locomotion, speed walking. The escalade couldn't keep up with that, even on a straight-a-way.

"I'll meet you on campus, Marcus. I'll check my mailbox and see if any of my students need any help. Once Marcus started the ignition, Elmo took what appeared to be one awkward step, then blurred into the distance. Marcus drove at a leisurely pace to the same destination. He reached the Oglethorpe campus gate and showed Professor Hoogle's parking pass. The security guard nodded and granted him entry to the faculty parking lot. Marcus placed the car in park and contented himself listening to the voices of an audiobook by S.A. Cosby while he waited for Elmo.

In half an hour, Elmo emerged from Hearst Hall's back exit. Two female students nodded appreciation and parted ways with Elmo. Marcus flicked the headlights on the escalade. In a blur, Elmo was at the driver's side window.

"I think I'll take a stroll down to the Zoo, Marcus. I'm in the mood for a sip from my favorite elephant's ears." He nodded absently, "Nice and fresh."

"I'll meet you there in say 30 minutes, sir?" Marcus asked.

"Brilliant, Marcus. Brilliant."

* * *

Marcus rolled up to a darkened Zoo facility. Several young men loomed around the parking lot and made themselves scarce when the escalade pulled up. Once again, Marcus flicked his headlights to signal his arrival. Elmo made a more languid approach to the vehicle and entered through the right back door. Marcus noted the heads of the homeless pop up at Elmo's retreat to the car. He wondered if his employer feasted on more than elephant ears this night but said nothing to his master.

"Let's go for a ride Marcus. I don't enjoy the comforts of this fine carriage often enough. How do you indulge in entertainment in here?" Elmo asked.

"Well, we have a state-of-the-art sound system. There are a variety of music selections to choose from, sir." Marcus stretched lanky fingers toward the touch screen. "Classical, sir?"

"I overheard some of my students talking about some new age music. Who is The Weeknd?" Elmo asked. "Are they Wrap musicians?"

"Yes, sir. Something like that I believe." Marcus searched for a sample selection of The Weeknd's latest work. After a few minutes, Elmo said, "Enough of that. What else do you have?"

Marcus ran through a few ballads that he thought the nineteenth century gentleman might enjoy. Elmo seemed to tap his knee to every second or third tune but ultimately, he said, "Anything other than music, Marcus. I seem to remember years ago that there were… what did they call them again?" Elmo searched his memories. "Radio shows. Do you have any of those?"

"They don't make many radio shows anymore, sir, but I have something similar that I've been listening to. I'd better warn you, it may be a little racy for your tastes."

"Marcus," Elmos drawled. "I hunt and feed on the terrified for my supper. What could, as the kids say, gross me out?"

The gritty, yet eloquent prose of S. A. Cosby enthralled Elmo and entertained Marcus with travails of Beauregard Montage so much so that they lost track of time and space. Two hours later, the escalade's fuel gage signaled low gas. Marcus found that he was off somewhere in rural Georgia where the streetlights seemed sparse. He could count the yellowing streetlights at the rate of changing scenes of the audiobook.

"Sir, I'll have to refuel. Please stay in the car," Marcus said. He wanted to add, *stay out of trouble.*

Panning his gaze left and right, Marcus saw too many confederate flags and red caps for his taste and safety. *These folks around here are not likely to bite their tongues about their beliefs, religious or political.*

There was no credit card reader slot at the pump. Marcus sighed. *Guess I'll have to go in to pay.* He heard music playing from the door. Nothing like he'd been playing at the college campus. He jogged over to the convenience store end of the establishment and found the cashier.

"Pump 5?" the young man asked. "That's $50 dollars even, sir."

Marcus started to voice a complaint about the price but thought better of it. He peeled off two twenties and a ten and offered a simple, "Thank you," to the young man. Marcus glanced around the store for a snack to munch on the way back but nothing on the shelves suited his taste.

He nodded once more and jogged back to the car and climbed into the driver's seat. "It's nearly 3 am, sir. We'd better hurry back if we're going to beat the sunrise."

Marcus turned around to hear Elmo's response only to find his ward gone. Marcus broke into a sudden cold sweat. He climbed between the SUV's seats in the vein hope of finding Elmo cuddle up in the mock coffin with which he had customized the vehicle.

Empty!

Marcus opened the car door and hung his head. He raised it and faced the source of music and revelry. Marcus spat a rare profanity and trotted past a row of tricked out Harley's back to the other end of the building. He opened the door to find Elmo Hoogle surrounded by baseball caps, bandanas, sunglasses, and motorcycle helmets chatting up a storm.

"Oh, how I love to go fast! The rush of wind on my face, the tingle at the roots of my hair…"

The chuckle rounded the club like the Wave at a Braves' game.

A bearded man hollered, "Sounds like you got a need for speed." And chuckle grew into raucous laughter.

"I do. Indeed, I do." Elmo looked around not realizing that many were good naturedly laughing at him, not with him.

The big guy with the beard tightened his bandana, handed his helmet to Elmo and led the crowd out to the parking lot. He straddled his bike and beckoned Elmo to do the same.

"Sir, I don't know that this is such a good idea." Marcus wrung his hands as he implored his employer not to go through with these antics.

"He doesn't have a heart condition or nothin' like that, do he?" The biker asked Marcus sincerely. "I'll just ride him to that there light yonder and back again. Give 'im a little thrill, ya know?" He said with a wink.

"No. I guess he doesn't have a heart condition.

A blonde, just past her prime, helped Elmo adjust the helmet, fastened the strap, and proffered some last-minute advice. "Now you hold on tight, darlin'. Don't let old Red shake up your bones, hear me?"

"Don't' get him too excited." Recalling a favorite 1980's TV show, Marcus wanted to add: *You won't like him if he gets too excited.*

Red confirmed that Elmo was safely seated and had a firm grasp around the biker's waist revved the engine. "Hold on, Elmo. 'Cause away we go!"

The whooping and hollering excited Elmo who joined in to the best of his ability waving his hand in the air as they popped a wheely. Before leaving the parking lot.

All Marcus could do was shake his head and cross his fingers. Good to his word, Red peeled off at a reasonable speed, turned at the closest streetlight, almost out of sight and rode back to the parking lot popping a second wheely upon triumphant return.

"That was BRILLIANT Marcus." Elmo declared. He faced Red and his girlfriend and said, "Let's do it again."

Charleen patted Elmo on the shoulder twice and said, "Cool your jets cowboy, that's enough for one night. You better let your friend get you home. Don't let the sun catch you up."

The advice sobered Elmos. Made him check his pocket watch. Marcus wondered if she knew how true her words were.

"Yes, sir. We had better get going." Marcus ushered Elmo to the Escalade. "We have a long ride a head of us."

Elmo turned to the crowd and gave a bow that, under any other circumstances, would be deemed a curtain call at the end of a great performance. Elmo and Marcus both disappeared into the big black riding machine and vanished into the night.

*   *   *

Marcus pulled up to the house as the early light of dawn began to hint at day's arrival. With all the excitement from the night before, Elmo was likely to do some serious walking after sunrise. Elmo dosed in the back seat, declining Marcus' urging that he take refuge in the onboard casket. Marcus took the opportunity to apply the sun blocking cocktail to his master's face before he became day restless when he heard something tumble to the floor in another room. Marcus was instantly alert and on his toes. Elmo sat torpid, unmoved by the disturbance.

Marcus hefted a butcher knife as he skulked through the kitchen. He would need it if Elmo's assistance were necessary with a home invasion. The place was dark everywhere except Marcus's own bedroom where the noise originated. Marcus moved as stealthily as a sixty-five-year-old man could toward the light when the intruders sprung the ambush.

"What's up old man?" The light skinned man said in an unctuous tone. "Nice place. Cluttered though. We gonna' give the place a makeover. Like they do on that HGTV show."

"Didn't yo' mamma ever tell you not to run with sharp objects." The Big man grabbed the knife by the business end and held it tight.

"Hey, Boone Doc, be careful." Ray laughed. "He defendin' his castle here."

"All these musty books all over the place. This joint a fire hazard." Lean and wiry, the tattooed youth had yet to shave the newly grown peach fuzz on his chin. "Could go up just like that." He snapped his fingers.

Berry prowled the parlor like a lion stalking a gazelle then sat in a wing chair and crossed his legs like he owned it. "What you think young blood?"

The youth narrated his assessment of bric-a-brac. "Just a bunch of old shit."

"Not old, Ray. Antique!" Berry annunciated the word with a faux British accent. "Jackson?"

"You right Berry. Some of this stuff could go for a sweet piece of change." The third man, Jackson quiet until now, seemed to be calculating the inventory. "With the right fence, we might could get 5 maybe 10K for this shit."

"We need to know what we got first." Berry concluded. Shifty eyes narrowed to slits and focused on Marcus. "What's your name, old man?"

"Marcus. Marcus Coke."

"Well, Mark the knife, why don't you start cataloguing our treasure here for us?" Berry commanded. "Start with this floor and then we'll go upstairs. I already know there's more old shit—antiques up there we need to… relieve you two gentlemen of."

Ray furrowed his brow for a moment and said in a lightbulb moment from remnants of an interrupted education, "Tisk, tisk. Never end a sentence with a preposition, Berry."

They laughed. All but Marcus.

"Alright schoolboy. We takin' a day off work. Starting a new enterprise. Import/Export."

Jackson shoved Marcus. "Grab you a notebook and a pen. Start writin' down all this paraphernalia and your best guess for the dollar value."

"You take the first shift, Jackson. You keep him honest of the estimates," Berry said, flashing teeth rimmed in gold. "Ray, you wrap Mr. Marcus' boss real pretty, huh?" Berry tossed Ray a role of duct tape.

"I'm going to take a nap." Berry raised his feet to the otto-man, crossed them, and propped a pillow behind his neck. He was sawing wood before Marcus got half-way down the first page.

By 4:30 pm the thugs had changed watch three times. Berry got up from his third nap of the day to review the register. The accounting was impressive. And apparently honest. The grand total must have been over $30,000 already.

Jackson grinned and slapped at the list. "And we ain't even got to the upstairs or downstairs junk yet."

"Good junk." Berry appraised. He grinned, obviously calculating the split in his head. "You got anything to drink in here, Marcus?" He drawled out "Marcus" as if he were a dog, he was teaching to play fetch.

"Master Hoogle keeps his spirits upstairs in the bar." Marcus waited for direction and glance at the grandfather clock.

"What you thinkin' old man?" Ray eyed Marcus suspiciously when he caught him checking the time.

"The clock, sir. It's worth another ten thousand dollars on the open market."

"Holy shit, how'd I miss that?" Jackson declared and jotted the grandfather clock down on the list.

"Men, this calls for a drink. Let's retire to the drawing room." Berry intoned.

Ray scrunched up his face, "What's a 'drawing room'"?

Berry smiled and spread his hands, "I don't know, but I've always wanted to say that!"

The three men with Marcus leading the way climbed the stairs to Elmo's study.

"So, this is the good stuff, huh?" Berry said appraising the room.

"The Master's best, sir."

"Why don't you mix us all up some fancy drinks, Marcus," Berry ordered. Before Marcus could begin tending bar, Berry gripped his arm. "Wait a minute. Why don't we invite old Elmo to the party?"

Jackson chortled, "What's his whole name again? Elmo Hoogle?" The bandits all broke out into a raucous laughter.

"Ray, bring his ass up here!" Berry ordered. "Give him a drink. For making our pockets this fat, he earned one."

Marcus counted, 5:10. *It won't be long now.* He fixed four drinks. He added sherry to each glass.

"What do you call these little things, anyway, Marcus?" Berry asked.

"These are called Smart Toddies, sir."

"Why these stupid little glasses? We not playin' Barbies tea party."

"I don't think—your palates are prepared for these drinks." Marcus almost cracked a wry smile, "They are an acquired taste."

Berry assessed the man servant. "Let your boy Elmo show us how it's done, Mr. Smart Ass." He took one of the identically prepared drinks at random, not in the order they were mixed. "Let's have Elmo here make a toast."

Elmo took the sherry glass as offered and grinned as he parted his lips and sipped.

"Creepy." Ray whispered. "Hey, what's up with him, Marcus man? He got Old timerz or he just retarded?" The humor had faded from the young man's voice as he awaited the answer. "He walkin around here like he some kinda of zombie or some-thin'. What's up with that?"

"My master is… special, sir." Marcus offered a half smile. "But he does love his Smart Toddies. I doubt you young men could keep up with him."

"Bullshit." Berry drew the word out defiantly. "Oh, we gonna git our drink on now!"

"No old dust bag gonna out drink the kid." Jackson pounded his chest.

They all drank at the same time. The choking started immedi-ately. Berry and Jackson threw their glasses to the floor and clutched their throats as the formaldehyde burned their throats. Ray couldn't breathe. He wasn't a drinker. He was turning blue around the lips. The boy crushed the delicate sherry goblet in his hands, setting forth free rivulets of blood down his arm as Ray, too, clawed at his own throat.

Marcus checked the time on the cuckoo clock. Quarter to six. The sun was getting low, and he smiled a triumphant smile. Elmo's eyes popped opened.

Berry had fallen to his knees, but managed to recover a func-tional airway before Jackson or Ray. He drew a 0.38 from his waist band and raised the barrel towards Marcus.

"Mutha Fuck—" the curse died on his lips.

A blur swept past Berry, spoiling his aim and knocking the weapon from his hand.

Elmo had Ray by the arm and slurped the running blood from the laceration. Ray fainted. Berry scrambled for the lost gun, found it and aimed at Elmo. He fired at the space Elmo had just occupied but was no longer. Fangs out, Elmo tore into Berry's neck and drank voraciously. The big man went limp. Jackson had recovered enough to seize a fire poker and swung it desper-ately from side to side in defensive fashion. In a flash, Elmo was on him, broke both the man's wrists and wrested the weapon away from the second thug. His thirst sated, Elmo took the poker and drove it up under Jackson's chin and through the top of his head.

Elmo looked at the young Ray, pale and motionless in a heap on the floor.

"What have I done?" Elmo cried in anguish. "What have I done?"

Marcus went to comfort his distraught ward when strong hands restrained him.

"Let him be Marcus. He needs this." Charleen stood there in the middle of the parlor as if she had been there all along. "It's cathartic."

"William! Oh, William." Elmo wailed. "What have I done?"

"That's not William, Professor. I am." Red stood beside Charleen, head bowed submissively.

Marcus felt confused. "What?"

"Elmo couldn't face what happened a hundred thirty years ago." Charleen shook her head. "And I couldn't forget it."

She guided Elmo and Marcus to a sofa. "You see, William had a rare disorder. Polycythemia Rubra Vera."

Marcus asked, "What!?"

"Too much blood." Red said. "I was but a lad in my father's house. I had this rare disease. The doctors didn't know what to do. When Lady Charlotte heard about it, she made a bee line to our estate to 'comfort' me." She mesmerized everyone in the house. Everyone except Professor Hoogle. He fought her with every fiber of his being. Finally, they struck a bargain. Professor Hoogle offered himself to endure the curse of the vampire if she would not take me. Of course, it was too late for me to go completely free." Red looked sympathetically at Elmo. "So, she agreed that she would never turn me. But she would have to siphon off some of the vampire blood every few weeks. She turned Elmo, but before she made him what he is, he vowed to take this curse and walk it out into the sun and end it forever rather than take a human life."

"I remember." Elmo mumbled, his eyes clearing. "That rueful smile you gave me. You thought I could never do it. No vampire can intentionally end their own afterlives, no matter how noble."

Marcus lips tightened, "Yet here he stands. The day walker. Who I have to protect from the sun's kiss every day."

Charleen nodded. "You were our best hope to restore him to his right mind and allow him to take his place in the family."

"He couldn't face the failure of not being able to protect his student. So, he goes forth every day to bleach the vampire blood form his veins and continue to educate the young bright minds that might still grow into what Duke William should have been."

"It hasn't been so bad, Professor." Red cradled Elmo's head in his arms. "I grew up. I had children and I survived a disease that all the doctors told my father would kill me."

"And Lady Charlotte?"

"Charleen?" Red asked, "I love her. I take care of her while she sleeps, and we cut up like drunken pirates most nights with our friends."

Marcus asked, "All those bikers, vampires?"

"Heavens no darlin'" Charleen said. "They're just friend's for now. When time passes and we don't change, we move on so as not to raise too many questions. We've been watching Elmo all these years. Making sure he remained safe. That was our bargain. Mine, Red's, and Elmo's."

Charleen caressed Red's beard. "It's nice to have friends."

Red nodded, "Real friends."

Marcus scowled a gaze about the room then smiled, "You know, they say the measure of real friends is whether or not they help you move bodies."

Welcome to Happy Haunts: Secrets and Lies
By
Aziza Sphinx

I woke to Sunshine gently caressing my right cheek. And no, this wasn't from the bright yellow ball illuminating the world on the other side of the wooden blinds. I welcomed that sunshine on these cold winter mornings when a light dusting of the white stuff clung to the green prickles of the fir trees and Jack Frost slithered up my spine. Instead, I opened my eyes to peer at the half-melted away face of my confidant and permeant shadow.

What a way to start the day. "Do you mind?" Appreciating this morning's wake-up call after the sun decided to grace us with its presence, I rolled over to stare at the aging wooden rafters forming a reversed V above my head. They'll need to be replaced this spring, less I end up with an unplanned skylight.

"Rise and shine sleepy head. Time to start a good morning."

Sunshine floated an arm's length away from the bed, just out of my reach. I cut my eye in his direction. "Far from a good morning."

"Oh please. You're such a drama queen before your morning tea."

"And you're like Satan's little helper poking me with a stick knowing the hole there is already red, puss-filled, and protruding." The covers flew over my head - not my doing but his - as the room warmed flowing his departure.

Most described our relationship as love/hate. Personally, I love to hate the spirit lingering in my humble abode. Or at least on days like this when he delivers a message of visitors. I suppose I should appreciate the warnings. His tips give me time to get things in order before the real work begins.

"You should get a move on," he bellowed from the other side of the wall, "your new guest shall arrive in exactly one hour."

Guest. Singular. No mother and father mourning the loss of a child? No harem of women seeking the truth about the demise of the man shared among them? These types of visitors periodically grace my home, summoned here by those with unfinished business. When this place calls, the beckoned answer.

Not too many people visit my neck of the woods to spend a night or two in Happy Haunts. North of the bustling Atlanta, my cottage in the woods is off the beaten path and, for the most part, cut off from the outside world. Only within the last year did indoor plumbing and phone service become a staple. I preferred to be hidden away. My long-paid-for old, haunted house in the woods was tucked away from prying developer eyes. But it didn't mean I didn't want a few modern amenities, so I bit the bullet and took the proceeds from my unique clientele for both necessary repairs and a handful of upgrades.

Sliding out of the bed, donning the goose down slippers strung together with a strand of leather well past its prime, I padded my way across the bedroom ignoring the slobber-filled greeting from my husky, Chopin. I showered quickly and dressed in a wool sweater, dark blue jeans that hugged my curves, and a pair of fur-lined boots.

Sunshine greeted me with a look of distain. "Took you long enough. He's coming up the drive."

"He?" I prepared the teapot before tossing a couple of logs into the fireplace and setting it ablaze. A sudden chill passed through me, an indication that the one my visitor sought had arrived.

There she was, standing before the bay window, her pigtails tied up with lace ribbons on either side of her head. She stared out of the window opposite the drive, her attention focused on the flakes falling from the sky. Something hung loosely from her right hand. Possibly a tie or leash.

I joined Sunshine at the other window, gawking at the strapping young man dressed in all black as he passed a few bills to the driver. His long, lean body sent something fluttering in my neither region, something I hadn't experienced since taking the plunge and walking away from my old life to continue my family's legacy.

"Do I detect a bit of lust?"

I waved Sunshine off. "Jealous?" I would have punched him in the arm if he possessed a solid form.

"Who me? Why would I be jealous? You're the one stuck with me. I can leave whenever I choose."

His comment caught me off guard. "What do you mean?"

"An opportunity or two have crossed my path to skirt over to the other side. But you need me."

"I do not!" Pounding my fist into the stone countertop hurt like hell. I rubbed the now tender flesh before removing the whistling kettle and setting the table for morning tea.

"What is he doing out there?" Sunshine asked still watching our visitor like a lioness stalking her prey.

I too expected a knock on my door by now. Guess he needed some encouragement. I added milk and sugar to my cup of Earl Grey, drooping only a half of a teaspoon into the other mug, suspecting my gentleman visitor preferred a much stronger beverage. Sliding the picturesque door open – hopping out of the way before Chopin bulldozed me over – I greeted my guest with a steaming cup of tea.

"Good morning," I bellowed a few steps away as I approached hoping not to startle him out of his thoughts. He reached down, petting Chopin on the head. At least I had confirmation that he wasn't a serial killer.

He graciously accepted the cup of tea I offered as we stood side by side enjoying a gentle but fridge breeze. The snow stopped falling, the sun reflecting off the wall of white covering the sloped roof of the store house on the west side of my property.

I closed my eyes basking in morning glow. My love for this place began the first time my Nana brought me here. The air smelled fresh and clean, something hard pressed to find in the city. The blooming trees afforded shade for miles around, and the open field in the back was a little girl's flowery paradise. Even in winter, the quiet soothed my soul whether my living – or dead – visitors roamed my home.

"This place doesn't feel like its haunted," the man muttered.

I didn't know whether to be offended or not. "Is that what you've heard? That my home is haunted?"

"Isn't it? That is why people come here. To say their final goodbyes."

My blood boiled at his comments, and I abruptly turned on my heel to storm away.

"Wait. Please." The pleading in his voice cooled the sudden fury. "That was rude of me. I apologize. I'm just under a lot of stress."

"I can make him go away if you want," Sunshine whispered in my ear. "He wants a haunted house; I can give him a haunted house."

I continued towards the house, speaking under my breath, hoping my guest didn't think I was losing my mind. "Don't. If the house invited him then I need to help. Maybe you can be of assistance and see what you can get out of the little girl."

Sunshine huffed at my subtle dismissal, "Fine. But I've got my good eye on him."

I snickered before turning my attention to my guest. "Please come in when you're ready." I closed the door behind me, needing a moment to regain my composure. My hands busily put away the tea setting, poked the fire, and roamed over the contents of the fridge in search of breakfast.

Sunshine sat on the counter, his feet dangling inches above the floor. "She's not talking."

I eased over to where the little girl still stood, wondering what in the field captured her attention. "Hi." No answer. "My name's Angel. Can you tell me yours?" Still nothing. Past visitors tended to want to move out of this place as quickly as possible. Not all of the departed found me. Most moved along to their destiny without a second thought. The ones who roamed my cottage in the woods appeared with a specific message for those they leave behind. I wonder what her message is.

The door opened, drawing my attention.

"Once again, I'd like to apologize. I-it's just- you weren't what I was expecting."

Figures. With my hands on my hips, I responded to the assumption passed my way throughout my childhood. "And what exactly did you expect? Some old woman in rags tending to a house full of stray cats."

"I deserve that. And yes, I was expecting a much older woman."

"Well, this is what you get. Take it or leave it." Okay, so I didn't need to be rude, but occasionally uninvited guests crawled under my skin. Maybe my attraction to this broad shouldered, narrow-wasted, sparkling smiled, and virile young man was messing with my head. *Or maybe it's something else.*

"I'll take it. If you'll have me? I don't exactly know what I'm doing here."

I gestured for him to sit at the kitchen table. I claimed the seat next to him, my usual spot at the head of the table. "How about we start with your name and how you heard about me."

"Mason. Mason Amador. As far as how I heard about you, well, that's a little more complicated. You see, last night, I had a dream about a stone cottage in the woods covered with snow. I stood at the window, that window right over there," he pointed to the one where the little girl stared out of. "This place is just like the dream, all the way down to that blue-glass dreamcatcher on the wall."

I allowed him to continue with the details, and not just about the dream. He told me about how his wife recently passed, and his business was going under. Though she'd left him a hefty insurance policy, most of the money was now tied up in court with a family dispute. Then we moved to the real reason the gateway summoned him here.

"So, you see, my little sister, Belle, has been missing for a week, and we've pretty much lost hope. I'd heard whispers about this place in one of my circles over the years and figured, if she was," he hesitated, the words catching in his throat. "Well...you know. On the verge of crossing to the other side," his eyes roamed around the room searching for some portal to another dimension, "that she'd have one last message for me."

His sister did have one last message for him. Unfortunately, she currently kept that message to herself. "I'm no miracle worker. Sometimes these things take a day or so. And I can only deliver from the dead. If she's still alive."

"Oh, I understand. I just didn't know where else to turn. You're my last hope. If she hasn't come here, then my family will hold out hope that she is still alive."

Sunshine hovered over the now trembling man whose gaze mysteriously settled on the little girl at the window. *Somethings not right here.* He mouthed. A subtle nod in agreement, and I decided I needed more information.

"Can you tell me what your sister looks like? Maybe the last thing she might have been wearing?" Mason described the girl at the window down to the leash in her hand. As far as anyone knew, she'd run out the back door after the family dog. "I think I have what I need. I'll need a little quiet time to see if she's here." I stood, prepared to excuse myself. "Make yourself at home. I grant my guest free reign of the refrigerator. If you'd like to freshen up or maybe take a rest, the guest bedroom and bath are on the left side of the hall."

I retired to my bedroom, the day slipping away fast. Winter meant shorter days, and today marked the change of the cycle, the shortest day of the year.

"Still nothing from the little girl?" I asked.

Sunshine plopped down on the edge of the bed, the skin hanging from his face jiggling with his movements. I hoped one day he'd learn his name and finally be able to leave me be. I in no way believed he hung around because he liked my company. He was stuck here, just like all the others, to seek me out regardless of what he'd said earlier.

"Not a peep."

"This is highly unusual. Normally they come in here spilling their guts trying to spew as many details as possible before the portal sucked them into oblivion." I leaned back on the bed. Maybe with meditation, I could reach her.

"I'm going to try again. Maybe tell her my story. I'd hate for her to end up like me." He poofed away in that annoying way he did sometimes that sent chills up my spine. While he worked his magic, I'd work mine.

I must have drifted off because I woke to a heavy angry spirit invading my personal space. Mason towered over me, straddling me in the bed as he bound my hands. The knife in his mouth kept him for speaking, though he mumbled and grunted as he worked.

Assured with the security of my bindings, he removed the shiny weapon placing the pointed edge beneath my chin. "She is here, isn't she?"

"Mason, what are you doing?" The smack across the face came as a surprise, the burning of his handprint on my skin raising tears in my eyes. During moments like this I wish Sunshine was real, or at least a poltergeist with the ability to manipulate matter.

"Answer my question," he said through gritted teeth, "or I swear I will do to you what I did to her."

The panic set in then, my heart racing as my mind sought an escape plan. "Yes, Mason. She's here. But she refuses to speak."

"It doesn't matter," he climbed from the bed, walking a path from the head to the foot. "Can't leave any witnesses."

"Witness to what Mason? Did you do something to Belle?"

He was on me again, his breath hot and rancid as spit flew through the air with each word. "You know what I did. She told you, didn't she? She gave you all the gory details of what we've been doing all of these years. She asked for it you know. She wanted it as much as I did. But then she got pregnant and..."

His voice trailed off as the little girl entered the room. With each step, she aged right before my eyes.

I didn't want what he wanted. At least not at first. It hurt for a long time. Then one day it didn't. No one believed me. He was the good one. The one who'd brought fame and recognition to our family. They didn't believe me.

When her hand brushed across my face, I saw it all. The years of what he'd done to her. Even the time when he finally broke her, convinced her that this was her role in life. He gave her things, showered her with gifts to hide his guilt. People started asking questions when she turned up pregnant. Especially his wife. Oh my Goddess. He did it.

"Yep, he did." Sunshine stood next to the beautiful teenage girl with green hair and an innocent face, an innocence stolen by her own flesh and blood. "He knocked them both off to cover his tracks. That's why the oldest sister has disputed the insurance claim."

"I'm not a witness." I tried to sound as calm and rational as possible. Anything to keep him from becoming more agitated. I just need to distract him long enough to reach the hidden silent alarm button beneath the divide in the headboard. "I'm just a crazy lady who lives in isolation in a haunted house in the woods that the townspeople fear of being a witch. No one in the town or anywhere else is going to believe me."

"You're lying to me!" He started to pace again, "Don't you dare lie to me. They won't find you. No. You said it yourself, you're out here and no one comes unless the house calls them."

He was right. I could be here dead for days or even weeks before anyone came my way. I didn't visit town often, and especially not during the winter months when ice – my greatest enemy – coated the roads.

Help me, I mouthed, hoping either Sunshine or Belle hand an idea. I just needed a half of a second and I could push the button. The two spirits joined hands, a white light emanating from their combined spirits until it filled the room. Mason's pacing came to a halt his head swiveling around as Belle called his name again and again. I took advantage of the distraction, pressing the button and praying the sheriff made it out to the house before I met my maker.

"Where are you little heffa? I know you're here. And stop calling my name." The echoing of Mason's name continued until his anger sent him over the deep end. Then he turned that blind fury to me, ripping my sweater down the middle.

"Tell her to stop." He sliced my shoulder, "tell her to stop or I swear you will live to regret her interference."

"I have no control over the dead. I can talk to her, but I can't make her do anything." He reached for the button on my pants as he pressed the tip of the knife just below my ear. I felt the trickle of warmth as he broke the skin. "Please," I tried to wiggle out of his grasp. He dug the blade deeper. "Please don't do this."

"Give me one good reason why I shouldn't. It not like anyone can hear you scream."

The chanting grew louder as Mason managed to get the button undone and started on the zipper. "Why are you doing this? What did I do to you?"

The glass shattered to my right. The knife burned as it sliced through my neck. So, this is how it ends. All of those lives. Maybe now I'll get to see what the other's who'd paid me a visit saw. I wondered if they'd be waiting for me as the darkness washed over me and the light faded away.

* * *

"Stop playing dead. I'm the only one who gets to be dead in this duo."

I'd know that voice anywhere. "Sunshine." A warm hand patted mine.

"Angel?"

My eyes fluttered open, coming to rest on a young detective who'd visited my home a few months back hoping for help on another missing person's case. With my guidance, they'd found the child's body and his murderer. After that case, the sheriff suggested I install the silent alarm, just in case I became someone's target.

"Carson? What happened?" His hand on my arm indicated that I shouldn't try to move.

"Your guest tried to murder you."

"Oh, my Goddess." It all came rushing back. The metallic taste in my mouth. The ringing in my ears. Even that ever described warm white light. My hand reached for my neck; Carson stopped it before I ripped the bandage way."

"I wouldn't do that. You've got a pretty nasty gash. You're the proud recipient of 45 stitches and a pint of my blood."

"Guess that makes us blood brother and sister." I chided. Carson already knew more about me than anyone else in town. We'd spent many summers running through the field behind my house until my Nana decided that it was unladylike for me to frolic in a field with the opposite sex. He and I worked on a case or two since I'd taken ownership, me being his secret weapon against mass murders who never seemed to pick our town.

"Yeah. It does. I thought I was gonna lose you there for a minute. That guy was a real piece of work."

Sunshine waved in my direction, indicating that he needed to speak with me privately. "You know I couldn't go out like that. Remember, we're supposed to die in an avalanche I cause screaming your name in the throes of passion on Valentine's Day." It hurt to laugh.

"Yeah, well, I'm holding you to that." Carson stood. "I'll let the sheriff know you're awake. He wants a statement."

"Thanks." Sunshine waited until Carson closed the door. "She's gone."

My heart lifted at the revelation. "I'm glad. She deserves some peace."

"Don't ever do that again."

"What?"

"Go towards the light. You are not allowed to die before I learn my name. Deal?"

His hand brushed against my cheek; his cold presence both comforting and grounding. "Deal. Besides, I've got a business to run. Happy Haunts needs to start living up to its name. Happy face for a happy place. Death is my suitor, and the spirits are counting on me to deliver."

Fae Falling
By
Kortney Y. Watkins

The portal opens.

I am in utter shock that it actually worked. I'm going home. Though I've never been there, *Ryndpha (*said like *rind pa)*, I can feel the magical summons pull me towards the bright rainbow-esque light like a pop can to an industrial magnet. Moments ago, I had willed the door to the hidden world to open to me, to obey my bidding. But now it is I who have no choice but to harken. Just feet from the once-barren and lonely tree lay the gray-blue body of Lake Lanier that shimmers with the multi-colored reflection of the portal and me, legs dangling, ten feet in midair. I must look insignificant and frail to the ethereal beings of the firmament—above the above. Scared and pitiful, no doubt. But I also know that I have never looked so beautiful. So *me*. So... *fae*.

I turn away shyly to my right in the opposite direction from my reflection where another shining thing very much out of place glitters. My birth token hangs on the branch nearest the ground. It had been a feat to reach it with me being my standard clutzy self and it being—well, a tree. Don't judge me. Not all fae navigate well around all elements of nature. Or, at least that's what I'd been told. Read mostly. Well, still told if you count the gypsy I'd met at a harvest carnival I snuck into when I was ten. Okay. So, maybe that person wasn't a gypsy. Who knows? What I'm trying to say is some mystical looking person in a wench-looking getup with silky shawls, head wrap, long curly hair, and hoop earrings as large as the many bangles on both her wrists told me that not all fae are graceful or fair in *Awbete*. That's what she called this world. *Awe-beet*. Needless to say, that as a ten-year-old I was *awestruck*. Get it? Okay, fine. Even to me, that sounds like the lamest joke ever. I'll stop now. Maybe.

The birth token begins to vibrate and morph. It is like looking at liquid mercury having the time of its life. The silvery substance works its way in lines and then pushes outward forming something resembling my old gypsy's crystal ball. The moonlight-like orb pulsates rhythmically from its solid pewter chain, and I can feel the portal's power feeding it and consequently supporting me. I am still up in the air and instinct tells me that I will remain this way for the duration of whatever is going on.

It hits me as I slyly glance back to my left again. The sun, past dusk's apex, turned the watery mirror of this hidden foreshore from blue grey to dark stone washed denim. It's a dismal sheet of darkest blue with patches of white where the modest waves break distantly and clap back against the gravelly beach. There are no sunset colors here. Locals at the Last Village Tavern (a play on the ghost lore of underwater towns now covered by Lake Sidney Lanier) told me that in this part of the lake there was an ever-present gloom. And true that. Many people had died in this lake since the Army Corps of the late 1940s and every year since completion of the dam. Atlanta local news consistently reports warnings and cautions during peak season. I'm sure the networks had saved many by their almost-weekly warnings, particularly in the summer peak season. But the warnings will never save everyone. Humans tend to be drawn to the divine, whether for their benefit or detriment. Humans also tend to be headstrong, trusting in their desires and faith, not logic. Nonetheless, many an Atlantan will praise the benefits of the beloved reservoir. But in fairness, just as many are loathe to participate in that lake's life. Edward Geter, the owner of the Last Village Tavern made sure to intimate to me that, "This lake is cursed!"

They are right to feel this way, of course, but for the wrong reasons. No evil ghouls or phantoms of long ago haunt the forest or patrol the lake's shores. The graveyards of the towns were re-located before the completion of the dam. So, no. No hauntings here.

This area, however, is ancient land that even predates the indigenous peoples. What humanity feels here, in this sacred space is space itself. It bends and twists in on itself in ways that humanity could never comprehend. Time configures itself in loops and spools around the space, shunning linear understanding. It feels unnatural in a mundane world. It is, in effect, otherworldly. But what humanity never recognizes is the reason behind the tingling of their sixth sense. Whether navigating the undercurrents of the lake or traversing through its surrounding forest, each person is faced with a *trial*. And the trial takes the form of an encompassing, dense mist. True fear in its most potent and aggressive form that mutates.

The mist ascertains and then exploits the fears of mortals. What humanity often fears is what *possibly* lurks in the dark they encounter, whether it's actually present or not. Make no mistake, heaven and hell are real. Angels and demons are real. Spirits of light and maleficence are real. Yet, the authentic experience of the supernatural is far less common than Hollywood would have the masses to believe. It takes a human with the ability of a seventh sense to even have an experience where there is more than just "a bad feeling". Senses eight through ten would land you bona fide experiences of the supernatural. The rare human might go off the charts at their max of eleven. Those are called fae-friends. They are the humans that possess "the gifts"—basically, the ability to live alongside higher beings in God's hierarchy, which often vibrates highest in His cosmic choir.

So, this trial determines if one belongs in the fae realm, or in the case of a human, if one is deemed worthy by being blessed with *the gifts*. The mist is designed to be both a safeguard and deterrent, a rewarder and punisher. A win of worth earns the seeker clear vision and peace in safety. No fear of possibilities crouching in evil darkness. Those born with the *right* or the *grace* would see what was really there—the fae or rarer, fae-friend.

The spectral images of Halloween fantasies flicker weakly here and there around me like a set of tea light candles on a windy day. They are cheap, cheesy illusions that 1970's Hollywood would have been proud to claim. No advanced *CGI* here. The closer I get to *Yrwehehi—pronounced like your way he*—the portal housed in the sacred tree, the more crude and feeble the flicks appear. But I still find myself unnerved. Apparently, Hollywood has gotten to me after years of watching creature-features and the mist senses this. It isn't really quite sure what to do with me.

It's not the illusions, of course, that set me on edge; what sends ripples of mini-mountains up my arms and down my back is knowing that I was one of the creatures that humanity would fear if it knew that I don't belong to them. Conversely, I hold the same fears for fae society. There is always this feeling of *judgment,* and it sucks. In my mind's eye, every rock and every tree judge me. "Her?" they ask. "She?" queries others. "Just look at her! Fair for human. Common for fae." And when I slipped or stumbled on my trek to the sacred tree, I swore I heard hushed tut-tutting.

But through it all, I continue my best to entertain you, my live, fake, pretend-since-I-was-five studio audience. You know how I cope—or at least you should by now. Acting like someone is watching makes one feel less alone, less insignificant. And bad things don't happen to important people, do they? Isn't that the book way, the movie way? Isn't that what happened when my family...the car crash, the——. Well, someone didn't think they were that important anymore. To keep them alive on Awbete. I guess someone thought I was important because I survived alone. So, I was either important or I was the butt of someone's sick joke. For the sake of my sanity, I still choose to believe the former. Even now. Twenty-seven years later. And the studio audience says...*awww*!

I'm looking at the sky now. I don't know what happened, but it feels like the lights suddenly go out in my mind's sound stage. I can hear the hollow clicks and clacks of electronic devices being shut down. My stage desk with my signature "I love Cereus" mug feels desolate, an abandoned piece of iconography that's sad in its present state. And what about those empty rows of seats where so many sat to watch with anticipation my successes and failures, my loves and breakups, my partying and sad attempts at promiscuity, my journey towards here? Where is my make-believe backup to share this burden? Will none of you answer me?

"Answer me!" I scream aloud. There's not even an echo. My cry is consumed in the vacuum of this void. To my own ears I sound desperate and hollow. And now I realize that my anchor to Awbete has been severed and I'm not quite sure if I exist in time anymore. But I feel the weight of the darkened sky and feel more the gravity of being alone. And I'm too tired after twenty-seven years to imagine more. So, I give in. Reality sucks. I sigh in defeat.

*   *   *

It seems like dawn when I come to present consciousness. I'd be lying if I said that it was the next morning. Time and space have been stripped away from me like my last lover's lusty rip at my clothing. I am too empty to look left or right and somehow, I manage to recline as if I were lying on my bed back in my rental townhouse in Kirkwood. But I know that I am even higher off the ground than before. The top branches of Yrwehehi appear closer from this vantage. Yet, I have no desire to look anywhere but in front of me. The fact is either direction is my mirror—one for how I look in the nexus of Awbete and Ryndpha and the other for what my birth token will mold me into being. I recognize that now.

Somewhere deep inside I knew that I was changing into whatever my birth token decided it would ultimately be. Caught up in my own doubts and self-pity, it was a thought that I'd been too scared to embrace. But at this point, I figure I have nothing to lose. So, this epiphany wanders in my present awareness as casually as a traveler at a gas station store. *I wonder if I'll have wings.*

As the last weak ray of what I assume is dawn's light kisses my cheek good morning, I hear trumpets in the distance. The music is stately and reserved, yet celebratory and glad all at the same time. The beautiful melody approaches ever-closer and I enjoy the moment of it, half thinking I've finally lost it and half grateful for the distraction. The unison of many marching feet adds a bass line to the music and I think it's the greatest mashup ever. Get the right DJ and this would've been an instant hit in the Euro-clubs, or better, the pop-up parties in New York, Vegas, or South Beach. With this train of thought, I can feel the tugging of a smile at the corners of my lips, but can't manage to do more than that. Exhaustion doesn't begin to indicate my level of tiredness. At least I've still got humor.

The tune fills my space and enters the core of my being, enveloping me like a child's favorite blankie. I feel safe in it. Familiar with it. And it seems like hours before my cradle of comfort stops rocking its child.

"Huvah!" yells a reedy masculine voice.

"Huvah!" the resounding reply goes. I didn't have to be on the ground to feel powerful vibrations. You know the intensity you physically feel when a gong sounds? Okay. Imagine that times ten. But here's the catch. The sound wasn't earth-shattering, more like earth-loving. Every being within its wake drinks it in like ice-cold lemonade in July's summer heat, quenched but left wanting—needing—more. It's pure power in the healthiest way.

Of the few things that I remember about my mother, I distinctly recall the words she had spoken to my two older brothers who had tortured a poor snail to death just days before the accident. She had looked eerily both calm and scary. Karan Layscape said simply, *"Power can do two things, Jack and Charlie. It can destroy, or it can heal. If you were the snail, what would you like someone to choose for you?"* I think that question stuck more with me than my brothers. But my father always said that out of us three kids, I was the most like mom.

A new rumbling breaks me from the spell of my reverie, and I know that *they* are around and under me. But I daren't look. My fear and trembling come from the realization that this could all come to an end, and I don't want it to. I need to feel safe. So, I just continue to look heavenward and pray for the moment not to end too soon.

"Where is she in the process, Jastfitch? Is she yet ready?" The voice had undeniable force, the kind that made others quake in fear of denying its owner what he wanted. I shudder inwardly at my clear sense of inferiority.

"No, my Lord. But…" The hesitation of whom I assumed was Jastfitch, the owner of the first voice I heard, rose half an octave higher. The silence that ensues is potent, a frenzied sense of nervous energies which wait as a collective.

"What? Speak," commands the lord.

"My Lord, this one is…different. She is only *part* fae, yet…yet full of *power*."

"Speak plainly, Jastfitch," the lord's voice rumbles with slight impatience.

"Sire," Jastfitch replies in a near whisper. "This child is of *royal* blood."

Even the bugs stop in awe. It's funny how you don't know what complete silence is until everything stops moving—breathing even. My own breath is shallower than my fifth grade b.f.f., Mitzy, who was ever-obsessed with anything fashion or gossip related. I hold as still as possible.

"Royal blood," the lord repeats flatly, as if his mind was as distant as the sunshine in this shadowy land. After a brief pause, I notice an almost imperceivable crunch of footsteps, which would never have been heard by me had it not been for the utter silence. They get louder in approach until at last they stop to the right of me, yet not quite beneath me, but close enough that I can feel the lord's body heat radiating and warming my stiff back, which had gone frigid for remaining so long in my immobile state.

Jastfitch's voice sounds closer now as he reports to his lord, "It appears as if the transition is not quite complete. If she is a princess, her next stage will begin soon. We cannot move her until then and only at moon's peak."

In my peripheral vision, I see the lord twitch and I'm not sure if his perception of me is desirable or deplorable. One would think that a possible princess would be desirable, but maybe not. And also, why the freak would a *lord* be part of a welcome party for someone assumed to be a commoner? More, did my parents know we had royal blood? And if they did, why weren't we with our people? Isn't royalty always supposed to have some kind of clout, some kind of advantage in a society?

I mean with all the wars and human ills, Awbete sucks! Who in their right mind would want to live in this existence if there was another option, a better option? But does that also mean that if my parents did know we might be special that our home world would still reject us and if so, why? The whole purpose of this venture was to not only get answers about my past, but also—*hopefully*—find someplace where I could finally belong. Because I for darn sure never fit here! This last thought is a scream in my head.

I take a mental breath from questioning state-turned-tirade as the anxiety overwhelms me. The drumming of my heart drowns out all other noise, save a high pitch ringing in my ears. I have questions. *Tons* of questions. My mind is reeling from all the new uncertainties, and I search for some kind of knowledge to ground me. All I can come up with is the realization that destiny has entered stage left and there would be no going back to who I once was for good or ill. It's the "ill" part I never considered, assuming that connecting with my heritage would make my f'd up life better, not worse. Complete, not lacking. Well, damn.

* * *

They say that caterpillars are lucky. You know, because they turn into pretty, winged things. But what can never be understood by anyone and anything other than a caterpillar is how much the process hurts. I mean, I was always afraid of giving birth. You see the TV shows and the movies and hear the horror stories of being ripped quite literally in special, sacred spaces, and you're like, "Surrogate, please!" I think now that I've experienced this, I am quite ready to have a brood.

The lord's inspection now over my birth token decides to become a new sun, which means that I also am, since I'm its mirror. And I mean it's burning *hot*. I swear my skin is melting away like that scene from *Raiders of the Lost Ark*. But I had followed the rules, didn't I? So, what the freak?! Why am I being rewarded with the eighth tier of hell—you know, the basement level past the first seven levels where even Satan won't go. I. Followed. The. Rules.

I had refused to look directly at those things—those better beings—that I knew my eyes were unworthy to behold. I had resolved to look ever upward, just appreciative to be in the presence of glorious wonders. That's enough for a simple girl from Atlanta by way of Evanston, Illinois. My life has been rough, and I have experienced unbelievable things, both supernatural and not. There were always consequences for not following the rules, hence my affinity for them.

I'd also learned long ago to just deal with whatever life threw my way. I'd learned to be content with my lot and to find whatever shred of happiness I could within it. Some days sucked. Others were better. All were more than my family experienced who lay cold and buried in the ground for decades now. Don't get me wrong. I'm not that every-day-is-a-gift kind of girl who wears the adage on a *Keep Calm* shirt or has that plastered on a rainbow coffee mug. But I am that girl who gets that some people have it easy and others have it hard. The reason doesn't matter. Fairness doesn't matter. But of the little of life that I could control, I wasn't going to take the complete theft of any potential happiness laying down, especially if I followed the rules. That resolve had come like a peal of thunder on the first day of middle school.

I had been through a hard summer of another relocation to the same situation. After being in half a dozen neglectful and abusive foster homes, I decided that I was going to have some kind of joy, even if I had to steal it back. That attitude, observed my last foster mom, was why I would do well in life. I loved her. She loved me, though she didn't adopt me. But the love was there. And it renewed my faith in people. She was the first, last, and only foster parent who *gave* me joy. From her, I didn't have to steal mine back. I loved her. Did I say that already?

As I'm thinking about her and our lost relationship, I recognize a shift in my pain. Either the sun is starting to wane or my missing relationship with Sharon Blake, my beloved foster mom, is a more painful thing than my transformation. Something inside me suspects it's a bit of both.

"Partoch."

"Yes, my lord," replies a peppery feminine voice.

"She's beginning to cocoon."

What?! I knew that he was talking about me and I knew that anything was possible. Clearly. But to speak of me like a nature conservationist may speak to a group of field-trip students unnerved me just a bit, to say the least. And exactly what did he mean by "cocoon"?

"The litter is ready, my Lord," interjects Jastfitch. "Shall we proceed with the removal of her birth token?"

"Not yet, Jastfitch. Partoch," he continues. "You will be her keeper."

"My, Lord!" both Partoch and Jastfitch chorus together, one in shock and the other in horror.

I imagine that the lord must have given a commanding look or silenced them with a grand gesture of the hand. It is silent again. The murmurs spurred by the lord's declaration, from what I assumed was the entire fae party, had instantly hushed.

"Partoch," the lord continues. "You have failed your office utterly. You were told that there may be a chance of redemption. Now, you must prove yourself, just as she," I feel a stirring breeze, which I assume originated from a gesture towards myself.

"But forgive me my Lord," Jastfitch says after a beat in careful protest, ensuring that his tone shows humility and respect. "Was it not through Partoch's negligence that Princess Reice was stolen from her people to begin with? Was it not *Partoch* who knew the thief had notions of romance for someone who was never intended for a hand so low as his? Was it not Partoch who—"

"Enough," snaps the lord. "I know full well Partoch's role in what transpired. More than you do," he adds that last part quietly. "Partoch will redeem herself in full after all of this time and then forever. Her debt is unending."

While conversation took place, a humming sensation filtered throughout my body, the vibrations more than ticklish, shy of discomfort. I imagine my cells pulsating to a new rhythm, far different from my human form. And then it happened. I can feel something fibrous oozing out of my feet and legs and then torso and arms like a *Chia Pet* on steroids, slowly pushing off my socks and hiking boots, ripping my jeans and underwear, then my tank and flannel overshirt. All of that had started to accelerate by the end of the lord's speech such that I am now completely butt naked. My heart starts fluttering a bit at the fact that the only things left from Awbete are me, my naked self, and I along with my birth token.

"Look! See!" says a chorus of voices and I know that they were witnessing the spectacle of my disrobing. I hope they enjoyed the free show. I'm also so very thankful that I had the presence of mind to dip into the lake, slick some deodorant on, and change into all new clothes before I attempted to open the portal. Originally, I had been thinking that a solemn occasion like this warranted a good scrub down. You know. Just out of respect for what I was about to do. Now, God, now all I can do is be so thankful that I didn't treat my endeavor like something common. No crusty anything here. Thank you!

Yet, I could feel my face still flush with humiliation. But the fibers that began pouring out of my entire body and my head acts as coverage, a thin layer of silk that masks my shame. Here's the deal. I was always told I was pretty, even though I'm not the *Cosmo* model type. I am, however, the plus-size model type and though there is always a market out there for BBWs, I assume, possibly wrongly, that this isn't that crowd. At least the cocoon binds my curves to rolling grasslands instead of many mountains and valleys. Maybe. Perhaps it will work like a waist trainer?

It's not that I don't like my body. I truly do. But I grow weary of everyone else assuming that I don't and being constantly offered dieting tips and exercises from the latest fad. Thus, a simple, magical solution would be welcome—if I don't have to do the work that is. Magic has to be good for something, right? Hell, that burning sun from moments ago might've helped release some water weight with all the sweat I produced. I'm just saying.

Though I had yet to lay my eyes on these beings of glory, I can't help but associate them with all of the images that are in children's fairy tale books and art, and movies, and…and jeez everywhere! They are supposed to be beautiful beyond compare, even in their oddness. Tall or petite, the pretty ones are always characterized as thin. Not that I just had to fit in or anything, but a part of me wanted to start my new life off without being too much of an outsider. I suspect that based upon my background and the conversations that I've heard thus far, I was never going to completely fit right in. Particularly, if I have to prove myself.

Next I know, I hear a loud applause complete with roaring cheer all of the sudden and I can feel something indescribably delicious emanating around my body. The last speech I hear comes from the lord.

He roars in quiet approval, almost like a prayer, "Oh my, Reice, she's going to be beautiful. Just like you were." A reassuring weight found itself where my left arm was covered in silken layers like a cast on a broken appendage. "Fall to slumber, fae child. You are safe now and will wake in your long-awaiting home."

*   *   *

The light is pretty. There's this ethereal quality to it that could make one imagine that life was indeed a dream that went along merrily, merrily. I'm giddy and filled with child-like wonder. I lift both my arms and reach skyward, contorting my fingers to play with the rays of light streaming in front of me at a gently sloping angle and those floaty things that embrace the spirit of randomness. The short dark hairs on my arms are reddened and my skin glows honey-gold. Good Lord. I'm pretty. Before, it was just a fact that I was told. Now, it is a fact that I *know*. There's no vanity in this thought, just an acknowledgment of what is. And it comforts me that I've really accepted myself. Even if I was ugly or average, it would still be just fine.

I heft myself up, ready to move. Every cell in my body is tingling, my muscles and organs vibrating, but I notice that there is a rhythm to it that's unfamiliar-ly familiar, if that makes sense. How can I describe it? You know that thump-thump, thump-thump sound your heart makes? This is more like ping-ping-ping-ping but sped up faster than you could say it. I tilt my ear in the direction of a similar sound and I realize it's a plant. I don't see the plant, mind you, but I know that it's a plant. And I can hear its rhythm, too. I won't even try to explain the sounds coming from the plant. Not because I don't want to bore you, but because I don't think a human could ever really understand.

And it hits me. I'm no longer able to be mistaken for human. I never was fully and certainly not now. Walking among them will require an effort in disguise.

Then memory assaults me like bait for a pack of piranhas. Is that what they're called? Or are they called a school? I mean, those fishies are more wolf than guppy, but that's just my opinion. The crazy thing is, my musings are stilling as fast as they came, the memories start to make way so that I process the last event of my life that I can remember. I suppose I'll have to retrace my steps to see how I got here.

Let's see. *Step one*. The love of my life, Xavier, decided to leave me for his yoga/spiritual coach via text message. *Step two*. I fall apart for about two hours. *Step three*. I look at myself in the bathroom mirror, tear streaked, splotchy faced, and near hyperventilating. *Step four*. I literally take my right hand and slap myself in sheer disgust. *Step five*. The shock makes me see the light. *Step six*. I run out of the bathroom and down my townhouse stairs to the coat closet and retrieve my medium, purple paisley four-wheeled suitcase and haul it and myself back upstairs, puffing all the way. *Step seven*. I gather my notebooks of all of the knowledge that I gathered about the fae, my secret stash of funds—about twenty-five hundred dollars-worth from an old, large pickle jar in the back of my guest room slash office closet in the corner. *Step eight*. I throw it all in the suitcase along with four pair of jeans, five shirts, two sweaters, and my favorite pair of sneakers along with a week's worth of underwear. Anything else would have to be bought on the road. *Step nine*. I climb into my compact SUV and get on the road with absolutely no clue what my specific destination would be. I just knew it was time to find love, to find home. *Step ten*. I meet Caroline Greer in the surprisingly clean ladies' room at the FastTrack truck stop six hours after my life-altering text message and change course yet again.

* * *

Caroline was a lovely hot mess to the mundane eye, but very well put together from a psychological perspective. Her bridge-taped glasses would make a Harry Potter fan wanna scream *Reparo*! But make no mistake that the plump pale hippie with unkempt silver hair that hung to her hips and moon shaped ear-rings of turquoise and solid hammered silver from a tourist-trap gallery in Sedona, Arizona had it together.

"Who was he?" she said.

"Sorry?" I replied a little taken aback.

"Who. Was. He?" she reiterated, slow and forceful. I stared at her reflection in the mirror that we both faced, my hands still dripping with soapy water. She stared back, defiant. "I know your type," she continued. Pretty girl. Super smart. Extremely dumb." That last part made me bristle. The thing is, I knew ex-actly what she had meant and she knew I knew it, too. "Finish washing your hands," she commanded like the practiced mom and grandma I figured she was.

I sighed deeply and did her bidding, slightly marveling at the lack of sink mold absent from the base of the faucet. In tones that indicated internal groaning, I said as poised as I could mus-ter, "He was the one I thought was the one." Tears threatened to well up as definite and all-consuming as Lake Lanier had been to its surrounding area. She was silent a moment before she sighed, too. A soft and practiced hand rubbed my right shoulder in that way that decades of motherhood do to the women who've earned the title and the honor.

As the first drop of the oncoming emotional torrent spilled forth, I gripped the faux marble sink edge for support and leaned my head forward until the mirror caught it in an embrace of pity. It provided a welcome chilliness against my fevered forehead and my eyes met themselves face-to-face. They were brown, beautiful, and barren with the burden of continuously adding an-other infertile charm on my long string of uncountable losses. This last failure I would call *racehorse*, for my hope had been that he'd be the one to see me to the finish line.

238

"Honey. *You* should be the one he *knows* is the one. Let's get you something to eat." She handed me a business card after I dried my hands and then my poor tired, red-ringed eyes. It read:

Caroline Greer,
Certified Life Coach.
Online by appointment.
"Make this day count, because you do!"

I snorted in a way that said, *Isn't this ironic?* "I'm Cereus. Cereus Layscape." She extended her hand, and we shook like a master to an apprentice. She was my Kenobi and I her Luke.

Caroline and her husband who was a retired CPA went across country in their insanely cute tiny home, which was hitched to a Ford F250. They lived simply, but meaningfully. That was the way I had always wanted to live. While her husband Charlie was off doing God-knows-what in the massive truck stop complex, she took me to one of several lines at the mini-fast food restaurant counters, insisted I eat, and paid for my meal.

"I hope you're not running away," she said chewing her sandwich.

"It's more like running towards something" I replied Caroline grunted and nodded.

"Just don't think that running towards something is always the solution either. I have a belief," she took a swallow of Fanta Orange and then continued, "that God in his infinite wisdom put all of his creation on a massive racetrack. No matter the twists and turns, it will ultimately lead back to the place on the track where you are supposed to be. So, one really can't run away. You can only find your place somewhere else. Get it?" Caroline took another swig of pop and didn't really wait for me to respond. She looked at me seriously then and said, "Don't run, Cereus. Walk, float, flip, skip. But always with purpose." I could feel my eyebrows arch in a quizzical reaction, but Caroline laughed in a nasal kind of way. "You'll get it one day."

I had awoken the next morning in a very nice and new Holiday Inn Express, not entirely sure about my last twenty-four hours of life, but certain that I would *skip* to my next stop in purpose. I had gone to *step eleven* then: pull out the notebooks and make a map. The Holiday Inn was my home for the next week, the little desk against the wall cluttered with papers and drawings, scotch tape and scissors, maps and copied text from the notebooks. All the crime solvers and detective lovers would have been proud. But I made my map to open doors, not close them. I guess I could say that I was more in line with archaeologists. The birth token that I had managed to keep, despite the theft that ran rampant in some of my foster homes, started to glow around my neck. I could see its light illuminating on a particular spot: an out-of-the-way portion of Lake Lanier that had once been another lake proper. Like other lakes and towns around it, everything had been merged or submerged. That point on the map looked small and inconsequential. I smiled.

*   *   *

With these memories now properly categorized, the rest flowed without bombarding me and I marvel at how much had happened since the journey first began to where I am now, which as I look around me, I realize that I am home—not the home I thought I was going to, that I was sure that the fae lord was inferring I was going to, Ryndpha—but home, home. As in my home in Kirkwood. Gentrified in recent years, the small shops and cafés with a mix of the old flavor of the neighborhood had spoken to my bohemian soul, which made it the closest thing to a home on Awbete as I could possibly get.

I find myself to be in my bed, but in a flowing white gown like the kind women from the European Middle Ages wore. If I had my choice, it would have been garb straight out of ancient Nubia. But I didn't dress me. That burden fell to someone else and out of sheer respect for clothing the naked without assistance from said naked, I think I'll shut up about it.

My hair rests below my breasts in intricate braids and flowers, the curly tendrils of 3 B/C hair adding richness and interest. How goddess-like! But once again I am pulled back to the mundane when I look to my right to find my now well-worn purple paisley suitcase, standing near my bedroom door, one wheel askew. My solo thought: *tragic*. I scoot to the edge of the bed and stand up, stretching and then walk to my open bedroom door. The sound of soft snoring makes me pause. But I'm not afraid, just curious. If I'm honest, a tiny part of me wants to berate myself for being "that girl". You know, the stupid one in all the horror movies who has the audacity to want to be rescued after the shock that someone wants to kill her, even though all of the signs were there, even though if she were smart, she'd have run the other way. But like the trial I'd already gone through in the woods of Lake Lanier, I see the futility of such fears because I understand that I'm powerful. Like legit powerful. I can feel the untapped energy swirling in my body's core, just waiting for the right one to test me. If anything, I'm the predator now and it is f'ing awesome!

So, with confidence, I walk to my left to my guest room-slash-office, and I see a tall woman stretched out on my murphy bed. She is the color of darkest rum with even darker hair that gleams with blue and green highlights; it is insanely beautiful, and I know that she, like me, is not of this world. I don't feel quite so alone anymore. Not like I had before, despite the many friends I made along the way.

She sits up suddenly, feeling my presence.

"Good morning, Princess." The voice is familiar, but I can't place it. She seems to be considering me thoughtfully.

"Good morning, uh…" I finish lamely.

"Partoch. My name is Partoch, and I will be your caregiver, teacher, protector, and more from now on." I shift from my right foot to the left, taking all of this in and knowing that I already knew these things.

"*Partoch*," I repeat, rolling the "r" like she had.

"We both have work to do, Princess, before we can return to Ryndpha."

"You mean *home*," I reply.

"No, Princess. *Home* is what you *are*, what you carry always as your *right* you. Your transformation was you finding yourself, thus your home. You—how do mortals say in Awbete? Ah yes, you 'fell in love' with yourself. Higher beings live no other way."

"Are you sure your name isn't Caroline?" I ask after a brief pause. Partoch looks at me ruefully, but I still smile then she joins me in the motion.

"Ready yourself, Princess. Work is always rewarding, but also hard." I nod at Partoch to express my acceptance of my fate and my birth token hanging between my breasts vibrates and shimmers my twinned response.

Partoch nods back sagely and smugly, "As in your first lesson that falls upon you now. Stretch before you fly."

My shoulder blades rip apart from their proper human places on my back as sudden as lightening appears and fades in the maelstrom. The crackling sound of severing muscle, tissue, and skin rents the air like New Year's Eve crackers at a long-awaited festive party. It hurts, but if I could survive the cocoon, I could survive this. So, I grit my teeth and zone out, vaguely aware of the thick streams of blood flowing down my back that adds a tickling sensation to the harmonious pains. I am quite sure that my gown is ruined. But I am also quite sure that I now have wings. And my body replies to my thoughts by the three feet extension in either direction, which creates a strong wind in the tiny guest bedroom, knocking down the framed diploma of my Master of Arts degree in Humanities. It hits the wooden floor, the glass cracking, though not quite shattering. I had taken pride in earning that degree. But now it represented so much more than my previous hopes and dreams. Now it represents the fragile veneer of a life I used to have, whose purpose was to act as place holder for an accomplishment worth sacrificing everything for. I marvel at how little I knew and still don't know of true possibility. Awbete's pervasive colonial, capitalist culture encourages its people to invest their time and efforts in things that are considered probable and plausible, not possible. Possibility is hard to quantify and thus adds no tangible value to the system that most, though not all, operate in. Partoch's explanation of "home" already has me excited about thinking and existing differently. My heart had always told me that there had to be another, better way. Maybe not a perfect way, but *better*.

I had still have those burning questions from earlier, though. Chiefly, why hadn't I always been with my people? A surge of uneasy energy makes my wings shiver.

Partoch simply looks at me as if she can read my mind. I wouldn't be surprised if she could. Her left arm reaches toward me, but her hand falls a foot and a half short of my heart. "Now Princess, stretch before you fly."

I feel it, smell it, taste it, hear it, need it before I see it. A portal opens up behind me and though it isn't Ryndpha, it is a safe world for our kind, fae kind.

I turn around slowly with seriousness of mind and carefreeness of my soul's glee. Two moons glitter in the distance of an over-crowded starry night that boasts sparkly constellations and swirly masses of galaxies never glanced before by human eyes.

"I was born here." Partoch makes a mild sound of assent, hearing the wonder in my declaration.

In front of me lays a vast ocean, its water thicker than Awbete's. Instinctually, I know it to have substance and the lifeforms within the ocean's loving, slow waves caress and rock them all to happy complacency. To be content with birth, life, and death.

My eyes adjust to the distance, and I can just make out a never-ending foreshore with trees of gold, silver, ruby, alexandrite, emerald, and sapphire. Upon it many figures stand gazing at me expectantly. They are beautiful, as opalescence is in that ethereal kind of way.

"Ghosts?" I query Partoch.

"No", she responds. "Our highest self. Free from the confines of the mundane."

"Heaven, then…" I try to process.

"A heaven, or rather haven for our kind." Partoch is now just behind me. Her wings are spread out, too.

"I guess this means that you are a princess, or do I assume too much that the royals are the ones with wings?" My peripheral vision caught the indigo russet colored pattern of her wings, not quite fully feathered, but more like a baby chick's.

"A much lower princess than yourself."

"Oh…," I breathed. I know she will explain it to me in due time. But frankly, it doesn't really matter to me. I'm not alone anymore and never would be again. She will be mother, aunt, sister, and friend all rolled into one. I am grateful. It is more than enough.

"I am your aunt, not your mother," she clarifies. This fae woman could definitely read my thoughts. "Look," she points, and my eyes follow to a singular destination on the shore. My pupils narrow and at last I discern the gift my aunt has given me. If atonement was what she has to work toward, she has a magnificent start in my humble opinion.

"Aww!" I gasp as the emotion rents my lungs.

Partoch moves around me with cat-like grace and agility. Though the portal proves to exit upon an infinity-like realm, my guest bedroom is what it is. "I go to be with my sister, brother, and nephews for a while. Will you stay or go?" My aunt cocks her head to the side and smiles sweetly, turning her beautiful ebony face towards peace. "You must stretch before you fly. You must fall before you rise. You must live before you die. You must let go the mundane before ascending to the prize."

With words of wisdom deposited on her pupil, my aunt takes to the air. I follow, my wings fully feathered and glittering like crystalline prisms, outshining the moons, stars, galaxies—and only fading in second best light to the opalescence of my long-awaiting family. I am whole. I am home.

The ATLiens

Jessica Cage

Jessica Cage is an International Award Winning, and USA Today best-selling Author. Born and raised in Chicago, IL, writing has always been a passion for her. She dabbles in artistic creations of all sorts but at the end of the day, it's the pen that her hand itches to hold. Jessica had never considered following her dream to be a writer because she was told far too often "There is no money in writing." So she chose the path most often traveled. During pregnancy, she asked herself an important question. How would she be able to inspire her unborn son to follow his dreams and reach for the stars, if she never had the guts to do it herself? Jessica decided to take a risk and unleash the plethora of characters and their crazy adventurous worlds that had previously existed only in her mind, into the realm of readers. She did this with hopes to inspire not only her son but herself. Inviting the world to tag along on her journey to become the writer she has always wanted to be. She hopes to continue writing and bringing her signature Caged Fantasies to readers everywhere.

Gerald L. Coleman

Gerald L. Coleman is a philosopher, theologian, poet, and Science Fiction & Fantasy author. He was born in Lexington and now makes his home in the Atlanta area. He did his undergraduate work in philosophy, english, and religious studies, followed by a master's degree in Theology. He is the author of the Epic Fantasy novel series, The Three Gifts, which currently includes *When Night Falls* (Book One), *A Plague of Shadows* (Book Two), and the upcoming *When Chaos Reigns* (Book Three). His poetry has appeared in: *Pluck! The Journal of Afrilachian Arts & Culture, Drawn to Marvel: Poems From The Comic Books, Pine Mountain Sand & Gravel Vol. 18, Black Bone Anthology, the 10th Anniversary Issue of Diode Poetry Journal, About Place Journal, and Star*line Vol. 43, Issue 4.*

His speculative fiction short stories have appeared in: The Cyberfunk Anthology: *The City*, the Roaring Lion Anthology: *Rococoa*, the Urban Fantasy Anthology: *Terminus* and *Terminus 2*, the 2019 JordanCon Anthology: *You Want Stories?*, *Dark Universe: Bright Empire, Cyberfunk!* by MVMedia, the Jordan-Con 2022 Anthology: *Neither Endings Nor Beginnings*, and *Whether Change: The Revolution Will Be Weird*. His essays appear in the polish language Con-Magazine: *KONwersacje*, *Apex Magazine 127*, and the Hugo nominated Fanzine: *Journey Planet*. He has been a Guest Author at DragonCon, Boskone, Blacktasticon, JordanCon, Atlanta Science Fiction & Fantasy Expo, SOBSFCon, The Outer Dark Symposium, World Horror Con, Imaginarium, and Multiverse. He is a Scholastic National Writing Juror, a Co-founder of the Affrilachian Poets, an SFWA member, a Rhysling Award Nominee, a recipient of The Hero of the Horn Award at JordanCon, and a Fellow at the Black Earth Institute. He is currently working on new editions of When Night Falls, A Plague of Shadows, and writing book three in epic fantasy series. And his newest poetry collection is entitled, *On the Black Hand Side*. You can find him at Geraldcoleman.com.

John Darr

John Darr is a native of the state of Georgia. As a graduate of Columbus State University with a B.A. in Communications, and with work on an M.F.A. degree at Howard University in Washington, D.C., he had over twenty years of experience as an author, screenwriter, independent filmmaker, educational television producer, screenwriter teacher, and technology specialist. His current projects include two YA Urban Fantasy book series; The Jonah Blackstone and Forest Heights series. He's currently working on a third adult Fantasy/Science Fiction series, Omega Quest, as well as completing the screenplay adaption of the first Jonah Blackstone book, The Protector's Ring.

Ashleigh Davenport

Ashleigh Davenport loves writing urban fantasies about monsters that bump in the night in more ways than one and the women who love them. Always working on one writing project or another, she fuels her late-night writing sessions with chocolate and bacon. You can find all things, Ashleigh, through https://linktr.ee/AshWritesLots.

L.M. Davis

L. M. Davis is a speculative fiction author who writes about shapeshifters, aliens, immortals, and witches. Her novels include *INTERLOPERS*, *POSERS*, *FORGERS*, and *skinless*. Davis is also a scholar of African American and Native American literatures and cultures, with particular interest in the speculative production of these communities. Currently, she is working on several projects including two novels and multiple ventures for television and film. She is the writer and director of the award-winning short film, "Fevered Dreams."

Milton J. Davis

Milton Davis is an award winning Black Speculative fiction author and owner of MVmedia, LLC, a publishing company specializing in Science Fiction and Fantasy based on African/African Diaspora history, culture, and traditions. Milton is the author of twenty-one novels and short story collections and editor/coeditor of ten anthologies. His short stories have appeared in several anthologies and magazines, most notably Black Panther: Tales of Wakanda, Slay: Stories of the Vampire Noire, Obsidian Literature and Arts in the African Diaspora and Tales from the Magician's Skull. Milton's story 'The Swarm' was nominated for the 2017 British Science Fiction Association Award for Short Fiction and his story, Carnival, was nominated for the 2020 British Science Fiction Association Award for Short Fiction. He is a recipient of the 2022 East Coast Black Age of Comics Convention Pioneer Lifetime Achievement Award.

Edward Austin Hall

A native of the Gulf Coast, Edward Austin Hall routinely refers to himself as an "Alabama escapee." He attended Tulane University in New Orleans and earned a Bachelor's degree in English there. Since then he has lived in Atlanta, Georgia, where his employers have included the *Atlanta Journal-Constitution* and *Newsweek.*

With novelist Bill Campbell, Hall co-edited the 2013 anthology *Mothership: Tales from Afrofuturism and Beyond*, which *The Magazine of Fantasy and Science Fiction* suggested might be "one of the most important sf anthologies of the decade." That estimation resonated in 2021, when *Mothership* appeared in a story headlined "Sci-Fi Has Changed A Lot In The Past Decade—These 7 Reads Will Show You How," which ran on NPR.org's main page.

As a writer/editor/developer of roleplaying game books, Hall co-created *Hunter: The Reckoning* for White Wolf Game Studio in 1999 and contributed to that rpg's 2022 fifth edition. He also worked in his three capacities on the forthcoming game *Blackbirds.*

In 2020, Gumbohaus released Hall's first novel, *Dread Isle.*
Twitter: @edwardahall
Facebook: @DreadIslander

Robert Jeffrey II

Robert Jeffrey II is a writer who has contributed to the worlds of comic books, video games, tabletop RPG's, and prose fiction. He currently works for video game developer Blowfish Studios as a game writer on the upcoming Phantom Galaxies, an open-world mecha space opera action RPG.

He has over 17 years of experience as a comic book writer and is a graduate of the DC Comics 2017 Writers Workshop. His portfolio includes work for 133Art Publishing, Subsume Media, RAE Comics, DC Comics, the Centers for Disease Control, and many other clients. He is the recipient of the 2008

Miller Brewing Company A. Philip Randolph Messenger
Award/ Journalism Award of Excellence in the field of
AIDS/Health, and the 2021 Glyph Comics Award for Best Story
(Changa & the Jade Obelisk #1.)

Alan Jones

I am an Atlanta native, first generation off the farm. Under-
grad and MBA from Georgia State University. I work as a
FinTech consultant for various clients. As a former Wall Street
consultant, my past clients include, CDW, JP Morgan, Honda,
Vanguard and the US Dept. of Energy.

I was a staff writer for the Technique at GA Tech, the Signal
at GA State and an IT columnist for The Atlanta Tribune.

I've published three full length speculative fiction novels (To
Wrestle with Darkness, Sacrifices, Heretics), four short story
collections ("So..." vols 1 thru 4) and one travel devotional (The
Consultant's Devotional). I have two new novels in development, the first of which should be available by the end of 2022.

Kyoko M

Kyoko M is a USA Today bestselling author and a fangirl.
She is the author of The Black Parade urban fantasy series and
the Of Cinder and Bone science-fiction series. The Black Parade
has been reviewed by Publishers Weekly and New York Times
bestselling author Ilona Andrews. Of Cinder and Bone placed in
the Top 30 Books in Hugh Howey's 2021 Self Published Science Fiction Contest. Kyoko M has appeared as a guest and pan-
elist at such conventions as Geek Girl Con, DragonCon,
Blacktasticon, Momocon, JordanCon, ConCarolinas, and Multi-
verseCon. She is also a contributor to Marvel Comics' Black
Panther: Tales of Wakanda (2021) anthology. She has a Bachelor of Arts in English Lit degree from the University of Georgia.

Violette Meier

Violette Meier is a happily married mother, writer, folk artist, poet, and native of Atlanta, Georgia, who earned her B.A. in English at Clark Atlanta University and a MDiv at the Interdenominational Theological Center. She is also a certified herbalist, a life coach, and an educator.

The great-granddaughter of a dream interpreter, Violette is a lover of all things supernatural and loves to write paranormal, fantasy, and horror. She is always working on something new.

Her books include:

Out of Night, Angel Crush, Son of the Rock, Archfiend, Ruah the Immortal, Oracles, Tales of a Numinous Nature, Hags, Haints and Hoodoo, Loving and Living Life One Day at aTime, Violette Ardor: A Volume of Poetry, This Sickness We Call Love: Poems of Love, Lust, and Lamentation, and two children's books.

To learn more about Violette and her eerie antics, visit her website VioletteMeier.com.

Balogun Ojetade

Balogun is Master Instructor and Technical Director of the *Afrikan Martial Arts Institute* and Co-Chair/Founder of *Blacktasticon*, the largest gathering of Black science fiction and fantasy creators and fans in the South.

He is the author of 42 bestselling fiction and nonfiction books and gamebooks, contributing co-editor of three anthologies: *Ki:Khanga: The Anthology*, *Steamfunk* and *Dieselfunk* and contributing editor of the *Rococoa* anthology and *Black Power: The Superhero Anthology*, Director and Fight Choreographer of the feature film, *A Single Link*, the short films, *Rite of Passage: Initiation* and *The Dentist of Westminster*; and the music video *Forward Motion* and co-author of the award winning screenplay, *Ngolo*; co-creator of *Ki Khanga: The Sword and Soul Role-Playing Game*, creator of the comic book series *Jagunjagun Lewa* and co-creator of the graphic novel series, *Ngolo*.

Glenn Parris

Glenn Parris writes science fiction, fantasy, medical mystery, and comic book fiction. Author of *The Underside of Darkness* for Marvel's Black Panther: Tales of Wakanda, *The Renaissance of Aspirin*, and the dark fantasy short stories, *The Tooth Fairies, Quest for Tearhaven, Unbitten: A Vampire Dream, The Sleepwalking Dead* and the speculative science fiction novel, Dragon's Heir, the first in a trilogy called *The Efilu Legacy* by Outland Entertainment in 2022. He has been a panel guest at the Planet ComiCon, ThrillerFest, TremediCon, DragonCon, BoucherCon, Creatures, Crimes and Creativity, Georgia Writers conference, and scheduled for the World Fantasy convention in November.

Aziza Sphinx

Writing professionally for over 20 years, Aziza Sphinx sees the world through peach, pecan, and a canopy of weeping willow trees. Family matters, and not just blood, for those who care for us are the truest who stand and fall during the winding road. When the hills and valleys of the literary journey summon and the pen becomes mightier than the sword, this is the world Aziza Sphinx breathes for. www.azizasphinx.com

Kortney Y. Watkins

Kortney Y. Watkins is a poet, short-story writer, novelist, and educator. She lives for love, waits on the moon, and hopes for the sake of humanity; every slash of a pen and stroke of a key is dedicated to exploring those things often done, less considered. She resides in the Atlanta metropolitan area amongst loving kin and friends.

More from MVmedia!

Atlanta. ATL. The Rising Phoenix. The City too Busy to Hate. The
Black Mecca. Capital of the Deep South. There, between flitting
shadows and full moons, exists another world filled with dark
creatures, demons, and immortals. Only a thin veil separates the
Atlanta you know from this mysterious realm. Nine brave authors risk
it all to reveal the crossroads of Southern charm and the Black
Fantastic. Y'all ready? https://www.mvmediaatl.com/product-
page/terminus-tales-of-the-black-fantastic-from-the-atl

For more exciting novels and anthologies, visit us at MVmedia, LLC, the Best of the Black Fantastic!

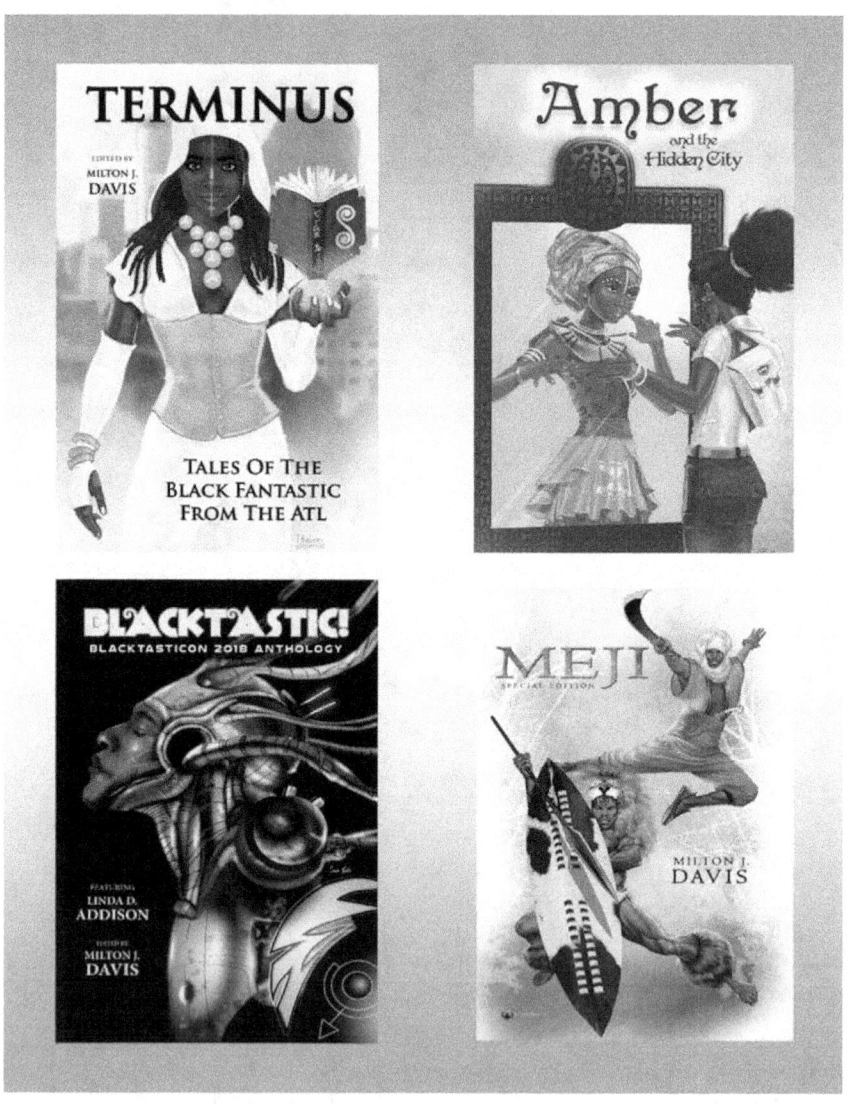

www.ingramcontent.com/pod-product-compliance
Lightning Source LLC
Chambersburg PA
CBHW052029020726
47501CB00004B/1328